HER WINTER OF DARKNESS

A Veronica Lee Thriller: Book Three

Melinda Woodhall

Melinda Woodhall
Visit my website at www.melindawoodhall.com

Printed in the United States of America

First Printing: September 2020
Creative Magnolia

For Tilly

CHAPTER ONE

Heavy footsteps pounded overhead as Astrid Peterson curled her body into a fetal position on the small, hard cot and wrapped thin arms around her legs. She flinched as an angry shout echoed in the room above, then squeezed her eyes shut against the harsh light coming from the bare bulb above her.

The man who had brought her to the underground bunker called it a safe room, but Astrid knew she was anything but safe as long as she was at the mercy of her hard-faced captor.

Forcing her eyes open again, Astrid studied the series of marks she'd scratched on the wall beside the cot. Each mark represented an endless day of anguish and regret.

How could I have been so stupid? Why did he have to pick me?

The Professor had seemed so innocuous and helpful. His brow had wrinkled into fatherly concern at her distress, and he'd offered to show her around campus, explaining with a reassuring smile that most freshmen got lost their first day of classes and that he would help her find her way.

Thinking of that terrible, fateful day, Astrid wondered where she would be now if only she'd kept on walking. If only she'd listened to all those warnings not to trust strangers. Would she be in class listening to a lecture, instead of trapped in an underground bunker listening to a madman's ravings?

Astrid stared in numb despair at the hundreds of marks on the wall. The tiny scratches didn't lie. Almost two years had come and gone. She'd been taken in late summer. A year had slipped by, and another was halfway through. Snow would be thick on the ground outside.

Her heart squeezed at the thought of a winter white landscape like the one she'd grown up in, but she pushed away the memories of her family back home. That would only make her cry, and she'd already shed enough tears for a lifetime.

Stifling a scream as the hatch in the ceiling swung open without warning, Astrid turned to see the retractable ladder drop down into the middle of the little room. She braced herself to face the Professor's rage but instead saw Skylar's slim legs descending.

The girl's silvery blonde hair was pulled back in her usual braid, and her eyes remained downcast as she set Astrid's lunch on a small table. The girl then looked up to where the Professor was staring down through the open hatch.

"You'll stay in the safe room today, girl," the Professor called down to Skylar, sounding distracted. "And keep that one quiet. I have important business to attend to."

Skylar blinked up at the man's weathered face and cold, green eyes, then turned and opened the little door that led into the adjoining room without responding. The Professor watched Skylar's slim figure disappear into the other room with narrowed eyes.

Astrid braced herself for the usual threats or reprimands, but the Professor's face disappeared, and the hatch fell shut with a thud.

Listening for the click of the lock that would let her know the Professor was really gone, at least for the time being, Astrid suddenly realized that the ladder was still hanging in the middle of the room. Her gaze lifted to the ceiling, and she held her breath.

He didn't lock the hatch, and the ladder is still down.

She waited, wondering if he was planning to come back, but the only sound she could hear was the Professor's big boots stomping away across the floor.

Astrid's heart began to pound in her chest at the faint sound of a door slamming. After all this time, had the Professor finally made a mistake? Or was he trying to trick her into disobeying his rules?

A shiver of fear rolled up her spine at the memory of what the Professor had done to the last girl who had broken his rules.

Moving to the thin wooden door that separated the two small underground rooms, Astrid knocked softly before opening it to reveal Skylar sitting in a straight-backed chair.

The younger girl looked up guiltily from the book she was holding. Astrid saw that it was her own paperback copy of *Pride and Prejudice*. She'd had it in her bookbag the day she'd met the Professor.

"Sorry," Skylar stammered. "I know this is yours, but I-"

"It's yours now." Astrid's voice was breathless with the thought of escape. "Do you know why the Professor is so angry?"

Skylar hugged the book to her chest and shrugged.

"He saw something on his computer that made him mad," she said, swallowing hard. "I haven't seen him that mad since...well..."

The girl's soft voice trailed off as a shadow passed over her pale face. Shaking her head as if to clear the disturbing memory, Skylar lifted the book and opened it to the page she'd been reading. Her lips began to move silently as her eyes focused on the page.

Skylar had once again retreated into the inner world where she seemed to live most of the time. Studying the small, bent head, Astrid felt a tug of pity. Best to let the poor girl find escape in her book. Reality would come crashing back soon enough.

Turning in the doorway with a sigh, Astrid stared at the ladder, nervously twisting a long strand of strawberry blonde hair that fell over her thin shoulder. Was the ladder a chance for escape, or a trap?

She looked back at Skylar with a worried frown, then closed the door firmly between them. If it was a trick, it wouldn't be fair to subject her to the Professor's wrath. She couldn't risk putting the girl in mortal danger.

But this may be my only chance to get out of here...to get home.

Crossing to the ladder, Astrid found herself climbing up before she could decide what she'd do once she got to the top. When her head brushed against the rough wood of the hatch, she hesitated only a moment before lifting a trembling hand. With a firm push, the hatch lifted several inches to reveal a view of the sunlit room above.

Astrid had been taken up to the ground floor before, but she'd never been left up there on her own, and she'd never had the opportunity to look around for a means of escape.

Now her scared eyes darted around the room, and she scurried to the wide windows, momentarily stunned by the blinding white of the snow falling on the already covered lawn beyond.

Tall, snow-capped trees could be seen behind the tall security fence that encircled the big property. She imagined the miles of frozen, unforgiving forest that waited past the fence.

The Professor had warned her often enough that the ranch was in the middle of nowhere. He'd assured her that if she somehow managed to escape, the mountain lions, grizzly bears, and grey wolves would be sure to find her before any people would.

She'd considered his threats to be just another ploy to keep her docile, but the daunting view out the window caused her heart to drop. Once she was outside, where would she go?

Pushing away the disturbing question, Astrid began to move toward the room's only exit. From what she could remember, the door opened to the foyer, offering a way out through the big house's front door.

Before Astrid could cross the room, a familiar *ping* caused her to freeze in place. She turned her head to see a laptop computer open on a sleek, glass-topped desk. The sound she'd heard must have been some sort of alert. The same kind she'd often used as a student to remind her she needed to leave for class.

She hurried to the desk, suddenly lightheaded at the possibility of using the device to communicate with the outside world. If she was lucky, she'd be able to call for help. The nightmare of the last few years might be over.

Staring down at the brightly lit screen, Astrid saw that the Professor had left a web browser window open to a news site. She read the headline above the featured video report.

The Shameful Truth About Human Trafficking in the Sunshine State.

Her blue eyes widened as she realized the Professor must have watched the video. Perhaps that's why he'd gotten so angry.

She quickly scanned the website but didn't recognize the name of the news station. She'd never heard of Channel Ten News in Willow Bay, Florida.

Before she could stop herself, Astrid reached out a trembling finger to tap the smooth surface of the laptop's trackpad.

The screen came to life as the video began to play. A reporter stood in front of a swaying palm tree, her long dark hair lifting in the gentle breeze as she faced the camera with a serious expression.

"Public outrage is boiling over as an ever-growing number of women and children in South Florida are being exploited or forced into servitude and captivity by organized trafficking networks."

The reporter's grim expression matched her sobering words.

"I'm Veronica Lee, and this is the first in a series of investigative reports Channel Ten will present on the scourge of human trafficking in our community, as well as the efforts local and federal officials are making to combat the problem."

Astrid tapped again on the trackpad, trying to silence the woman's loud voice, terrified that the Professor would slam into the room at

5

any minute as the reporter gestured to what appeared to be a police station behind her.

"Local police departments throughout the region are teaming up with the FBI's Human Trafficking Task Force to combat this rising threat to the most vulnerable members of society."

Finally managing to stop the video, the room fell into silence as tears sprang to Astrid's eyes. It seemed like the earnest young reporter had been speaking directly to her.

Maybe if I can reach that reporter, she'll send someone to find me.

Astrid hesitated beside the desk, hope and fear blooming in her chest. Should she spend precious time attempting to send a message, or would it make more sense to run now, while she still had the chance to get away?

And what if the Professor had set her up? What if it was part of some kind of sick test to see what she'd do?

The demented bastard is trying to trick me. He's probably outside right now waiting for me to run so he can chase me down like the others.

But the possibility that the Professor was setting some kind of twisted trap couldn't stop her now. This might be her only chance to escape, and if she had any hope of surviving the harsh conditions outside the compound, she'd need help.

Sinking into the chair in front of the desk, Astrid clicked on the email icon. An error message flashed across the screen.

Facial Recognition Failed. Try again or enter password to access email.

Holding back the wave of panic that threatened, she navigated back to the web browser and studied the Channel Ten News page.

Jumping at the sound of a car door slamming outside, Astrid glanced toward the window with frightened eyes but could see nothing beyond the white blur of falling snow.

She looked back to the screen and clicked defiantly on the *Leave a Comment* option under the video. With shaking hands, she began to type, determined to let someone out there know that she was still alive and that she and Skylar needed help.

Footsteps pounded up the porch steps as Astrid clicked on *Submit Comment* and jumped up from the chair to scurry through the doorway into the darkened hall beyond. She could hear the Professor stomping his snow-crusted boots on the doormat outside.

Holding her breath, Astrid crouched behind a thick winter parka and heavy woolen scarf hanging on the coatrack by the door. The door swung open, letting in a burst of frigid air and a spatter of snow.

The Professor's shadow fell across the floor in front of Astrid as he stopped on the mat just inside the door, stomping his feet again to knock off the remaining snow on his boots. Astrid peeked out just as he raised an arm to pull a thick woolen cap off his head.

Desperate to get through the front door before the Professor had the chance to lock it behind him, Astrid jumped forward to grasp the big steel-plated door with both hands.

Using all her strength, she slammed the heavy door into the Professor's shocked face, sending him stumbling backward. He bellowed as he lost his footing on the slippery hardwood floor and landed hard on his back.

As the Professor lifted a hand to his bloodied face in disbelief, Astrid grabbed the parka and scarf off the rack and darted past him. She'd almost made it out the door when a powerful jerk on the jacket wrenched her backward. She hit the ground with a painful thud as the Professor grabbed for her.

She looked down to see his gloved hand close over her thin wrist. It was the hand that was missing two fingers. The one he always concealed inside a glove. Anger surged through her at the hated touch of that hand on her skin.

I can't let him put me back underground, or I'll never get out again.

Releasing her hold on the parka, she grasped the three fingers gripping her arm and gave a savage twist. The Professor's hand fell away as Astrid scooted out of reach and onto the porch.

The shock of frigid air on her bare skin stole her breath as she flew down the steps onto the icy driveway, her bare feet stinging as she ran past a white pick-up truck parked just inside the still-open gate.

If I can just get through the gate and into the trees, I can hide.

She wouldn't think of what she'd do after that to stay alive in the frozen forest. First, she had to get away from the Professor. Only then could she figure out how to protect herself from the other dangerous predators that may be prowling nearby.

Daring to take a look behind her as she slipped through the gate, Astrid gasped in terror. The Professor was emerging from the door of the house. The front of his shirt was covered in blood, and he held a big rifle in his hands.

The Professor raised the sleek weapon, aiming it in Astrid's direction just as she dropped to the ground and sank into a thick bank of snow. A bullet whizzed by, grazing a spindly pine tree behind her.

Astrid ignored the growing pain in her feet and forced herself to stand and run toward a clump of fir trees to her left. The thick needles of the firs would provide cover from the Professor's shotgun and offer shelter from the wind and snow that whirled around her.

At least the snow will help hide my tracks.

The fleeting hope vanished as Astrid looked back to see a deep trail in the snow behind her. Only a blizzard would be able to hide her tracks from the quickly moving predator behind her.

Pushing through heavy clumps of prickly branches, Astrid plowed onward, moving quickly. After ten minutes of forging relentlessly through the snow, she stopped, leaned against the thick trunk of an old pine tree, and looked down at her red, aching feet.

The pain was beginning to fade into a numb heaviness. Frostbite would soon set in. After that, Astrid knew it would only be a matter of time until she succumbed to the elements.

She'd have to take shelter soon if she had any hope of survival. Luckily, Astrid had grown up in a country with long, harsh winters, and her father had taught her how to make an emergency shelter to ride out an unexpected snowstorm.

But poor Papa never thought I'd be in a storm without shoes or a coat.

She dropped to her knees and began to arrange fallen branches around the base of the pine tree. The crack of a twig close by made her stop and listen. Heart thumping, Astrid maneuvered herself so that her back was against the tree trunk.

Drawing her legs up to her chest, she huddled against the rough bark, her ears straining to hear any sound that might mean the professor had found her hiding place, but she heard only the soft whoosh of the wind through the trees.

Maybe the Professor has given up. Maybe he's back at the house now.

The thought of the house and the room underneath it made Astrid think of Skylar. A guilty ache started in her stomach.

I've left her all alone with the Professor. But what else could I do?

She hadn't had a chance to take Skylar with her, and she certainly couldn't go back now. Astrid had seen what her captor did to girls who ran away. He would dispatch her without mercy or remorse.

If I survive this, I'll go find help. I'll send someone back for Skylar.

Just then a loud, haunting howl rolled through the forest, causing the hair to stand up on the back of Astrid's neck. The howl had sounded close by. Too close for comfort.

That had to be a wolf. The Professor must have been telling the truth.

Watching her breath puff around her in a frosty cloud, Astrid tried to stay calm. The snow had stopped falling, and what was left of the sun was sinking quickly in the western sky.

9

The wolf is probably more scared of me than I am of it. Right? That's what Papa always told me. That wild animals just want to be left alone.

But her kind, decent father had never known that an animal like the Professor existed. And he had grown up half a world away in Sweden. How could he know what the wild animals in America would do to a lone woman in the wilderness?

Thoughts of her father were interrupted by the crunch of boots on snow. Astrid flinched as a cold voice sounded beside her.

"I warned you not to run, girl. I told you what would happen."

Springing up from her hiding place, Astrid was surprised to find that her numb feet were still able to support her as she headed deeper into the forest. Hope filled her chest as she neared a heavy clump of spruce trees.

I'm going to make it.

Astrid's last thought was followed by a deafening crack. A single gunshot echoed through the forest as the brilliant white world around her exploded into darkness.

CHAPTER TWO

The Channel Ten newsroom felt uncomfortably warm despite the late January chill outside. Veronica Lee shrugged off her jacket and frowned at the computer screen on her desk. The next report in her trafficking series was ready, and thanks to Finn Jordan's help the production was flawless.

So, why does it feel like something's wrong?

Clicking on the finished video file, Veronica watched closely as the report began to play again. She knew every shot and every word by heart. The in-depth investigative report focused on a disturbing increase in trafficking activity in South Florida, revealing evidence of a newly formed crime syndicate with ties to several small towns in the area, including Willow Bay.

Veronica had been satisfied with the script she'd written, and with Finn's work behind the camera. It had all come together smoothly. Everything appeared to be just as she'd planned.

So, what's bothering me?

Leaning forward, Veronica held her breath as the interview segment began. It had been the most difficult part of the project to shoot, and the most sensitive.

A young trafficking victim had agreed to be interviewed on the condition that her identity would be concealed. The woman on the screen remained hidden in shadow as she began to recount her ordeal at the hands of the men who had exploited her.

During the original interview, the woman's frightening tales of intimidation and violence had made Veronica's stomach turn. The shame and fear that filled the trembling, broken voice had shaken Veronica to her core.

Now, in the finished report, she could hear only the clear, smooth voice-over Finn had used to disguise the woman's identity.

That's it. That's what's wrong with our report. We can't hear her voice.

Veronica slumped back in her chair. The detached voice in the finished report diminished the story's impact. It couldn't convey the true horror of everything the woman had endured.

"The look on your face is telling me you aren't happy with it."

Veronica jumped, startled to see Finn standing at her shoulder as the video ended. She opened her mouth to assure the young videographer that the report was fine, then hesitated.

Why should she be happy when the woman they'd interviewed was still too ashamed to show her face in public, and too scared to tell her story in her own voice? How effective had their investigation been if the heart of the story had been silenced?

"You did good work, Finn. You always do..."

Veronica hesitated, knowing her disappointment wasn't rational. News stories rarely had satisfying endings. Sliding her eyes back to the screen, she pictured the woman behind the shadows.

"It just feels...*wrong* to have the victim in this story hidden as if *she's* ashamed while the criminals responsible are still out there."

Finn considered her words, then shook his head.

"We've got to protect our source, Veronica. Fair or not, that always has to be our number one priority. You know that."

He took in her downcast expression and his voice softened.

"Cheer up. Our series isn't over yet. These guys will make a mistake soon enough. Once they do, we'll be there."

Holding out a piece of paper, he cleared his throat.

"I actually came to see you about something else. Not sure it's the best timing, but I thought you'd want to see it. Just in case."

"In case what?'

Veronica narrowed her eyes, staring at the printout without taking it from Finn's outstretched hand.

"In case it's not just some kind of sick prank. But it probably is."

She heard doubt in his voice.

Plucking the paper from his hand with a sigh, she saw it was a printout of a viewer comment from the Channel Ten News website.

The words made her heart skip a beat. She raised wide green eyes to stare at Finn, then dropped them back to the paper.

Please help me. My name is Astrid Peterson. I am a victim like the women in your report. The Professor has me and Skylar and he won't let us go. Please send help before it's too late. He's coming back now, please hurry.

Veronica studied the words for a long beat, then turned to her computer and opened the web browser. She ignored Finn's curious stare as she navigated to the FBI's website for missing persons.

"What are you doing?"

Ignoring Finn's question, Veronica typed the name *Astrid Peterson* into the search field and held her breath. Within seconds she was staring at a picture of a lovely young woman with long strawberry blonde hair and smiling blue eyes.

The report below the picture identified the woman as twenty-three-year-old Astrid Peterson, a coed reported missing from her college campus in Montana almost two years before.

"Oh, damn." Finn moved closer, studying the screen. "If this is someone's idea of a prank, they are seriously messed up."

Scanning the information included on the FBI missing person's page, Veronica saw that Astrid Peterson was from Sweden and that she'd been in the US on a student visa. The young woman had only been in the country a few months when she'd gone missing.

"What are you two working on?"

13

Veronica looked up to see Hunter Hadley's tall figure approaching, followed by Gracie, Finn's white Labrador retriever. The smile on Hunter's face faded as he registered Veronica's strained expression.

"You look like you've seen a ghost. What's happened?"

He circled around to stand beside Finn, who made room as he gestured toward Veronica's screen.

"We got a comment on the station's website from a viewer who claims she's being held against her will by some professor."

Finn held up the printout, then pointed at Astrid Peterson's photo.

"The name she used matches a woman on the FBI's missing person website. But anybody can access the site, so maybe-"

Snatching the paper out of Hunter's hand, Veronica stood to face Finn, impatient with his skepticism.

"I hope it is just a sick joke, Finn," she said in a tight voice. "But I plan to take it seriously until we find out for sure."

She turned to Hunter, who was standing close enough for her to smell his cologne. It was the one she'd gotten him for Christmas, and the familiar scent immediately calmed her nerves.

"We need to find the computer that was used to send this comment," she said, clutching the paper and heading down the hall. "If we find the computer, we just might find Astrid Peterson."

* * *

"No luck," Jack Carson said, stepping into Spencer Nash's office with a rueful shake of his balding head. "Whoever submitted that comment on the message board used a VPN to connect to the internet. My buddy says there's no way to track it back to a specific person or a physical location."

Veronica stared at the older man in dismay. Jack always seemed to have the answer to any technical problem, and he knew everyone in town. It had taken him only minutes to get a specialist from the news station's internet service provider to call him back.

Half an hour later he'd gotten his answer, but it wasn't the one Veronica had been hoping to hear. The IP address linked to the comment was a dead end. She was back to square one.

Looking at the other men in the room, Veronica sighed.

"That's a shame," she said, still holding the printout as she prepared to stand. "I'm not sure this is much to go on, but maybe the FBI will have better luck than we did."

"Hold on a minute, Veronica."

Spencer lifted a well-manicured hand to smooth back his neat thatch of blonde hair. The station manager motioned for Veronica to stay seated as he leaned forward.

"That message was sent to Channel Ten, not the FBI," he said slowly. "And that may mean that this person, whether it's Astrid Peterson or someone else, may not want the FBI involved. Maybe they have information they want to share with the press."

Raising an eyebrow, Veronica considered Spencer's words. Before she could respond, he spoke again, warming to his theory.

"You found the FBI missing person's page in just a few clicks, right? So why wouldn't this woman have contacted the FBI directly? Why reach out to us?"

Jack Carson leaned against the doorframe and nodded.

"And the computer used a VPN to mask its location," he agreed. "So, the person could be trying to hide from the feds or the cops."

The men's words sounded logical, but Veronica wasn't convinced.

"I think you're all forgetting something."

She crossed her arms over her chest and lifted her chin.

"That comment was posted under *my* report asking *me* for help. I think Astrid Peterson watched the report and saw that I'm trying to help women like her. It gave her the courage to reach out, and I'm not about to let her down now."

15

Pushing back her chair, Veronica stood and crossed to the door. As Jack Carson stepped aside to let her pass, she stopped and looked back into Spencer's office.

"I'm going to do everything I can to find Astrid Peterson," she said, her eyes finding Hunter's handsome face. "I plan to start by contacting the WBPD and the FBI. I'll take any other help I can get."

Hunter's approving gaze sent a warm flush through Veronica as she turned and walked back to her desk. She could always count on him to have her back when she was working on a difficult story. That was one of the many reasons she'd fallen for him.

Back in front of her computer, Veronica read the printout one more time. This time her eyes stopped on the other name in the comment. Wherever Astrid Peterson was, she wasn't alone. A girl named Skylar was with her, and they both needed help.

CHAPTER THREE

A cool wind whipped Nessa Ainsley's red curls around her face as she climbed out of her black Dodge Charger. The light blanket of grayish clouds had parted momentarily, allowing the weak winter sun to make an appearance. Lifting her face to the sky, Nessa relished the warmth of the sun on her skin, already dreading the stale, artificial atmosphere inside the police station.

She'd made it halfway across the parking lot when her coat pocket began to vibrate. Without breaking her stride, Nessa pulled out her phone and glanced down to see Veronica Lee's name pop up on the little display.

Suspecting she knew why the investigative reporter was calling, Nessa dropped the phone back into her pocket.

Veronica must've heard that the WBPD is joining the FBI trafficking task force. She'll want a statement, and I just don't have the time.

Willow Bay's chief of police had been surprised the week before when Special Agent Clint Marlowe called to invite her little department to be involved in Operation Stolen Angels.

The objective of the newly formed task force was to infiltrate and ultimately bring down a crime syndicate that had recently started operating in South Florida. The unsavory group trafficked in illegal narcotics and young, vulnerable women.

Nessa suspected that Channel Ten's series of reports on trafficking in the area had drawn the FBI's attention, and may even have persuaded them to include Willow Bay in the operation.

Whatever the reason, she had gladly accepted the invitation, and was on her way to meet with the man heading up the task force.

Before she could get through the station's door, Nessa's phone pinged with a text message. Reaching into her pocket again, she saw that Veronica Lee wasn't going to give up so easily.

Need to speak to you urgently. Please call ASAP.

Shaking her head at the reporter's persistence, Nessa was about to tap on Veronica's number when the door to the station opened and Detective Tucker Vanzinger's wide shoulders filled the doorway.

"Where have you been, Chief?" Vanzinger looked over his shoulder as if someone may be listening in. "Agent Marlowe's already set up in the briefing room and he's getting a little antsy."

Nessa stuck the phone back in her pocket and hurried after Vanzinger, bypassing her office and following the big detective's figure down the narrow hall and into the briefing room.

Special Agent Clint Marlowe stood at the front of the room. His shirt sleeves were already rolled up, and he'd thrown his suit jacket over the back of a chair.

"Morning, Agent Marlowe, morning Detectives," Nessa said, trying to rein in her southern accent. "Hope I didn't keep you all waiting too long."

"I'm sure you must be very busy, Chief Ainsley."

Marlowe's voice was brisk.

"I appreciate your team's willingness to jump into the operation on such short notice. I know you've had your hands full lately."

Despite his reassuring words, the agent's dark eyes followed Nessa with undisguised impatience as she took off her coat and settled into a chair at the long table. She waited for Vanzinger to take a seat next to his partner, Detective Simon Jankowski, then nodded.

18

"Okay, we're anxious to get started," she said, leaning back in her chair. "Tell us all about Operation Stolen Angels."

Turning to the whiteboard behind him, Marlowe gestured to a poster-sized map of Florida he'd affixed to the board. Stickers of various colors had been placed on the map, and several cities had been circled in red marker.

"As you know, there's been a steep increase in trafficking activity throughout South Florida in the last few months."

Marlowe tapped on the map for emphasis.

"The red stickers indicate reported or confirmed incidents of human trafficking and the blue stickers indicate drug trafficking."

Nessa leaned forward to study the map as Marlowe continued.

"We've noticed an unusually high density of incidents outside the normal geographic areas we'd expect. Most crime organizations start up in one of the bigger cities. Places with international airports and maybe even seaports. Places like Miami and Tampa."

Gesturing to the map, Marlowe turned to face Nessa.

"What do you notice about this pattern, Chief Ainsley?"

Nessa sat up straighter, feeling like a student being called on in class. Luckily, she thought she knew the answer.

"Looks like the incidents are clustered in the smaller towns and cities," she said with a frown. "Places like Willow Bay."

"Exactly," Marlowe said. "And we need to understand why."

Jankowski stood and moved closer to the board. The detective crossed thick arms over his chest and rubbed the stubble on his chin.

"It seems like these guys are avoiding the big cities altogether," he murmured, tracing a line of stickers with a long finger. "Maybe they're just trying to stay off the radar of the bigger police forces."

"That's certainly a possibility," Marlowe agreed, "which is why we need to involve the local police in these smaller towns whenever possible. But we think this pattern could tell us a lot about this specific organization."

19

Looking over at Nessa, he pointed to her coat.

"Where'd you get that coat, Chief Ainsley?"

Nessa shrugged, confused.

"I've had it for years," she admitted. "Ever since I lived up in Atlanta. Not much need for a winter coat down here."

"So, you probably got it at a store. Maybe in downtown Atlanta, where everybody goes to shop. But if you were buying that coat today, you'd probably start online. Maybe find out if the coat you want is available, and if there's free shipping, right?"

Nodding in agreement, Nessa thought she knew where Agent Marlowe was going.

"So, you all think this organization is soliciting customers online? That they don't need to be in the big cities anymore to find buyers?"

"That's the theory," Marlowe agreed. "If a local group is running things, they probably want to stick close to home. Maybe stay in a town where they have the right connections. Perhaps be in a position where they can smooth over any concerns or questions that arise."

Vanzinger sat up in his chair, suddenly interested.

"Hold on, now, Agent Marlowe. Are you saying you suspect that someone in Willow Bay is involved with this group? Maybe even running it?"

The faint creases between Marlowe's eyes deepened as he considered Vanzinger's question.

"If you're asking if we have a specific suspect in mind, then the answer is no, Detective. But if you're wondering if we suspect that someone in this town or one of the other towns on this map could be involved, then the answer is yes. That's why we need your help."

A hesitant knock on the door stopped Vanzinger's reply. Officer Dave Eddings stuck his head into the room.

"Sorry, Chief, but someone's asking to see you. Says it's urgent."

"We're in the middle of a meeting, Officer Eddings. Who is it?"

Giving Marlowe a nervous glance, Eddings cleared his throat.

"It's Veronica Lee, Chief. Says she's been calling you, and–"

"Okay, tell her I'll be right out."

Once Eddings had closed the door behind him, Nessa turned to Marlowe, ready to apologize for a further delay, but the agent spoke up first.

"Veronica Lee? Isn't she the reporter who's been investigating trafficking in South Florida?"

Surprised by the question, Nessa nodded.

"She's covered some of the big cases we've handled recently."

Nessa felt suddenly protective of the young woman who had been through so much in the last year.

"And she can get herself into some pretty risky situations trying to get her story. I better talk to her and find out what's going on."

She stepped into the hall, almost colliding with Dave Eddings.

"Here she is, Chief," the young man said, his face flushed as he turned to present Veronica, who was following close behind him.

"Sorry to interrupt you, Nessa, but this can't wait." Veronica's voice was strained. "I have information about a missing person."

Nodding at Eddings, Nessa put a hand on Veronica's arm.

"That's all, Dave. You can go now."

The officer disappeared down the hall just as a deep voice spoke behind Nessa. Agent Marlowe stood in the briefing room doorway.

"Thought we'd take a break while you're busy out here," Marlowe said, stopping short when he saw Veronica.

Nessa decided good manners prevailed, even when time was short.

"Agent Marlowe, this is Veronica Lee, an investigative reporter with Channel Ten News. Veronica, this is Special Agent Clint Marlowe with the FBI."

Marlowe raised his eyebrows at the formal introduction but gave Veronica a curt nod.

"I've seen your work, Ms. Lee."

"And I've heard about your trafficking task force, Agent Marlowe," Veronica replied, looking over Marlowe's shoulder into the briefing room. "Does this mean the WBPD is now officially partnering with the FBI?"

Figuring the news would spread quickly around the small town, and that the FBI's presence in Willow bay would be hard to conceal, Nessa knew it would be pointless to deny it.

"Nothing's official unless it comes out of our media relations office," Nessa replied cautiously, trying to gauge Marlowe's reaction. "But *off the record,* I can confirm that the WBPD is cooperating with the FBI as part of the larger national effort to combat trafficking."

"That's what I'd heard from my sources," Veronica said, nodding her approval. "And I'm glad Willow Bay is finally getting some serious attention, but right now I need to talk to you about something else that can't wait."

"Sounds like my cue to leave," Marlowe said. "I'll go get a cup of coffee and leave you to it."

Veronica reached out a hand to stop the agent before he could move away down the hall.

"Actually, you might be the one I should be talking to, Agent Marlowe," she said, dropping her hand to reach into her purse. "You see, someone posted a comment to the Channel Ten message board."

Pulling out a piece of printer paper, Veronica held it toward Marlowe. The agent took the paper and scanned it. His expression didn't change as he looked up and handed the paper to Nessa.

The words on the page sent a shiver up Nessa's spine.

"According to the FBI's missing person website, Astrid Peterson was a foreign exchange student from Sweden. She disappeared from a college campus in Montana almost two years ago."

Veronica's voice was grim.

"As far as I can tell, she's never been heard from since."

Nessa read the words on the printout again, then looked up at Veronica. Doubt creased her forehead into a frown.

"Could this be some kind of...of..."

"Some kind of sick joke?" Veronica finished for her. "I guess it could be, but that's not what it feels like to me."

Veronica's voice wavered, betraying her distress as she continued.

"I've interviewed quite a few abused and exploited women during my trafficking investigation, and this sounds all too real."

She looked to Marlowe.

"We can't just dismiss the claim without at least trying to find out if it has some merit, can we, Agent Marlowe?"

"Of course not," he replied without hesitation, taking out his phone. "I'll take a picture of the comment and send it over to the Bureau. We'll get the right person working on this right away."

Surprised by the agent's quick reaction, Nessa put a soft hand on Veronica's shoulder. She wasn't ready to pass this one off to the feds so quickly.

"I'll ask Detectives Jankowski and Vanzinger to look into it, as well," she said. "If Astrid Peterson did write those words, she chose to reach out to our local news station for help. I want to know why."

* * *

It was lunchtime when Nessa finally stepped out of the briefing room and headed to her office. She turned a corner to see Detective Peyton Bell standing in the hall outside an interview room.

Willow Bay's newest detective greeted Nessa with a distracted smile, her face tense as she prepared to open the door.

"Where's Detective Ingram?" Nessa asked as she approached. "Don't tell me he called in sick again."

23

"I almost wish he had." Peyton rolled her eyes. "He's in there interviewing a girl picked up for shoplifting earlier today. Let's just say it isn't going very well."

Checking her watch, Nessa was tempted to let the detective handle the matter without her help, but something about Peyton's choice of words stopped her.

Willow Bay's only female detective didn't make a habit of asking for help. If she'd raised a problem to Nessa's attention, even casually, it was probably something important.

"Okay, what's going on?"

The blunt question seemed to catch Peyton off guard. She combed nervous fingers through her dark pixie cut, obviously hesitant to say anything that might cause further discord between her and her partner.

Nessa didn't blame her. Detective Marc Ingram wasn't easy to work with on the best of days. If he thought Peyton was complaining about him to his boss, he would make his partner's job very difficult.

Silently cursing Mayor Hadley for bringing Ingram back into the department after she'd fired him for gross negligence, Nessa offered Peyton a reassuring smile.

"Tell me what's really bothering you. Don't worry about Ingram."

"It's not Ingram I'm worried about," Peyton replied with a shake of her head. "I'm worried about Ruby Chase."

Nessa cocked an eyebrow.

"Who's Ruby Chase?"

"She's the girl in there with Ingram." Peyton's amber eyes glinted with anger as she looked toward the door. "He's giving her a hard time because he doesn't buy her story, but I'm not sure she's lying."

Resisting the urge to look at her watch again, Nessa nodded.

"Okay, so what's her story?"

"A convenience store on the west side detained her for shoplifting, and the uniforms that picked her up say she resisted arrest. Apparently, she started yelling about men chasing her."

Nessa raised her eyebrows.

"I don't understand why you guys caught the case. As far as I remember, shoplifting isn't a major crime."

"No, but trafficking in narcotics is," Peyton replied with a sigh. "The girl had quite a stash on her when she was booked. She insists the drugs aren't hers. Says she was transporting them for the men who were chasing her. Claims these guys were forcing her and other girls to make deliveries. Ingram's convinced she's making it up."

An uneasy feeling settled in Nessa's already upset stomach.

"And you're trying to figure out if she's a criminal or a victim?"

"Exactly."

Wishing she'd taken the time to eat breakfast that morning, Nessa decided lunch would have to wait a little while longer.

"You go join the interview. I'll watch from behind the glass."

She headed toward the observation room next door. She wanted to see for herself if Ruby Chase was lying.

CHAPTER FOUR

Peyton Bell opened the door without knocking and slipped silently into the interview room. Ingram didn't look up as she sank onto the chair next to him. He kept his small, close-set eyes fixed on the silent girl sitting across the old wooden table.

"So, tell me again. Why'd you spend time strolling around a store shopping if you were in fear for your life? Why not call the police?"

Jet black eyeliner and a thick coat of mascara made Ruby Chase appear older than her eighteen years. Peyton studied the stubborn set to her small pointed chin and imagined she could still see a trace of the little girl Ruby had been only a few years before.

"I was hungry," Ruby muttered. "And why should I run to the cops? I knew you guys would never believe me."

"You took the food because you were hungry?" Peyton asked, ignoring the razor-sharp glare Ingram threw in her direction. "Why hadn't you eaten?"

Ruby's blood-shot eyes shifted to Peyton.

"Ask *him*." She pointed a listless finger at Ingram. "I've already told him the whole story, but he thinks I'm lying."

"So, tell *me*," Peyton said, leaning closer. "What happened?"

Drawing in a shaky breath, Ruby folded her arms over her chest. Peyton noted multiple bruises and scratches but didn't see any track marks. She kept her expression neutral as Ruby began to speak.

"Diablo's men were busy unloading a big truck this morning and left the gate open, so I took off while I had the chance. I was trying to stay out of sight, but I got hungry. And it was cold outside. I thought the store would be warm."

"Who's Diablo?"

Peyton felt Ingram tense beside her. She knew he wanted to be the one asking questions. He didn't like her jumping in and taking over.

"Diablo's the boss, I guess," Ruby said with a shrug of her small shoulders. "You know, the head honcho. Everybody there was scared shitless of the guy."

"Can you describe him?"

Clenching his fist on the table, Ingram turned to Peyton.

"Thank you, Officer Bell, but I'll ask the questions from here on out if you don't mind."

Peyton lifted her hands in mock surrender, hiding her anger at his outburst. It was never acceptable to argue in front of a suspect. The thought raised the question that kept playing in Peyton's mind.

Is Ruby Chase a suspect, or is she a victim?

Studying the girl's pale face, Peyton was inclined to trust her own instincts. Ruby's story had stayed consistent, and underneath the tough act, Peyton could see she was truly scared.

A rap on the door stopped Ingram's next words.

Nessa appeared in the doorway, her face drawn and serious under the harsh overhead lights of the little room. She motioned for Peyton and Ingram to join her in the hall.

"You trying to ruin this interview?" Ingram hissed as soon as the door had shut behind him. "I was about to get a confession, and–"

"Be quiet, Detective Ingram," Nessa snapped. "I've been watching the interview and it's clear your *technique* is not working with this interview subject. We need to gain her confidence, so she'll share any details she knows about the men who supplied her with the drugs."

A red flush spread over Ingram's thin face. His eyes narrowed into angry slits as he looked back and forth between Nessa and Peyton.

"Fine. You two play softball with this street kid and see where that gets you. But don't say I didn't warn you."

Spinning on his heel, Ingram strode down the hall and out of sight. Peyton watched him go with a mixture of relief and dread. He was gone for now, but Ingram was still her partner, and she knew the matter was far from over for him.

"Ruby Chase mentioned a man named Diablo," Nessa said, obviously not too concerned about Ingram's angry departure. "We've got to find out who this guy is."

The police chief checked her watch as she spoke in a hurried voice.

"If this Diablo guy really exists, and if he is the *head honcho* of a group of men trafficking in drugs and girls like Ruby claims, we may be able to do more than just support the FBI with Operation Stolen Angels. We could be the department to successfully close it out."

"Operation Stolen Angels?" Peyton frowned at Nessa. "Is that what Jankowski and Vanzinger have been working on with the FBI?"

Lowering her voice, Nessa gave a reluctant nod.

"That's the name they've given the trafficking task force," she admitted. "But I shouldn't have said anything. I don't want information about the operation shared outside the assigned team."

Peyton swallowed back more questions. She would love to be assigned to the joint operation with the FBI, but she knew Nessa would never assign her and Ingram to the task force. In fact, Peyton was sure Nessa had been thinking of Ingram when she'd said she didn't want information shared outside the team.

"You go back in there and try to gain Ruby Chase's confidence," Nessa said, already moving down the hall. "And let me know what you can find out about Diablo."

* * *

28

Ruby kept her head down when Peyton entered the little room. She had curled up on the chair, pulling her legs under her and wrapping her arms around herself as if trying to get warm, even though the building was well heated against the chilly day outside.

"Detective Ingram had to take care of another case," Peyton said, keeping her voice neutral. "So, now it's just you and me."

Waiting for a reaction, Peyton noticed a slight tremor in Ruby's hands. She thought about the bag of pills found on the girl when she'd been booked.

The bag had been sent to the lab for testing, but Peyton figured it likely contained Oxycodone or Hydrocodone. Both drugs were highly addictive, and sudden withdrawal could be agonizing.

"How long have you been hooked?"

When Ruby didn't respond, Peyton tried again.

"Did you start taking pills before or after you got mixed up with this gang? Is that how you ended up there? Did they offer you pills?"

"Sure, blame the victim," Ruby muttered. "That's what Diablo's men said you'd do. Guess they know how the system works."

Trying to catch Ruby's eyes, Peyton leaned forward.

"I'm not blaming anyone, Ruby. But it looks to me like you need help, and I can't help you if I don't know what happened."

Ruby glanced over at Peyton. The pain on her pale face confirmed Peyton's suspicions; the girl was an addict, and she was scared.

"If you tell me the truth, I promise I'll do whatever I can to get you help. Now, where did you get the drugs?"

Dropping her eyes, Ruby swallowed hard before answering.

"I was helping load the truck like I said before, and I took my chance to get out. I just stuck the bag I was holding in my pocket."

"Okay. So, where'd you go after you ran out?" Peyton asked. "I mean, you ran through the gate and then what?"

Ruby hesitated as if trying to remember.

Or maybe she's thinking up another lie.

29

A sheen of sweat began to form on Ruby's forehead as Peyton waited for a response, and the tremor in her hands worsened.

"The place was in the middle of nowhere," Ruby finally said in a hoarse whisper. "It was like a prison compound or something. There was even barbed wire on the fence, and all the doors had locks on the outside."

Dropping her feet to the floor, Ruby sat up straight in her chair. Her hands tightened into fists on top of the wooden table.

"When I ran out, I was in some kind of forest. I couldn't hear anyone shouting or chasing after me, but I was scared. I ran through the trees until I got to a little road."

Her voice faltered as if she was finding it hard to remember.

"I...I followed the road until...well, until I found a place to hide out. But I got hungry. That's when I went to the store."

Trying to keep the skepticism out of her voice, Peyton nodded.

"Okay, so you took some food at the store, and that's when you were stopped for shoplifting. Why didn't you ask for help then? Were you afraid they'd find the drugs?"

Ruby shook her head in frustration.

"No, I forgot all about the bag in my pocket," she said, pushing a strand of dark hair off her damp forehead. "But I was scared the people in the store might know Diablo. That they might call him, and that his men would come for me."

"But...why would the people at the store know Diablo?"

The words came out sounding more like an accusation than a question, and Peyton winced as Ruby turned away.

"I'm sorry, Ruby. What I meant was, what made you suspect the people at the store would know Diablo or his men?"

"The other girls said Diablo knew everyone in town."

Her words sent a ripple of concern through Peyton.

"How many other girls were at this...this compound?"

Ruby shrugged.

"I don't know. Girls would come one day and be gone the next."

"And they told you Diablo knows lots of people in Willow Bay?"

A shadow crossed Ruby's face as she looked up at Peyton, holding her gaze as if searching for some truth in the detective's eyes.

"They said Diablo had people working for him everywhere," she finally said. "They said he even had some cops working for him."

Recoiling at the girl's words, Peyton sat back in her chair, stunned at the possibility she'd gotten caught up in another case where the integrity of the force was in question.

She tried to hide her dismay, but the memories washed through her, and she had to drop her eyes and turn away.

Her first job as a police officer had been with the WBPD, but it had ended in shame and regret after she'd witnessed an innocent man go to jail. She'd decided to leave the department rather than speak up against the corrupt detectives in the department, and that mistake had taken its toll. Some days she still struggled to stay sober.

But now she was back in Willow Bay and working for the WBPD as a detective. Nessa Ainsley had taken over as the chief of police, and she ran a clean department. This time things were different. Everything had been going well.

Peyton had even made peace with the man who had been wrongly convicted because of her silence. The thought of Frankie Dawson serving time in prison brought a hot flush of shame to her face, and Peyton stood and crossed to the door.

"I'll get us some water," she said in a hoarse voice, not meeting Ruby's eyes. "I'll be back."

Once outside the door, Peyton leaned against the wall and forced herself to take a deep breath. The need for a drink was overwhelming, and water wasn't going to quench the kind of thirst she had.

Walking straight to Nessa's office, Peyton knew she should tell the police chief what Ruby had said about Diablo. If there was some kind of connection between the department and the traffickers they were investigating, the chief needed to know.

But when she got to the chief's office, Nessa wasn't alone. State prosecutor Riley Odell sat across from the police chief. Both women seemed tense as they turned to see Peyton standing in the doorway.

Nessa looked up and waved Peyton into the room.

"Come on in. We could use a break from...*this*."

Gesturing toward the papers and folders spread out on her desk, Nessa sighed as Riley nodded toward the chair next to her.

"Yes, please tell us something that will take our minds off this motion to dismiss. We need to clear our heads before meeting with Judge Eldredge."

The prosecutor offered Peyton a smile, taking off her glasses and tucking a glossy strand of dark hair behind one ear.

Peyton glanced down at the desk, her eyes falling on a familiar name on one of the folders. Nick Sargent's case had been going on for months, and it had taken up much of Nessa's time.

"Still trying to tie up the Sargent case?" Peyton asked, finding herself stalling for time. "I thought it was pretty much airtight."

"Judge Eldredge doesn't see it that way," Riley said with a grimace. "He's considering a motion to delay the trial again. It seems Sargent can't find a lawyer to take on his case in Willow Bay after all the *sensationalized press coverage of recent events*, as he puts it."

Turning to Peyton, Nessa took a cleansing breath.

"Enough about Nick Sargent for now, I want to hear what you found out from Ruby Chase. Any luck? She tell you anything useful?"

Peyton shook her head, then swallowed hard. She glanced at Riley's alert expression and felt her heart drop. How could she tell Nessa that Ruby had implicated her department in a trafficking scheme while sitting in front of the state prosecutor?

"Ruby Chase is coming down hard off whatever she's been on," she heard herself say. "I think she's gonna need rehab before we can get anything useful out of her."

Considering Peyton's words, Nessa hesitated, then turned to Riley with a thoughtful frown.

"We've got an eighteen-year-old girl in custody who was picked up for shoplifting," Nessa explained. "When we found narcotics on her, she claimed to be a victim of some sort of trafficking gang. Says they're using girls to transport drugs."

"And you're thinking she could be a potential informant?" Riley's eyes lit up with interest. "Or maybe even a witness if we ever get this group into court?"

Nessa nodded.

"Trouble is, she's clearly an addict, so we're not sure how reliable her story is, or how convincing she'd be as a potential witness."

"Maybe if we get her some help, she'll be able to tell us more," Peyton said, pushing Ruby's comment about Diablo having connections with the police force to the back of her mind.

Peyton's words seemed to please Riley, who nodded her approval.

"Okay, I'm willing to give it a try," Nessa agreed. "As long as she goes into a facility in the area where we can keep tabs on her. I just don't know how quickly she could get in somewhere."

Frankie Dawson's face drifted through Peyton's mind for the second time that day.

"Leave it to me, Chief. I think I know somebody who can help."

CHAPTER FIVE

The lobby at Hope House was quiet as Frankie Dawson pushed through the front door. He rubbed his hands together with a relieved sigh, grateful to be inside the warm building after his brisk walk through the chilly afternoon.

A slim black woman in a pink suit crossed the lobby, greeting him with a wide smile. The Hope House name badge that hung around her neck identified her as Dr. Regina Horn.

"I appreciate this, Doc. You're a real pal."

Frankie looked around the room, hoping in vain to see Peyton Bell's dark hair and bright eyes coming toward him.

"I'd say you're the real pal, Frankie." Reggie arched an eyebrow. "And Peyton's lucky to have a friend like you. Not many people would drop an important case to do a friend a favor."

A flush of heat worked its way up Frankie's neck at her words, and he wondered if it was obvious to everyone that he had fallen hard for Willow Bay's newest detective.

I'm making an idiot out of myself in front of the whole damn town.

Reggie's phone began to buzz in her pocket, saving Frankie from having to respond to her comment. He only hoped Reggie wouldn't tell Pete Barker about him skipping out on his latest assignment.

The other half of Barker and Dawson Investigations thought he was still tailing Garth Bixby around town. They'd been hired to collect evidence that the sleazy political aide had been cheating on his wife.

If Reggie tells Pete I was here, he'll go batshit. But how could I say no?

Frankie turned to look out the window with forlorn eyes. He'd been wanting to ask Peyton out on a real date for months, but every time they talked, she just went on about what a nice guy he was and what a good friend he'd been.

It doesn't take a rocket scientist to get the message she's trying to send. Peyton likes me all right, but only as a friend.

Part of him wished he could just forget her altogether. And who would blame him? After all, Peyton had been partly responsible for him going to prison. And it was no thanks to her that he was walking around a free man.

The girl ran off to Memphis leaving me to rot in jail.

Scratching at the stubble on his chin, Frankie tried to block out the negative thoughts. After all, Peyton had tried to make amends, and she needed him if only to keep her company at her AA meetings.

He stared out the window at the gloomy sky like a lovesick teenager, not noticing that Peyton had come up behind him until she tapped him on the shoulder.

"Thanks for setting this up, Frankie. I really appreciate it."

He shrugged off her words and sighed.

"I know...I know. I'm a *really good friend.*"

Frankie's self-pity evaporated when he saw the girl standing behind Peyton. Her glassy eyes and pale, waxy skin told him she was the girl Peyton was trying to help.

"How you doing, Ruby?"

The girl didn't seem to register his greeting as she stared around the room. Peyton raised her eyes to his, and he had to force himself to look away as Reggie's voice sounded beside him.

"Peyton, good to see you. And this must be Ruby."

Introducing herself in a reassuring tone, Reggie led Ruby across the lobby, motioning to an alcove furnished with several comfortable-looking chairs around a television.

"Ruby, why don't you have a seat while we get your room ready."

Frankie and Peyton watched as Reggie helped Ruby settle into a chair. She walked back to them with worried eyes.

"Looks like she's in for a hard time," she said in a low voice. "Detox is never easy. It'll take time before she's in any kind of shape to give evidence or go through an interrogation."

"I understand," Peyton said. "And I don't plan on *interrogating* her, Dr. Horn. Nothing that combative. Once she's feeling better, I just hope to talk to her about the men who gave her those drugs."

Glancing toward Ruby's small figure, Frankie saw she had her eyes glued to the television, which was tuned to a special report on Channel Ten News.

He recognized Veronica Lee's long, dark hair, and moved closer to read the headline across the bottom of the screen.

Human Trafficking Victims Face Intimidation and Threats.

The reporter was conducting an interview, and as the camera panned to a young woman with her face in the shadows, Frankie strained to hear her response to Veronica's question.

"I'm still very scared, mainly for my family. They threatened to go after my whole family if I didn't do what they wanted. I tried-"

Frankie blinked as the screen went dark, then turned to see Reggie holding up a remote, having silenced the rest of the woman's words. Ruby was still staring at the blank screen, her kohl-rimmed eyes dark and sunken in her pale face.

Clenching his hands into fists, Frankie felt the familiar rush of anger at the men who preyed on vulnerable women.

Why do these bastards always target girls like Ruby...or like Franny?

The image of his younger sister flashed through Frankie's mind, adding a hot stab of pain and regret to his anger.

"These scumbags are really starting to *piss me off*."

Peyton turned wide eyes to Frankie, startled by his outburst. She tried to put a hand on his arm, but he shook it off, embarrassed by her look of pity and tired of playing the fool.

Avoiding Peyton's eyes, Frankie dug in the pocket of his jacket and pulled out a stick of gum. He tore off the wrapper and stuck the gum in his mouth. Chewing hard, he crossed to where Ruby sat and knelt in front of her chair.

"Ruby?"

He waited for her big, brown eyes to turn toward him.

"My name's Frankie Dawson, and I'm a private investigator. I wanna help Detective Bell find the lowlifes who were bothering you."

Doubt creased Ruby's forehead, but she didn't look away.

"But we're gonna need your help, and that means you have to go through detox. You gotta stay here until you're clean."

Past experience with addicts had taught Frankie it was unlikely the girl would stay once things got tough. The urge to use again would be too much. The need for relief would be too strong.

She might even run back to the men who'd abused her if she thought they'd supply her with drugs she couldn't get elsewhere.

"You gotta promise me, Ruby," Frankie said. "You don't know me from Adam, but I know you. I know you want to get better, and I'm gonna help you. And Reggie and Detective Bell are gonna help you."

"But what about Diablo? What if he finds me?"

Wrapping her thin arms around herself, Ruby began to rock slowly back and forth, her eyes darting around the room.

"Who's Diablo? Is he one of the guys we're looking for?"

Ruby nodded slowly, keeping her eyes on Frankie as he stood and looked toward Peyton.

"Supposedly, Diablo's the leader," Peyton murmured beside him. "According to her, all the girls were scared of him. They claim the guy has important connections in Willow Bay."

He paused at Peyton's choice of words.

Supposedly...according to her...they claim...

Running a frustrated hand through his shaggy hair, he wondered what chance Ruby would have if the people trying to help her didn't even believe her?

"She's not making this shit up, Peyton." Frankie swallowed hard, trying to keep his voice down. "You may not want to believe it, but I think she's telling the truth, and that we're gonna need her to catch these guys."

"We?" Peyton's eyes narrowed. "Are you thinking you're going to be involved in the investigation?"

Frankie didn't answer as Reggie held up a hand.

"Ruby's room is ready. We need to get her into the back now, so you guys will have to finish this conversation later."

"Oh, I think the conversation is over."

Frankie's voice was hard, but it softened as he turned to Ruby.

"Remember what I said, Ruby. Stay here and get clean. You've got people who will help you, but first, you gotta help yourself."

He was almost glad to see her roll her eyes at his words as any typical teenager would. She was just a kid really, and unlike Franny, she still had a chance.

Waiting until Ruby had disappeared into the back with Reggie, Frankie headed toward the door, suddenly anxious to get back on Garth Bixby's trail before Barker found out he'd been slacking off.

"Wait, Frankie!"

He swung around to see Peyton hurrying after him.

"I wasn't trying to be rude, but I think-"

"I know what you think, Peyton," Frankie said, unable to hold back his anger. "You think I'm just some dumb PI that you can call when you want something and then kick to the curb once you got whatever the hell it was you wanted."

Frankie hooked a thumb toward the door before she could reply.

"Now I have an important case going on, so if you're done with me, I'll get back to it."

"That's not fair," Peyton protested, following him out onto the sidewalk. "You know I appreciate your help, but the investigation is already being handled by the task force."

Stopping at her words, he shook his head.

"What task force?"

"The FBI is running a joint task force with our department," she admitted. "It isn't my place to bring anyone outside into the case."

The buzz of the phone in Frankie's pocket reminded him again that he should be working. Barker was probably looking for him.

"The feds, huh?" he said, the anger in his voice fading. "Good. I'm glad. I just hope they hurry up and catch these scumbags before they find out Ruby's here."

Peyton didn't call after him as he again turned and headed toward downtown. The afternoon chill had deepened, and Frankie pulled the collar of his jacket up around his ears as he walked, trying to keep warm, and trying to clear all thoughts of Peyton, Ruby, and even poor Franny from his mind.

He was tired of thinking, and tired of a world where scared young girls were abused and left to die.

CHAPTER SIX

Skylar washed the last of the lunch dishes and began to sweep the kitchen floor, trying to block out the angry ranting coming from the Professor's study. He'd been on his computer most of the day, stopping only to swallow down a sandwich and a glass of milk before he'd returned to his desk.

His foul mood hadn't improved since the previous day when he'd burst into the safe room to accuse her of helping Astrid escape, his fisted hands sticky with blood as he'd stood trembling over her.

"See what your treachery has caused, girl!"

Unable to remember exactly what had happened next, Skylar suddenly wasn't sure his furious arrival had been real after all; maybe it had been another one of her terrifying dreams.

She'd woken this morning to the Professor's angry voice at the hatch, yelling at her to come up and bring in wood for the stove. She had seen that Astrid wasn't in her bed and that the food she'd brought down for her the day before was untouched.

Not daring to ask the Professor where Astrid had gone, or if she would be back, Skylar had gone about her usual chores, avoiding the Professor and his thunderous mood as much as possible.

Looking through the bars on the kitchen window, Skylar saw that yesterday's storm had left behind a smooth layer of fresh snow. The white lawn was undisturbed other than a single trail of footprints leading from the back porch to the big barn where the Professor parked his truck and kept his tools.

As she stared toward the big wooden building, an image flashed into Skylar's mind. The barn door was open, and vivid smears of blood stained a path through the white snow leading into the dark shadows beyond.

Squeezing her eyes shut, Skylar breathed in deeply, tempted to find refuge in the only place she was truly safe. The only place where the Professor couldn't find her.

The safe room in her mind had offered a way out in the past, but it had also caused her to forget. Skylar had lost long stretches of time hiding there; she feared that one day she might not be able to find her way out.

I need to find out what happened to Astrid. I need to know if she ended up like all the others. There were others, weren't there?

Memories struggled to the surface. Skylar pictured the frightened face of the young woman who had been brought to the safe room only days before Astrid had arrived.

The tiny blonde woman had seemed weak, maybe even ill, but she'd somehow found the strength to attack the Professor without warning, managing to knock him off the ladder and climb past him.

That woman had gotten as far as the locked front door before the Professor caught up to her. Instead of dragging her back downstairs as Skylar had expected, he'd unlocked the door.

"You want to go outside, girl? Then go on."

He'd shoved the woman onto the porch, watching with grim, hard eyes as she had started to run through the wide, snow-covered yard before lunging at the gate leading out to the world beyond.

"Get back in the safe room," the Professor had ordered Skylar, crossing to his study where the big gunrack hung on the wall. "Stay there until I come for you."

41

The gunshot had sounded before Skylar made it to the hatch. Creeping on shaky legs to peer through the bars on the front window, she'd seen the woman sprawled on the ground beside the fence, her open, unseeing eyes turned up to the endless sky.

Those eyes had stayed with Skylar, merging with shadowy images of the other women who had come and gone in years past. Images that haunted her dreams, but which often eluded her waking memory no matter how hard she tried to conjure them.

A creak of the floorboard behind Skylar snapped her back to the present moment. The Professor was standing behind her, his face red from exertion, and his eyes narrowed.

"Go down to the safe room. I'm going on a trip."

Questions rose in her mind, but Skylar knew better than to open her mouth. Anything she said would be treated with suspicion. If she dared ask where he was going, or when he would return, the Professor would assume she wanted the information to help her escape. He trusted no one and gave nothing away.

Walking toward the study, Skylar felt a sudden impulse to make a break for the front door. She could grab one of the guns on the rack. Maybe bring it down over the Professor's head and take the heavy set of keys on his belt. One of those keys opened the lock on the big gate. She could be outside the compound within minutes.

But what then? Where would I go? How would I survive the forest?

A hand settled over her shoulder, pushing her forward as if he could sense her rebellious thoughts. She looked down to see the Professor wasn't wearing his usual glove. Instead, a bandage had been wrapped around his three remaining fingers.

"Don't try anything foolish while I'm gone."

Pulling open the hatch, the professor stepped back and motioned for her to descend the ladder. She raised her eyes to his, sensing something was different. His voice was filled with anger, but she thought she could hear something else as well. Was it regret?

Skylar wondered again what the Professor had seen on the computer that had caused such a violent reaction. Whatever it had been, it had rattled him badly.

Her eyes must have betrayed her concern, and he scowled as he gestured again toward the opening in the floor.

"Go on, you'll be safe down there while I'm gone."

Lowering herself onto the ladder, Skylar had the unsettling feeling that once she got to the bottom, she would never set foot on the ladder again. She descended with a heavy heart, weighted down by the possibility that the professor would never return.

The Professor retracted the ladder then stared down at her, one hand on the hatch, ready to close the only means of escape from her underground prison.

"Whatever happens while I'm gone, don't leave the safe room. If you make it outside the wall, the cold or the animals will kill you."

It was a familiar warning. One he'd issued many times before. But this time his ominous words sent a shiver through her.

"Are you coming back?"

The hoarse words escaped before she could stop them. He paused, as if surprised, then nodded.

"I'll be back."

Instead of closing the hatch, he continued to stare down at her.

"You're different than the others," he finally said, in a voice she'd rarely heard him use. "You've been taught to be obedient and to follow orders. You know better than to run."

Nodding at his words, Skylar felt hope. Maybe he'd change his mind about locking her in the safe room. Maybe if she promised not to escape, he'd let her stay upstairs while he was away.

His next words killed any hope she had.

"So, remember, for your own safety, don't ever try to leave."

The hatch swung closed, shutting out the natural light and throwing Skylar into pitch-black darkness. She didn't bother to feel around for the chain above her as she made her way toward her small room. There was no need for light. She knew the way by heart.

Feeling her way to the little cot by the wall, Skylar folded herself into a fetal position and willed herself to go to sleep. Maybe she could sleep until the Professor returned.

And maybe if the Professor never returns, I'll be like the women in my dreams. The ones who sleep forever and never come back.

CHAPTER SEVEN

The Professor checked the lock on the hatch again, then stomped over to his desk, still cursing himself for taking out Astrid Peterson without thinking through the consequences. His shock and fury at the news he'd seen had clouded his judgment.

It isn't every day you find out the woman who ruined your life and betrayed you has come back from the dead. And that the traitorous bitch is safe and well and enjoying the sunny Florida weather.

But no matter how justified his outrage, the Professor knew he should have thought through the business repercussions before he'd destroyed what would have been a very lucrative transaction.

Dropping heavily into his chair, the Professor banged both hands on his desk, then winced as his bruised fingers throbbed under the bandage in response.

The stupid girl almost broke my fucking fingers.

Astrid Peterson's near escape had come at the worst possible time. After almost two years of effort, the Professor had finally admitted to himself that his attempt to tame her into compliance had failed, and he'd quickly found a buyer willing to pay a small fortune for her.

The young college student had been a rare find. She'd been the most valuable woman the Professor had managed to get a hold of in many years. She wasn't like most of the women he routinely trafficked in. She wasn't a wasted addict or a used-up pro.

45

The fresh-faced innocence that made Astrid so valuable had also allowed the Professor to lure her into his car and had led to her ultimate fate. She'd been naïve, and she'd ended up in the wrong place, at the wrong time, trusting the wrong man.

But the Professor knew he'd also been foolish. His excitement at catching such a valuable prize had clouded his judgment, persuading him to keep Astrid for himself, rather than sell her on right away.

I must be getting old and soft. I should have known better. After everything that happened, I still haven't learned my lesson when it comes to lying, ungrateful women.

Resisting the urge to pound the desk again, the Professor sucked in a deep cleansing breath, reassuring himself that he'd only done what was necessary to clean up his mistake.

Once Astrid got past the front door and the gate, what choice did I have?

Besides, he'd been worried that her defiant attitude would rub off on Skylar. He didn't want the younger girl to get any ideas.

Pulling the keyboard toward him, the Professor couldn't resist clicking through the pictures he'd saved from the Channel Ten News website. His teeth clenched as he studied the crowd of people cheering at the campaign rally.

He zoomed in on a familiar face, his chest tightening as he studied the face of the woman who had haunted him for so long. Only she wasn't dead, and she wasn't a ghost. The woman was alive and well in Willow Bay, Florida.

And while I've been freezing my ass off up here for decades, she moved to the sunshine state. Probably laughed the whole way down there, too.

Forcing himself to close the window, he navigated to the darknet message board he'd set up to communicate with his suppliers and buyers. Men whose business dealings required total anonymity.

It was one of his contacts on the darknet board who had suggested he visit the Channel Ten website. A reporter was stirring up trouble for his partners down in South Florida and he thought the Professor might want to check it out.

That was when the Professor realized that twenty-eight years earlier he had been deceived in the worst possible way. Even though he knew the pictures didn't lie, it was still hard for him to believe it.

My wife isn't dead...and our daughter is alive, too.

Refusing to let the rage take over again, the Professor scrolled through the darknet board, looking for the user that would help him put his plan into motion. The darknet board he'd started was increasingly active and allowed the Professor to act as a middleman, connecting potential buyers with sellers of illicit goods and services.

Most of the time he remained cloaked in the virtual shadows of the darknet, but sometimes he'd agree to be more hands-on, and his long-haul truck allowed the transport of particularly lucrative or interesting cargo from one side of the country to the other if needed.

Often storing drugs or weapons at the compound he'd escaped to in the Bitterroot Valley all those years ago, the Professor doubted anyone would blame him for bringing some of the human cargo back to the compound to wait until a buyer was found.

His eyes found the username he was looking for. Diablo had been posting to the message board for the last several months, and his boasts about his operation had caught the professor's attention.

Although the message board users couldn't be traced via their IP address, the Professor was skilled at getting users to reveal personal details that often allowed him to uncover their true identities.

Preferring to know exactly who he was dealing with, the Professor would spend hours following a lead, while at the same time making sure to divulge nothing about himself. He'd been in hiding for the last twenty-eight years, and he considered himself an expert at it.

He clicked on the post by Diablo that had alerted him to the Channel Ten News reports and typed in a reply.

Interesting video. Looks like you have a problem down there, but I may be able to help you. Of course, I'd need a little favor in return.

The Professor waited a few minutes, then logged off.

It might take time for Diablo to get back to him, but that was okay. He already knew the man's real identity, and he had enough dirt on him to ensure his cooperation, although he doubted too much pressure would be needed.

Based on what he knew about the man, the Professor was confident they could work out a mutually beneficial arrangement. And he had plenty of work to do in the meantime. The truck needed to be loaded, and he had a long drive ahead of him.

Shrugging on his parka and pulling on his gloves, the Professor made his way through the backyard toward the old barn. He went straight to the big chest freezer and opened the lid, looking down at Astrid's stiff, alabaster skin without remorse.

I told her not to run. She should have listened.

He closed the lid and fastened the latch, deciding he would need the moving dolly and loading ramp to get the heavy freezer into the truck. And with his damaged hand, it wasn't going to be easy, but in the end, his pain and effort would pay off.

Twenty minutes later the truck was loaded, and he sat in the driver's seat, ready to roll.

Reaching his good hand into his pocket, he pulled out two laminated school ID cards and studied them. The newer one was still in good shape, but the older card was cracked and faded.

He stared down at the woman who'd promised to love, honor, and obey him. It had taken him over two decades, but he was determined to keep the oath he'd made the last time they'd been together.

If you ever leave me, I swear I'll find you and I'll kill you.

CHAPTER EIGHT

Veronica peered through her bedroom window, grimacing at the hint of frost on the glass. Raised in South Florida, she'd never gotten used to the occasional cold spells that descended in January and February, and the overcast sky prompted a groan as she pulled her red coat off a hanger.

"I think I need a new coat, Winston. Our viewers must be getting sick of seeing me in the same old thing every day this week."

The big orange tabby blinked up at her from his spot on the windowsill, clearly content with his own thick coat of fur.

Grabbing her purse and phone, Veronica hurried down the stairs. She'd slept in later than intended after Hunter had joined her and her mother for a late dinner the night before.

The smell of freshly brewed coffee drew her to the kitchen, and Veronica found herself smiling as she entered the warm room, remembering Hunter's tall figure stooped next to her mother's tiny body last night as she washed and he dried the dishes.

Hunter had been coming over more often lately, and it felt good to have a man in the house after all the years of it just being her and her mother. The man she'd assumed was out of her league when they'd first met, had proven to be a natural fit with her little family.

"Morning, Ma. Aren't you late for school?"

Ling Lee smiled at her daughter over the front page of the *Willow Bay Gazette.* She was still in her bathrobe and her dark hair, usually pulled back in a neat bun, was loose around her small shoulders.

"I took the morning off to take care of some campaign business," Ling said, her eyes returning to the paper. "I'll go in after lunch."

Veronica was pleased to see her mother so content, and glad that she was taking her run for mayor seriously. The election was only a few weeks away, although Ling didn't appear to be at all worried.

Pouring a hot stream of coffee into a thermos, Veronica decided she'd have to eat breakfast on the run. Three days had passed since she'd talked to Nessa and Agent Marlowe about Astrid Peterson's disturbing comment, and she wanted to stop by the police station before heading into work.

Unable to get Astrid Peterson out of her mind, Veronica had spent hours poring over the news reports and researching the tragic story of the college student's sudden disappearance from her Montana campus. She was more certain than ever that the girl must have been taken against her will, and that she was still alive and needed help.

Veronica stepped out of the warm house into the chilly air, pulling her coat around her as she hurried to her Jeep. She knew the weather in Willow Bay was mild compared to most cities at this time of year, but that didn't stop her from turning the Jeep's heater to full blast as she backed out onto Marigold Lane.

Her phone buzzed as she prepared to turn onto Waterside Drive.

"Hi, Finn, what's up?"

"Hey, Ronnie, I just took a message from a girl named Ruby Chase. She says she has information you may be interested in. Something to do with the trafficking series."

Dread settled in Veronica's chest at the thought of yet another young girl who had a story of abuse and violence to tell. Ever since she'd started the special series, she'd been getting calls from women who'd been targeted by traffickers.

Women who were too scared or ashamed to tell their own family about their ordeal, but who desperately needed to tell someone their story, and who wanted to do their part in stopping other women from falling into the same trap.

"She asked you to go by and see her," Finn continued. "Apparently she's in rehab at a place downtown called Hope House."

"Yes, I know where that is," Veronica said, already steering the Jeep toward the exit lane. "I'll swing by there first. Then I plan to go by the WBPD and see if they have an update on Astrid Peterson."

Turning into the Hope House parking lot ten minutes later, Veronica parked in a Visitors Only space and hurried through the glass doors, wondering if she should show her press badge at the reception desk.

A familiar face smiled at her from the doorway of a large meeting room as a group of men took their seats in a wide circle of chairs. Reggie Horn crossed the lobby, her high heels clicking a hurried beat against the hard floor as she moved to intercept Veronica.

"It's good to see you, Veronica, but we don't allow press in the facility without prior arrangement. I'm sure you can understand; it's a privacy concern for our patients and their families."

"I'm actually here at the request of a patient, Dr. Horn. A girl named Ruby Chase called and asked me to visit her."

Reggie's face registered surprise, then concern.

"I don't know if that's such a good idea."

"I want to talk to her."

Hearing a quiet voice behind her, Veronica turned to face a young woman in faded jeans and an oversized t-shirt. She was pale, with dark circles under puffy eyes and fading bruises on her arms.

"Ruby, I don't think you're ready to give any interviews, and-"

"Maybe we could just talk," Veronica interrupted, watching as Ruby's eyes darted around the room. "I'll consider our conversation to be off the record. No cameras, and no mention on the news, I promise."

Reggie looked toward the meeting room with anxious eyes.

"Okay, I'm scheduled to lead a meeting now, but you two can sit in the rec room and talk. I'll check on you as soon as I'm done."

"Thank you, Dr. Horn."

Veronica glanced over the director's shoulder toward the meeting room and frowned.

"I didn't know Hope House also treated male patients."

"Well, our residential program doesn't," Reggie said, moving her small body in front of Veronica as if she was trying to shield the men in the room from view. "But we host NA and AA meetings here for anyone in the community who wants to attend. The attendees expect anonymity and privacy, of course."

Watching as Reggie returned to the meeting room, Veronica glimpsed the back of a large man perched awkwardly on a straight-backed chair. Something about him seemed familiar, but the door closed before she could get a clear view.

"The rec room's through there."

Ruby led Veronica down the hall into a brightly lit room. Several women sat around the television watching a talk show as Ruby made her way between the tables to a corner alcove.

Sinking into a comfortable chair next to Ruby, Veronica studied the girl's face, trying to see past the puffy eyes and bruises.

"So, how'd you end up here, Ruby?" Veronica asked, deciding it would be best to jump right in. "What's your story?"

Ruby dropped her eyes and hesitated as if wondering where to start, or maybe unsure what was safe to tell.

"Anything you say here stays between me and you, Ruby," Veronica assured her. "And I don't want you to say anything that makes you uncomfortable."

Nodding her head, Ruby kept her eyes on the floor as she began to speak in a trembling voice.

"I got hooked on pills back home. Things got...bad, so when I turned eighteen, I took off."

She crossed her arms over her chest in a defensive gesture and swallowed hard.

"I ended up trusting the wrong person and got picked up by Diablo's guys."

Veronica sat forward at Ruby's words. She'd heard many rumors about the ruthless leader of the trafficking ring operating in South Florida. So far Veronica couldn't be sure if Diablo was a real man, or just a myth used to scare the gang's victim's into compliance.

"This man...this Diablo. Did you ever see him?"

The question prompted Ruby to lift her eyes.

"I saw him, all right," she murmured. "He was yelling at the men to load the truck the day I managed to get out of the compound."

"The compound? What kind of compound were you in?"

Shrugging her shoulders, Ruby tried to explain.

"It was like a prison compound or maybe a military camp," she said, shaking her head at the memory. "There was a fence all around with barbed wire and everything. Some of the guys were walking around with guns."

Veronica felt a twinge of doubt at the image Ruby's words conjured. Could the traffickers have set up a secret prison camp in the area without being detected?

"Could you find the place again?"

"Oh, I never want to go back there." Ruby's eyes widened at the possibility. "Diablo would kill me if I did. Especially if he knew I'd been talking to you and to the cops."

"The cops?"

Ruby nodded, dropping her eyes again.

"I got picked up for shoplifting after I left the compound. I was just trying to get some food, but the cops found drugs. They wanted to lock me up, but Detective Bell brought me here instead."

"And you told the police about Diablo, and about the compound?"

An angry glint shown in Ruby's eyes.

"I tried, but they wouldn't believe me."

Rising from the chair, Ruby moved to the window. She wrapped her arms around her thin body and stared out toward the parking lot.

"I'm sorry they didn't believe you," Veronica said, feeling a guilty flush spread over her cheeks at her own doubt. "But I do, and I'd like to help stop these men before they hurt other women."

Ruby didn't respond.

"If you can describe what the man called Diablo looks like, we can make a composite drawing, and–"

A soft cry interrupted Veronica's words as Ruby turned around, her face deathly pale, her dark eyes filled with fear.

"I can't do this. I need you to leave. It isn't safe."

"What isn't safe?"

Scurrying toward the door, Ruby didn't stop or answer as Veronica called after her.

"Ruby? If you want to talk again, you can call me."

But Ruby had already disappeared down the hall.

* * *

Veronica left Hope House feeling as if she'd just failed an important test. Ruby Chase had wanted to tell her story, but something Veronica had said or done stopped her.

What was it that made her clam up and panic?

Parking her Jeep in the downtown parking garage, Veronica tried to bring her focus back to the task at hand. She needed to talk to

Nessa. Hopefully, the police chief had an update on the search for Astrid Peterson.

As she approached the police station, Veronica saw Peyton Bell standing on the sidewalk. The detective wore a black police-issue jacket and a thick woolen scarf. Her short hair had been tucked away under a dark knit cap.

Looks like Peyton hates cold weather as much as I do.

Veronica buttoned her red coat and stuck her hands in the pockets, wishing she'd remembered to bring her gloves.

"Detective Bell, how are you?"

Veronica gave an awkward nod, thinking that she'd never be able to repay the detective who had saved her mother's life when Ling Lee had been abducted the previous fall.

"I'm doing pretty good," Peyton replied, but her smile melted as she stared past Veronica.

Looking around, Veronica saw Detective Marc Ingram marching toward them. Peyton's partner wore a nasty scowl as he approached.

"Are you working on the joint trafficking task force?" Veronica asked Peyton, determined to ignore Ingram. "Has there been any progress that you can share with the community?"

"No comment, Ms. Lee," Ingram said behind her. "If you have any questions for the department, ask our media relations officer. She's right over there."

Veronica could see Tenley Frost standing outside the police station. She appeared to be deep in conversation with Nessa Ainsley, and Veronica suspected the media relations officer wouldn't be happy to see her.

Anticipating a cold reception, Veronica was surprised when Tenley looked up and waved a graceful arm in her direction. She left Peyton and Ingram behind, eager to speak to Nessa while she had the chance.

"Hello, Veronica!" Tenley called out in the friendly tone she usually reserved for on-camera press conferences. "How's your mother's campaign going?"

The question stiffened Veronica's back. Tenley was undoubtedly being friendly in hopes of getting information about Ling Lee's campaign strategy. After all, the woman worked for Mayor Hadley. She was bound to want to help her boss get re-elected.

"I'm sure it's going very well," Veronica replied, without a smile. "But since I'm a reporter, I don't get involved in the campaign for any candidate, even my own mother."

"Of course," Tenley said with a wink, smoothing back a glossy strand of auburn hair. "I just wanted you to know, *off the record*, that your mother has my vote."

Blinking in surprise, Veronica gaped at Tenley, then turned to see if Nessa had overheard the unexpected admission.

"Don't look so shocked," Nessa said, a wry smile lifting the corners of her mouth. "Anyone who gives a hoot about Willow Bay, or who knows what Mayor Hadley's really like, is planning to vote for your mother."

Tenley nodded her agreement.

"Especially anyone who plans to raise a daughter in this town."

The comment brought another smile to Nessa's face. She turned her light blue eyes to Tenley.

"How is that little angel of yours?"

A pleased blush turned Tenley's smooth skin pink.

"Little Avery Lynn is perfect." Tenley's happy smile faded. "Although, I have to admit this town is beginning to feel like a dangerous place to raise a daughter."

Veronica raised her eyebrows at the city's official spokesperson.

"I'm assuming that comment was also *off the record*?"

Without waiting for a reply, Veronica turned back to Nessa, her thoughts returning to poor Ruby Chase hiding in fear over at Hope House.

"Tell me, Chief Ainsley, for the record, do you think the women in this town are in danger?"

CHAPTER NINE

Nessa winced at Veronica's blunt question, knowing she couldn't tell the reporter that Willow Bay was unsafe for women without causing panic in the community. But she was also reluctant to make a blanket statement that there was nothing to fear. Either option could cause trouble down the line.

"Willow Bay is safer than other cities in South Florida," Nessa finally said. "Crime rates are much higher in Miami or Tampa."

The image of Agent Marlowe's map of trafficking activity flashed through her mind. The red and blue stickers had painted a grim picture. She could only hope the press wouldn't get hold of the map before the task force could make some real progress.

"I think that's my cue to leave," Tenley said, her voice losing some of its warmth. "I've got to get back to City Hall."

As soon as Tenley was out of earshot, Veronica turned to Nessa.

"Have you heard anything more about Astrid Peterson? Any update from Agent Marlowe or your detectives?"

"I've assigned the case to Vanzinger and Jankowski, but I haven't gotten an official report from them on their progress yet."

Noting the disappointment on Veronica's face, Nessa promised herself that she'd check in with the detectives before lunchtime. The sudden thought of lunch made her stomach lurch, and she wondered if she was coming down with a stomach bug.

Maybe one of the boys brought home the flu. That's all I need now.

"...and I'm glad it's not Detective Ingram."

Nessa frowned, realizing she'd missed Veronica's last remark.

"I was just saying I'm glad you assigned Detectives Vanzinger and Jankowski to the case instead of Detective Ingram," Veronica repeated. "I'm sorry to say, but I can't stand that man."

Looking around to make sure they were alone, Nessa leaned forward and lowered her voice.

"You don't have to be sorry," she murmured. "You aren't the only one to feel that way. And *off the record*, Mayor Hadley signed an iron-clad agreement with Ingram which allowed him back on the force against my advice."

Veronica rolled her eyes.

"Why doesn't that surprise me?" she asked, shaking her head in disgust. "That man doesn't ever seem to learn his lesson."

"Well, he's not the only one. Old Judge Eldredge mediated the agreement, so I don't have a hope in hell of getting it thrown out."

The frown on Veronica's face deepened.

"You mean the same Judge Eldredge that lets criminals like Nick Sargent walk free on bail?"

Nessa nodded, her own outrage bubbling up to match Veronica's.

"Yep, that's the one. But if we're lucky, Judge Eldredge will be voted out of office along with Mayor Hadley next month."

A high-pitched scream sounded somewhere in the distance. Nessa looked around in alarm as a man came charging down the sidewalk, his eyes bulging underneath a Miami Heat baseball cap.

"What's going on?" Nessa called out. "Are you hurt?"

"There's a woman sitting on a bench in Old Willow Square," the man gasped as he ran toward the police station. "She's...she's *dead*."

* * *

59

The woman sat on a wooden bench under a gnarled willow oak tree. She was bundled up for winter in a puffy black parka, black jeans, and black boots. A thick woolen scarf was draped around her neck, and a black knit cap covered her head.

Long strands of strawberry blonde hair had escaped the cap, falling over her shoulders and obstructing a clear view of her face as she appeared to stare down at a newspaper on her lap.

"Are you sure she's dead?"

The woman in front of Nessa nodded.

"She's stone cold. I checked her pulse just to be sure, but I used to be a nurse over at Willow Bay General until I retired last year, and I know a dead body when I touch it."

Hearing the whine of an ambulance siren coming closer, Nessa knew she had to focus on securing the scene. A crowd had started to gather, and she didn't want pictures of the poor woman's body posted online before she'd had a chance to figure out who the woman was, and what had happened to her.

She called over to Andy Ford, who was staring at the body with wide eyes. The young officer had been the first one on the scene, and he seemed shaken by the surreal sight.

"Officer Ford, call Eddings out here. You two can cordon off the scene while we wait for the medical examiner."

Footsteps pounded the pavement behind her. Vanzinger appeared at her shoulder, closely followed by Jankowski.

"What the hell?" Vanzinger murmured.

"We need Iris here as soon as possible," Nessa said, catching sight of the ambulance crew running across the square. "Unfortunately, these guys are way too late to be of any help."

The paramedics confirmed the retired nurse's assessment under Nessa's watchful gaze, taking care not to disturb the body before rolling the empty stretcher back to the ambulance.

Minutes later Wesley Knox appeared in the crowd using his thick arms and broad shoulders to make a path for Iris Nguyen. The petite medical examiner followed closely behind the brawny forensic technician. She wore white protective coveralls and carried the big black bag she always took with her to a death scene.

"We need to get a tent set up," Iris called to Wesley as she surveyed the scene. "And I want to take plenty of photos before we move anything."

Iris turned to Nessa with a grim expression.

"I think you need to get Alma Garcia and her team out here fast."

"You think this is a suspicious death?" Nessa asked. "Couldn't she just have sat down and had a heart attack or something?"

Raising her eyebrows, Iris shook her head.

"She wouldn't still be sitting upright if she'd suffered a sudden fatal event of some kind," Iris explained. "I'd say that her body's been staged and that whoever left her here didn't want her death to be discovered until he was long gone."

Jankowski hovered at Nessa's shoulder and cleared his throat.

"You want me and Vanzinger to take this one, Chief?"

She nodded slowly, her plan to ask him for an update on the Astrid Peterson case now forgotten.

"Yes, and you probably want to start by interviewing the witnesses who found her on the bench."

She pointed out the man in the Miami Heat hat and the retired nurse still standing in the crowd, then waited as a tent was erected around the bench. Once Iris was inside performing her initial exam of the body, Nessa waved Vanzinger over.

"I'm assigning this one to you and Jankowski, and I expect we'll need to give a press conference before the day is over, so we need to get feedback from Iris as quickly as possible."

"Speaking of the press..."

61

Following Vanzinger's gaze, Nessa saw Veronica Lee and a Channel Ten News cameraman setting up just outside the scene perimeter. A crew from Channel Six News snaked their way through the crowd just behind them.

Stress began to work its way up Nessa's back as she anticipated the media frenzy around the case. Her thoughts were interrupted by Wesley's deep voice from inside the tent.

"Chief Ainsley, can you come in here?"

Nessa ducked under the flap, her pulse quickening as she joined Iris beside the bench. The woman's parka had been removed to reveal the bluish flesh of her back, and Nessa felt her stomach heave as she saw the red, ragged bullet hole in the stiff, mottled skin.

"Looks like we may have found our cause of death," Iris said, as Nessa felt Vanzinger slip into the tent beside her. "And based on her internal body temperature and the lividity of her skin, I'd say she was frozen within hours of death."

"Frozen? Like, in a freezer frozen?"

Iris nodded.

"She's just starting to thaw. Decomposition hasn't even begun."

Circling to the other side of the body, Vanzinger bent to stare at the woman's face, still partially shielded by her curtain of reddish, blonde hair.

"So, you're saying someone shot her in the back, kept her body in a freezer, then staged her here on this bench so we would find her?"

He raised a long finger and lifted a strand of hair to reveal the woman's cold, stiff face. Suddenly dizzy, Nessa turned and felt her way out of the tent, lifting her face to the sky and sucking in a breath of cold, fresh air.

"You okay, Chief?"

Peyton Bell stood guard by the perimeter as the crowd continued to swell. Both women turned to Vanzinger as he charged out of the tent after Nessa, his face flushed a deep red to match his crewcut.

"Maybe I'm crazy," Vanzinger gasped, "but I'd say that woman in there looks an awful lot like Astrid Peterson."

"Who's Astrid Peterson?"

Nessa ignored Peyton's question as she stared at Vanzinger, her mind spinning with the possibility that the woman who'd disappeared from Montana almost two years before could have turned up on a bench in the middle of Old Willow Square.

"How sure are you?"

She watched Vanzinger pull out his phone and tap on the display. The color in his face drained away as he held up the phone to show her Astrid Peterson's image from the FBI's missing person website.

"Based on this, I'd say I'm pretty damn sure."

CHAPTER TEN

Peyton glanced down at Vanzinger's phone. A pretty woman with long, strawberry blonde hair filled the screen. The kind of vibrant young woman she'd expect to see on a shampoo commercial. Was that same woman inside the tent?

"Who is Astrid Peterson?"

Her eyes were still on Vanzinger's phone.

"She was a college student in Montana. Went missing about two years ago," Vanzinger said, sticking his phone back in his pocket. "The local police organized a search, called in the FBI, but they never were able to find out what happened to her."

Looking toward Nessa, Peyton was alarmed to see the chief of police swaying on her feet. She reached out a hand to steady her.

"Chief? Are you okay?"

Nessa nodded and straightened her shoulders.

"I'll be fine," she murmured, giving Peyton a weak smile. "I should have eaten something for lunch. And seeing that poor girl in there certainly doesn't help."

"I hope the FBI has Astrid Peterson's DNA on file," Vanzinger said. "If they managed to get a profile, we'll know for sure it's her."

Lifting a finger to her lips, Nessa motioned for the big detective to keep his voice down. Peyton looked around to see who might be listening in to their conversation.

The historic square was jammed with people trying to get a glimpse inside the tent, but no one seemed close enough to overhear anything they were saying.

Her eyes landed on the Channel Ten News crew shooting live at the edge of the scene. Veronica Lee stood in front of the camera holding a microphone and gesturing to the tent behind her.

"I don't want Veronica to find out the victim might be Astrid Peterson," Nessa said in a hushed voice. "Not until we're sure."

Peyton raised her eyebrows and turned to Vanzinger.

"How does Veronica know about Astrid Peterson?"

"Astrid Peterson submitted a comment on the Channel Ten website," he murmured. "At least someone claiming to be Astrid did. Said she was like the other girls in Veronica's reports and that she was being held by a man who wouldn't let her go."

Glancing back at Veronica, Peyton understood Nessa's reluctance. If the woman in the tent had reached out to the reporter for help, and subsequently been killed trying to escape, it would be a bitter pill for Veronica to swallow.

"If Astrid disappeared in Montana, why did she contact a reporter all the way down here in Willow Bay?" Peyton asked, her past experience as a detective on the missing person's squad in Memphis kicking in. "Maybe he was holding her down here, or has connections in the area?"

Vanzinger's eyes narrowed in concentration.

"Maybe leaving her here for us to find is the killer's way of stopping us from looking for her where she was taken."

He spoke slowly as if still piecing together the thought.

"Could be this is the guy's way of saying, *no need to look anywhere else, cause here she is.*"

"You could be right," Nessa said, her voice sounding stronger. "But, if my gut is right, I think he's telling us, *no need to look anywhere else, cause here I am.*"

The police chief's words sent a shiver of foreboding through Peyton as she surveyed the growing crowd.

Is the man who killed Astrid Peterson watching us right now?

It seemed that everyone in Willow Bay had arrived to watch the spectacle. Curious faces peered toward the tent, and onlookers held up cameras. Peyton tried to study each face, knowing that killers sometimes returned to the scene of the crime.

The sick bastard will want to enjoy the show.

Searching the throng for suspicious bystanders and unfamiliar faces, Peyton realized she knew almost everyone in the little square, which had been built up around an ancient willow oak tree in the heart of the town.

Peyton had grown up in Willow Bay, and she was beginning to feel like she belonged again. Her move to Memphis had been an attempt to run away from her mistakes, but after years of self-imposed exile, the little town, and her sick mother, had called her home.

She'd been disappointed to find the warm, small-town atmosphere still concealed an undercurrent of discontent and disillusion induced by the corruption and incompetence of the town's leaders. Perhaps small towns weren't so different than big cities after all.

The arrival of the crime scene unit caused a ripple of excitement, and Peyton watched as Nessa and Vanzinger waved senior crime scene technician Alma Garcia past the perimeter and into the tent.

Catching sight of Ingram pushing his way through the crowd, Peyton stepped back toward the perimeter, in no mood to deal with her partner's negative attitude.

"Detective Bell?"

Veronica Lee stood just across the yellow perimeter tape. Her bright green eyes and cheerful red coat seemed out of place in the grim surroundings as Peyton glanced up in dismay.

"I'm not authorized to give any statements or information about the crime scene," she said automatically, taking a step back.

"I actually wanted to ask you about another case."

Veronica's microphone was nowhere to be seen as she rubbed her gloveless hands together in an effort to warm them.

"This may not be the right time, but I'm wondering if you've had any luck finding the men who held Ruby Chase?"

It wasn't a question Peyton had expected, and she hesitated, unsure what she could say, and how much Veronica already knew.

"Has Ruby Chase contacted you? What did she say?"

Holding her breath, Peyton waited for Veronica's response. Had Ruby mentioned the gang's rumored connection inside the WBPD? Was that what the reporter really wanted to ask her about?

"She didn't say much," Veronica admitted, "But she did mention that she'd seen the gang leader. A man called Diablo. Several other women I've interviewed for my trafficking reports have talked about this man as well."

"I can't discuss Ruby Chase or reveal anything she told me in the course of the investigation," Peyton said, relieved that Ruby hadn't shared the rumor about the WBPD's connection to the Diablo syndicate with the reporter. "It's her story to tell."

Veronica hesitated, then nodded.

"Okay, I can respect that," she said, sticking her hands into her coat pocket. "But can you tell me what the WBPD or the FBI task force is doing to track down Diablo?"

A nasty laugh alerted Peyton that Ingram had found her. He stood a few feet away staring at Veronica, an amused sneer on his thin face.

"Are you falling for that old Diablo hoax?" he snorted. "Stories about Diablo have floated around ever since I joined the force. You pick up any street kid and they'll blame this boogey man for everything they've ever done."

Rolling her eyes at Ingram's remarks, Peyton shook her head.

"Regardless of what my partner says, this guy sounds real to me."

An angry flush colored Ingram's face at her words. He looked past her and lifted a skinny arm toward the crowd, pointing to Frankie Dawson, who was heading in their direction.

"Diablo's no more a real man than that loser's a real detective."

Peyton flinched as Ingram's angry words hung in the air. She met Frankie's eyes over Veronica's head, but he didn't smile or react as he pushed past her toward the front of the crowd.

Had he heard Ingram's insulting remark? Or was he still mad about the other day at Hope House?

"Frankie Dawson is one of the best investigators in this town, Detective Ingram." Veronica's voice was ice cold. "And one of the most decent men I know. Unfortunately, I've never heard a single person say the same about you."

Spinning on her heel, Veronica moved back toward the Channel Ten News crew. Peyton turned to see Ingram staring open-mouthed after her. She couldn't hold back a smile as she watched her partner stomp away. But her smile faded as she thought about the look on Frankie's face as he'd passed by.

Veronica's right. Frankie is a good, decent man. Maybe too good for me.

CHAPTER ELEVEN

Frankie looked for Garth Bixby in the crowded square, angry with himself for letting Peyton distract him from the Bixby case again. After he'd snuck off to Hope House earlier in the week, Barker had warned him that Barbie Bixby wouldn't hesitate to hire another firm if she decided Barker and Dawson Investigations wasn't up to the job.

Shoving his cold hands in the pockets of his oversized hoodie, Frankie searched the milling crowd, sure that the subject of his investigation had been in the stream of city workers who'd heard the sirens and swarmed through the doors, eager to witness whatever drama was unfolding in Old Willow Square.

Garth Bixby was Mayor Hadley's campaign manager, and Frankie had spent the morning shivering at his post outside City Hall, ready to tail Bixby if he left the building.

Glad for a chance to stretch his legs, Frankie had followed the rush of people heading toward Old Willow Square, keeping his eyes on Bixby's slick, gelled head until Peyton's slim figure had captured his attention. His feet had instinctively moved in her direction when he'd caught sight of her standing just beyond the yellow crime scene tape.

Only after he'd overheard Ingram's insult, and seen the look of dismay in Peyton's eyes, had Frankie remembered that she didn't want him involved in her investigations. It appeared that her weasel-faced partner Marc Ingram felt the same way.

Approaching the stately willow oak that dominated the square, Frankie circled the huge trunk of the tree that had been planted in the middle of town more than a century earlier.

The tree stretched up fifty feet into the crisp, winter air, while the branches, still bearing a respectable amount of leaves despite the season, cloaked the crowd below in frigid shadows.

A familiar figure suddenly appeared, emerging from the shade of the tree just as he'd started to turn away. Mackenzie Jensen's long, brown hair and cat-eyed glasses were hard to miss, even in a crowd, and Frankie had seen the Willow Bay Gazette's star journalist many times during the last week as he'd tailed Garth Bixby.

The sleazy politician had a habit of visiting the shapely young journalist on a daily basis, and she featured in many of the photos and videos Frankie had taken for Barbie Bixby's growing collection.

Following Mackenzie in the direction of the tent behind the perimeter, Frankie didn't realize the woman was heading straight for Peyton Bell until she called out a question.

"Can we get a statement, too, Detective Bell?"

Mackenzie raised her voice louder than was necessary to attract Peyton's attention, and Frankie felt sure the journalist wanted the people in the crowd to hear her.

"Or is Veronica Lee the only one who gets a special briefing? Tell me, is that because her mother's running for mayor?"

Frankie felt a pang of anger as he took in the startled look on Peyton's face, but he knew he couldn't step in and defend her from Mackenzie's verbal attack without drawing attention to himself.

I won't be any use on the Bixby case once Mackenzie Jensen notices me.

Suddenly Nessa Ainsley was standing in front of Peyton.

"Ms. Jensen, the WBPD has no official statement to give at this time," Nessa said in a cold voice. "In future, please address all questions to Tenley Frost, our media relations officer."

Glaring at Nessa with undisguised contempt, the journalist stood her ground, undaunted by Nessa's icy demeanor.

"Aren't you capable of answering my question yourself, Chief Ainsley?" Mackenzie asked. "I simply want to know why Veronica Lee received a private briefing from your detective while the rest of the press has to wait for the city to schedule a press conference."

Frankie winced at the venom he'd heard in Mackenzie's voice, but Nessa seemed unruffled by the journalist's question. She turned and waved to Andy Ford, calling out in a voice that betrayed no anger.

"Get Eddings to help you move the perimeter back a few yards, Officer Ford. I think we need a little more room here."

Frankie gave a silent nod of satisfaction and looked over to see how Peyton had reacted to Nessa's intervention, but the spot where she'd been standing was empty.

Catching a glimpse of Peyton's slim figure and dark cap of hair as she disappeared through the gate leading back to City Hall, Frankie once again found his feet moving in her direction.

Screw Garth Bixby. I need to make sure Peyton's okay.

He hurried down the path and through the gate. Spotting Peyton standing on the steps of City Hall, he decided to take a shortcut across the lawn. When Marc Ingram appeared behind her, Frankie had just enough time to duck behind a statue of the town's first mayor.

Peeking around the statue, he saw Peyton's shoulders slump as she noticed Ingram approaching.

"So, who's the dead girl?" Ingram asked. "Nessa wouldn't tell me anything, but I bet she told you."

"I don't think the victim's a local," Peyton said in a vague voice crossing her arms over her chest. "Vanzinger and Jankowski have caught the case, so it's not really our business, anyway."

"Victim? So, it is a homicide?"

"I assume so." Peyton's voice tightened in irritation. "Otherwise they wouldn't have called out the crime scene techs."

Inching closer to Peyton, Ingram dropped his voice, and Frankie had to strain to hear his next words.

"So, what's the deal with the street kid?" he muttered. "I heard she left with you the other day, and when you came back to the station you were alone. Where'd you take her?"

Frankie's body tensed as he waited for Peyton's response.

Please don't tell that schmuck where Ruby is. He'll screw it all up.

Leaning against the cold marble of the statue, Frankie resisted the urge to step out and tell the little weasel just what he thought of him.

If Peyton knew he was hiding there, she'd think he was stalking her. Besides, she was a grown woman and a seasoned detective. She could handle her partner without any help from an amateur like him.

"Chief Ainsley and Riley Odell decided that Ruby needed to go into treatment," Peyton finally said. "They want her to be fit to give evidence if needed."

"Evidence against who?" Ingram snorted. "Don't tell me they believe the bullshit she was trying to feed us about being force-fed drugs by some guy named *Diablo*."

Frankie frowned at the scorn in Ingram's voice. The man was obviously in serious denial.

"You think she just came up with that name out of her head?" Peyton asked. "And how do you explain the other women who have shared the same story."

"What other women?"

Ingram sounded confused.

"The other women who have talked to Veronica Lee," Peyton said, suddenly sounding tired. "She's interviewed women who have gone through the same ordeal as Ruby. Women who've named Diablo as the leader. How can you think it's some sort of coincidence?"

"So, you're going to believe some two-bit reporter who's desperate for ratings, and a street kid trying to beat a drug rap over Agent Marlowe and the FBI task force?"

Raising his eyebrows at the mention of the task force, Frankie tried to quiet his breathing. He wanted to hear what the feds were doing to help Ruby and the other women.

"What do you mean? What did Agent Marlowe say?"

"He agrees with me," Ingram said. "Diablo is a myth, not a man."

Before Peyton could react, Ingram jogged down the steps toward the sidewalk and the street beyond, his jacket flapping behind him.

"I'm going to check out the convenience store where they picked Ruby Chase up for shoplifting," he called over his shoulder. "See if I can find out the real story."

Peyton shook her head in frustration, then started down the stairs after her partner. Frankie wished he could call out and stop her, or maybe follow after her, but instead he only watched her go.

Reaching into his pocket, he pulled out his phone and tapped on Barker's name, then waited for his partner to answer.

"Where the hell are you?"

"I'm over by City Hall following Bixby," Frankie lied, walking back the way he'd come, his gait slow and heavy with disappointment. "Why, where are you?"

"I just got to Old Willow Square. I'm standing in front of the crime scene tent, and I have eyes on Bixby."

Frankie began to move faster, leaving the quiet grounds of City Hall behind as he plunged back into the throng of concerned citizens and curious onlookers clogging up Old Willow Square.

Weaving his way through the crowd toward the tent, Frankie saw Barker's wide shoulders and salt and pepper head of hair. His partner was standing only yards away from Garth Bixby.

The political aide wore a black leather jacket that had been tailored to flatter his leanly muscled frame and expensive aviator sunglasses

73

that concealed his eyes. He stood at the edge of the perimeter tape, chatting up Mackenzie Jensen.

"You been here long?" Frankie asked, slipping up next to Barker.

"Long enough to know *you* haven't been here."

Barker studied Frankie's downcast expression, then turned his eyes back toward a crime scene technician dressed in white coveralls and protective booties. The tech appeared to be taking soil samples from the area surrounding the bench.

"Lucky for you Bixby's been hanging around here, so you haven't missed much," Barker said, his voice softening.

After a beat of silence, Barker looked over.

"So, any idea who's in the tent?"

Shaking his head, Frankie leaned closer.

"I heard it's a woman who's not from around here. They haven't released her identity yet."

"Heard from who?"

Frankie put a hand on Barker's arm and tugged him toward the old willow oak, needing a break from the jostling crowd.

"I overheard Peyton Bell and Marc Ingram talking," Frankie admitted. "According to Peyton, the woman in the tent isn't a local."

Giving Barker a sideways glance, Frankie wondered if he should tell Barker about Ruby Chase, but his partner spoke again before he could make up his mind.

"I'd say if the girl isn't local, it's probable her killer isn't either."

"I've been watching the crowd," Frankie said, scratching at the stubble on his chin. "You know, to see if I could spot anyone suspicious that may have returned to the scene."

Barker nodded, his eyes scanning the crowd as he listened.

"I haven't seen any new faces," Frankie continued, his mood sinking even lower. "Just the same old suspects."

"Well, keep your eyes on Bixby," Barker reminded him. "Barbie Bixby isn't paying us to find whoever killed the woman in that tent."

Throwing a resentful glare in Bixby's direction, Frankie nodded.

"I've been sticking to the slimy bastard like glue. Barbie Bixby will get all the evidence she needs, and more than she can stomach."

"Evidence isn't always enough in this town," Barker murmured.

Frankie followed Barker's gaze, his eyes drawn to a man who stood a head taller than the rest of the crowd. The man stooped to speak to his companion, and Frankie scowled as he recognized Nick Sargent's handsome face.

"If evidence were enough to convince Judge Eldredge to make a fair ruling, that crook wouldn't be walking around like he's not got a care in the world."

Barker's words rekindled the old anger in Frankie's chest.

Around here the guilty walk free and the innocent get locked up.

Swallowing the bitter words that threatened, Frankie turned his head away. He saw that Channel Ten News was reporting live from the scene again. As Veronica Lee spoke earnestly into the camera, Hunter Hadley approached the crew, a white Labrador retriever close behind him. The newsman's arrival lessened the weight in Frankie's chest, and he decided it was time to shake his pessimistic mood.

See, it's not all bad. We've still got a few good men left in this town.

CHAPTER TWELVE

Hunter Hadley tried to keep his eyes on Veronica as she faced the camera and described the scene behind her, but Gracie kept pulling on her leash and pawing at the ground, clearly anxious about being in the midst of such a big crowd.

Kneeling to stroke the Lab's soft white fur, Hunter looked up to see that the crew had stopped shooting. He tried to calm the big dog, but she backed away and barked loudly, before again pawing at the ground in agitation.

"Gracie's signaling," Finn said, walking over to stand next to Hunter. "She must have caught the scent of the body in the tent."

"Right, I should have thought of that." Hunter kept a calming hand on the dog's back. "I'll take her back to the van."

Veronica appeared next to Finn and reached out to pet the Lab.

"What's wrong, girl? You okay?"

"She'll be fine," Finn assured her. "Gracie was trained as a cadaver dog by the army, remember? She's supposed to act like this whenever she's around a dead body."

"I remember, all right." Veronica smiled down at Gracie. "Her training helped save my mother. She's a hero around my house."

Catching Veronica's eye, Hunter gestured toward the tent.

"Any update on the deceased's identity or cause of death?"

She shook her head.

"A woman's body was found on a bench, but she hasn't been identified as far as I know," she offered. "We're assuming it was a homicide since the location is being treated as a crime scene, but again, nothing official from the WBPD or the city's press office."

"Not much to go on then."

Gracie barked again, and Hunter stepped back, ready to leave.

"I better get Gracie out of here."

Veronica put a hand on his arm to stop him. She looked toward the exit, and Hunter turned his head to follow her gaze. Nessa Ainsley stood by the gate talking to one of her officers, her face was drawn, and her expression grim.

"Actually, I was thinking maybe you could try to talk to Chief Ainsley. See if she'll give you the inside scoop."

Hunter raised an eyebrow.

"And why would she do that?"

"Come on, Hunter," Veronica teased. "You know Nessa has a soft spot when it comes to you. Don't pretend you haven't noticed."

Shaking his head at the idea, Hunter pointed behind her.

"Looks like Jack's calling for you to go back on the air."

Veronica didn't have time to protest. She crossed to where Jack Carson was ready with the live feed. Her report would interrupt whichever show was currently being broadcast, alerting Channel Ten viewers that all was not well in Willow Bay.

Following Gracie toward the gate, Hunter lifted a hand in greeting as Nessa looked up. He lowered it again when she quickly turned away, pretending not to have seen him.

I guess Veronica was wrong about Nessa having a soft spot for me.

He was about to keep walking, then decided something wasn't right. The look on Nessa's face when she'd seen him hadn't been one of annoyance at an unwelcome interruption.

She looked guilty as hell. Now, why would that be?

Nessa's startled reaction to his hand on her arm confirmed his suspicion. She knew something she didn't want him to find out. Something he wasn't going to like.

"Okay, Nessa. Tell me what's going on."

Hesitating only a moment, Nessa issued a heavy sigh and led Hunter through the gate and out onto the sidewalk, where there would be fewer people to listen in.

"I don't know why I'm telling you this, because I shouldn't be, but I figure you're going to find out soon enough."

Anxiety bloomed in his chest, but he remained silent.

"As you know we haven't officially released the name of the woman we found, and we won't be releasing it for a while."

Meeting his eyes, Nessa swallowed hard.

"But *off the record,* we have reason to believe the woman out there is Astrid Peterson, the missing woman who contacted Channel Ten. The one Veronica brought to our attention earlier this week."

Hunter stared at Nessa, suddenly understanding why she'd felt compelled to tell him. Veronica had been obsessing over Astrid Peterson for days, worried that the girl needed help, and unsure what she could do. The news that Astrid was dead would devastate her.

"I'm putting my neck out telling you this," Nessa said, running a hand through her red curls. "You can't tell anyone. After all, we could be mistaken. And in any event, we'll need to perform an autopsy and notify her parents in Sweden before we make any kind of official announcement."

Nodding slowly, Hunter tried to imagine Veronica's reaction.

"I'll have to tell Veronica," he said, feeling the anxiety in his chest growing. "I don't know how, but she'd want to know what happened to Astrid. She deserves to know."

Nessa paused, then nodded.

"Yes, she does. Just as long as you both remember that what I told you is off the record."

A loud voice boomed out behind Hunter. He turned to see Garth Bixby. His father's campaign manager produced a toothy smile and slapped Hunter on the back as if he were an old college buddy.

"This ought to be good for ratings, eh, Hunter?"

Backing away from Bixby, Hunter frowned in confusion, his mind still on Veronica and the news about Astrid Peterson.

"What should be good for ratings?"

"A murder in downtown Willow Bay. That'll send the ratings through the roof, won't it?"

Before Hunter could respond, Nessa cleared her throat and stepped around Bixby, her face a mask of dislike and disapproval.

"I'll see you later, Mr. Hadley," she said, not looking at Bixby before she hurried back through the gate.

"She's a cold one, isn't she?" Bixby muttered once Nessa was gone. "But I'm sure your father will find a good replacement once he wins this race. Just a few more weeks and all these signs will be filling up the city dump."

Kicking a booted foot at a *Ling Lee for Mayor* sign, Bixby produced another wide grin, then leaned close enough for Hunter to smell his expensive cologne.

"Don't worry, your father and I have a plan to win this election."

Hunter stared at the man in disbelief.

I guess dear old dad didn't tell his new campaign manager about the Hadley family falling out. Keeping dirty little secrets is a hard habit to break.

Although Hunter had considered himself estranged from his father for almost a year, Mayor Hadley refused to acknowledge the situation and liked to pretend everything between them was fine.

A shrill ring alerted Bixby to an incoming call, and he stuck up a finger as if to silence anything Hunter might be planning to say.

Deciding to make a quick escape, Hunter walked toward the big news van parked at the curb, urging Gracie to hurry.

"See you later, man!" Bixby called out from behind him.

Hunter didn't turn around; he was too busy rehashing what the obnoxious man had said about his father's plan to win the election.

I'd better go see the old man and make sure he isn't planning anything that'll hurt Veronica or her mother. They've been through enough already.

* * *

City Hall was practically deserted when Hunter and Gracie walked into the big building. They'd made it halfway down the corridor leading to the mayor's office when Judge Eldredge came into view.

The old friend of his father wore his usual sour expression as he passed Hunter, lowering his head in a curt nod but not slowing down.

Judge Eldredge is in a hurry. Must be heading to Old Willow Square like everyone else in town. Nothing like a dead body to bring people together.

Hunter was tempted to stop the judge and ask for a comment on his controversial decision to grant Nick Sargent bail and his pending ruling on a motion to dismiss the case altogether.

Continuing down the hall, Hunter pondered Judge Eldredge's handling of the case. Was it possible that the judge had been paid off? Based on the town's history of corruption and cronyism it wasn't hard to imagine him accepting a bribe.

Or could Nick have dirt on the old man that he's using as pressure?

The idea wasn't too farfetched, considering the charges against Nick involved extortion and blackmail. Hunter filed the idea away to research later. First, he needed to talk to his father.

The reception desk was unmanned as Hunter stepped into the outer office. Muffled voices could be heard through the closed door to the mayor's office.

Rapping twice on the door, Hunter waited for a beat, then pushed the door open without waiting for a response. His father's face lit up in a pleased smile as he caught sight of Hunter.

"Come on in, son. There's someone I'd like you to meet."

Mayor Hadley made no reference to the fact that Hunter hadn't visited his office in almost a year, or that they'd barely spoken more than ten words to each other in the months since.

His casual greeting made it seem as if they could have spoken only minutes or hours before, but Hunter wasn't surprised. His father had always been capable of incredible self-deception and wishful thinking, especially when it came to his only son.

"Sorry to interrupt," Hunter said to the man sitting across from his father's big desk. "But I was hoping to-"

"Don't be rude, Hunter," the mayor scolded. "I haven't introduced you to Special Agent Clint Marlowe yet. From the *FBI*."

Standing and moving around the desk to stand beside Hunter, the mayor tried to wrap an arm around his shoulders, but Hunter shrugged his father off and held out a hand to the FBI agent, taking in the man's tall, athletic frame, clean-shaven jaw, and poorly concealed firearm.

"Good to meet you, Agent Marlowe," Hunter said, noting the agent's firm handshake. "I'm Hunter Hadley, and I need to talk to my father for a few minutes. I'll wait in the reception area until you two are finished in here."

"Don't be silly. Agent Marlowe doesn't mind if you stay," the mayor said. "He's the man who's going to help me win this election."

Marlowe raised his eyebrows and turned to Hunter with a frown.

"I'm simply here to coordinate certain efforts between the FBI and the WBPD. We're cooperating on a task force, and-"

"This is my son, Agent Marlowe, and the head of the leading news station in Willow Bay, so no need to be coy," Mayor Hadley insisted. "This boy knows everything that goes on in town."

Ignoring the shock on both men's faces, the mayor forged on.

"Agent Marlowe is here to help our lame police department hunt down a criminal ring that's formed on our very doorstep. He and his men are running a top-secret special operation."

Meeting Marlowe's guarded eyes, Hunter thought he saw a flash of irritation, maybe even anger.

"So, you're heading up Operation Stolen Angels?" Hunter asked.

Marlowe hesitated, obviously reluctant to talk about the task force in front of a civilian.

"Information gets around quickly in a small town, Agent," Hunter said, then cocked his thumb over at his father. "Especially if you tell my father. He's not the kind to keep a secret for long."

The mayor scowled at Hunter's words.

"Agent Marlowe is here to bring down the crime syndicate your *girlfriend* keeps going on about every night on the news."

The irritation that entered Mayor Hadley's voice told Hunter that his father's old southern charm routine was now over.

"And he's going to do it before the election," the mayor snapped, "so that the citizens of Willow Bay will know I'm the *tough-on-crime* candidate."

"So, *that's* your big plan Garth Bixby was talking about?" Hunter gave an angry shake of his head, sending a dark curl falling over his forehead. "That's why you want to stop these traffickers? To make yourself look good, so you can win the election?"

Throwing his son a disapproving glare, Mayor Hadley no longer tried to hide his frustration.

"Of course. Did you think I was hoping to lose the election? Even you can't expect me to just give up and walk away."

Marlowe held up a big hand.

"Excuse me, Mayor, but I need to go. I have a lot to-"

"And it's about time I get some positive press coverage around here,' the mayor continued as if Marlowe hadn't spoken.

"I'd have thought you'd gotten enough coverage to last a lifetime after your attempted bribe was recorded," Hunter snapped back.

The mayor darted an uncomfortable look at Marlowe.

"As I explained at the time, my comments were taken out of context. It was all just an unfortunate misunderstanding. Which is one of the reasons I need some positive coverage now."

Moving toward the door, Marlowe held up his phone, which buzzed in his hand as he spoke.

"I better get back to work. Thank you for your time, Mayor."

"But we haven't finished discussing the press statement," the mayor protested. "I need your quote, as head of the task force."

Hunter cringed at his father's blatant display of self-interest.

"Here's a quote for you," he said between gritted teeth. "A woman has been killed in our community and our mayor cares more about his campaign than he does about finding the woman's killer."

A stunned silence followed Hunter's words.

"What on earth are you talking about?" the mayor finally said. "What woman's been killed?"

Realizing his father hadn't heard about the situation in Old Willow Square, Hunter shook his head and sighed.

"While you've been in here wasting Agent Marlowe's time, a woman's body has been discovered in Old Willow Square."

He shifted his eyes to Marlowe's stern face.

"A woman who just might be a possible trafficking victim."

The agent stiffened at Hunter's accusatory tone, as Mayor Hadley race toward the door.

"Is that what all those sirens were about?" he muttered, pulling on his coat. "I told my assistant not to disturb me, but this..."

And then his father was gone, disappearing through the door without another word to his son or to Special Agent Marlowe.

Hunter met Marlowe's eyes, his anger fading as he realized what he'd just said. The FBI agent would soon find out that the victim's identity hadn't been released. Hunter's statement that she was a possible trafficking victim would suggest the WBPD had leaked confidential case details. Nessa wouldn't be pleased.

But for the time being, Marlowe said nothing as he turned to the door and followed Mayor Hadley down the hall.

Staring after the agent, Hunter had no doubt where he was going.

Looks like the feds will finally find out what happened to Astrid Peterson.

CHAPTER THIRTEEN

The winter sun peeked through the clouds, painting Old Willow Square with patches of light, and giving Diablo an excuse to hide his eyes behind dark sunglasses. He watched with interest as the scene around him unfolded; the sheer audacity of leaving a dead body staged in the middle of town was impressive.

The Professor keeps his promises. I had better keep that in mind.

That had been his first thought upon hearing about the discovery of the woman. His contact from the darknet discussion board hadn't been trying to scam him after all. The Professor had promised to leave a present for Diablo in a place he couldn't miss.

And here she is, in the middle of town. Of course, I'd prefer her alive.

His initial admiration for the professor's brazen act suddenly gave way to a cold stab of fear. If the Professor could come to Willow Bay and do this, he could do pretty much anything he wanted.

How the hell does he know where I am?

Somehow the cold-blooded killer had discovered he was in Willow Bay. Diablo's darknet connection was no longer just a faceless entity out in cyberspace. A shiver passed through him at the thought that the killer had been standing only yards away from where Diablo was standing now.

Noting the tension and fear on the faces around him, Diablo tried to calm his own expression. It wouldn't do for him to show any emotion that might be used against him by the public. He had to stay strong and make it clear he had nothing to fear, and nothing to hide.

But the idea that he had finally gotten in over his head took root as Diablo watched the crime scene technicians scurry past him. He'd thought his foray into organized crime would be short-lived. A way for him to use his experience and connections to make a little quick money. He hadn't anticipated just how much money he could make, or how much he would enjoy his new role as a crime boss.

Giving up the perks of the position he found himself in wouldn't be easy, but the alternative now seemed clear.

Eventually, something always goes wrong. Someone squeals or someone else tries to take over. Maybe this is the time to get out for good.

Of course, the Professor wouldn't just let Diablo walk away into the sunset now that he'd set things in motion.

The Professor doesn't play around, and he wants to make a deal.

Tucking the thought into the back of his mind, Diablo buttoned his jacket and adjusted his dark glasses. The black jacket, along with snug black pants and sturdy leather boots, provided warmth against the chill that hung in the air.

While he wasn't the only one who'd taken advantage of the short burst of cold weather to bring out a rarely worn jacket and boots, he enjoyed the thought that his outfit matched the tough guy image he liked to project in his role as Diablo.

He'd always been hard and ambitious, but he had never been willing to let the rest of the world know just how far and how hard he was willing to go to get what he wanted. Today at least, his outward appearance reflected his true, dark nature.

Catching sight of a young woman standing in the crowd, Diablo felt his pulse race. Her back was turned to him, but the long dark hair was the right color and style.

Is that the little bitch that got away?

86

He kept his eyes pinned to the girl's slender figure, willing her to turn around. When she finally looked in his direction, Diablo wasn't sure if he should be disappointed or relieved that she wasn't the girl he was looking for.

The girl who had escaped the hideout while his men were loading the truck had been younger, and prettier. Although she'd already been hooked on pills when they'd picked her up outside Tampa, she'd still been fresh. The effects of addiction hadn't ruined her yet

She'd have made me some decent money if she hadn't run off.

For a minute Diablo couldn't remember the girl's name. It was hard for him to keep track of the girls coming in and going out. Most of them were easy to control using drugs or threats, or a combination of both. They all started to blend together after a while.

It's only the difficult ones that stick out. The ones like Ruby.

The name came to him in a rush, as did his fury at the thought that the girl had outsmarted his men. Clenching his fists by his side, he silently fumed at the losers he had working for him.

The men were too easy on the girls and too lazy with security. He'd tried to teach them how to deal with the girls properly. He'd explained that any sign of weakness gave the girls hope, and hope would give them the courage to try to escape.

Trying to educate the men who worked for him had proven useless. They were from the bottom of the barrel. Men who'd been leftovers from a Miami syndicate that had been busted the year before. Men who'd been too low within the now-defunct operation for the feds to chase down, although most of them had warrants out in Miami or Tampa.

But then again, these men had managed to escape the sting operation that had taken down the rest of their crew, and Diablo knew they were able to keep a low profile and keep their mouths shut. Otherwise, they'd surely be locked up by now.

All his men wanted was to make some money and stay out of jail. They were mercenaries, loyal to the almighty dollar, but not to him.

I have to remember that. If I start thinking I can trust one of these guys, I'll end up making a mistake. I'll end up like their last boss.

Dismissing the man who'd run the Miami operation, and who was now serving hard time up in Raiford, Diablo had decided to run things his way. He figured the guy had gotten caught because he'd gotten careless. He'd been sent away for decades, creating the perfect opportunity for Diablo to step in and build his own operation closer to home.

It had been easy to make use of the tall tales that had circulated in the area for years about a vicious underworld boss named Diablo. According to the rumors, the name had been given to a violent kingpin by the men who'd worked for him. They'd sworn their boss was as cunning and evil as the devil himself.

While the dreaded Diablo had once been a figment of the town's collective imagination, thanks to the man watching the crowd, Diablo was now very real and walking the streets among them.

The reputation of his fictional namesake had grown over the years, and Diablo had taken full advantage of the mystery that surrounded it. He'd used the name to instill fear in the women he wanted to control, and he couldn't let a girl like Ruby ruin his image.

Pulling out his phone, Diablo typed in a text to one of his men. They needed to find another girl to add to the Miami shipment now that Ruby had run off and couldn't be found. He suggested they pick a girl with less attitude, and with more to lose.

She'll turn up eventually. And when she does, I'll take care of her myself.

Diablo dropped his phone into his pocket and focused his eyes on Veronica Lee. Her reports from the scene of the crime would undoubtedly draw rave reviews.

Too bad she doesn't have a clue about what's really going on.

Although to be fair, Diablo wasn't really sure himself what the Professor's ultimate plan was. All he knew was that the man wanted a favor and that he'd promised he would deliver a favor in return.

There's only one thing I want right now, and I doubt the Professor will be able or willing to help me get it.

Although there were many women in town who had good reason to hate him, there was one woman he'd treated like a queen before she'd dumped him. A woman who was even now under the misguided impression that she'd gotten the better of him.

She actually thinks I'll be willing to just let her walk away.

Clenching his jaw, he recalled the ugly words coming out of the woman's beautiful mouth. Her mouth needed to be shut. Forever.

He still wasn't sure how he was going to pull it off, but he knew he'd find a way. Eventually, he'd take care of her, and he'd take back what was rightfully his.

A familiar voice drifted through the chilly air. Diablo turned his head, recognizing Mackenzie Jensen's curvy figure as she leaned provocatively over the perimeter tape to drill questions at a uniformed officer.

Poor dope doesn't stand a chance against a barracuda like Mackenzie.

The ambitious newspaper reporter had been useful in the past. If Diablo played his cards right, she could be useful again. As long as he was careful not to reveal too much and wasn't seen talking to her in public too often. People around the little town liked to talk. He didn't want rumors circulating about him and the young reporter.

She's sharp and sexy, but she'll fuck me over if she finds out I'm Diablo.

If Mackenzie knew his secret, she'd have no qualms about breaking his cover. It would be too tempting for her not to. Her thirst for recognition wouldn't allow her to sit on a big, juicy story, even if she was screwing around with the main subject.

Feeling his phone buzz in his pocket, Diablo dug it out and stared down at the display. His hunch was right; the Professor was still in town, and he wanted to meet.

CHAPTER FOURTEEN

Veronica waited for Jack's cue that she was off the air before lowering her microphone and letting out a deep sigh of relief. She'd spent much of the morning giving live updates and recording footage to use in later segments; her nerves were on edge. All she wanted now was a long drink of water and a few minutes to decompress.

"I'm going back to the van," she told Jack. "I need a break."

"Sounds like a good idea."

Jack studied her face with fatherly concern.

"Make sure to get some water while you're there. I'll stay here and help Finn get more footage of the crowd and the crime scene."

Keeping her head down, Veronica skirted around the edge of the square and out the gate.

She was still a few yards away from the big news van when she saw Hunter and Gracie approaching from the other direction. Her heart dropped at the grim look on Hunter's face.

As Gracie trotted up to Veronica and sat at her feet, Veronica bent to scratch the dog behind her ears. Her intuition was telling her she would need all the comfort the Lab could provide.

"Okay, Hunter, what's wrong?"

She raised her eyes to his, but he was looking down at Gracie.

"I just went to see my father. It seems he's hoping to use the FBI task force as a way to show the town *he's* tough on crime. As if he had anything to do with setting it up."

Veronica stepped closer, reaching out to put a hand on his arm. Hunter knew his father routinely used underhanded tactics. The mayor's tendency to bend the truth to suit his own self-interest was one of the main reasons they'd fallen out.

So, why was he so upset about this new revelation? And why was Hunter getting involved in his father's campaign strategy anyway?

"We both know we can't be involved in the campaign." Veronica tried to soften her words with a smile. "Even if my mother wasn't running against your father, we're still reporters, and we need to be unbiased so we can report objectively on the race, right?"

Finally meeting her eyes, Hunter sighed.

"You're right. I was just worried my father would do something that would end up hurting you or your mother," he admitted. "But that isn't what's really bothering me."

He pulled her toward him as if he wanted to comfort her, but Veronica backed away, suddenly scared.

"What is it, Hunter? What can't you tell me?"

"Let's sit in the van," he suggested, swallowing hard. "I don't want to do this out on the sidewalk."

Nodding in numb agreement, Veronica waited for Hunter to slide open the door to the back. She climbed inside the van and perched on a folding chair, staring at the racks of equipment and video monitors.

She picked up a bottle of water and took a long drink as Hunter settled in beside her, but her mouth was still dry when he turned to take her hands in his.

"Nessa told me something in confidence." His hands tightened around hers as he spoke. "It hasn't been confirmed yet, but she's pretty sure the woman they found is Astrid Peterson."

For a minute Veronica couldn't breathe. She stared at Hunter without moving, not knowing what to say.

"I know how much you wanted to help her."

"How could we let this happen?" she whispered, her throat tight and her mouth dry. "She needed help and we all just stood around and did nothing."

Hunter sat back and shook his head.

"This isn't our fault, Veronica. The man who killed Astrid Peterson made sure no one could find her. He's the one to blame."

Knowing his words were true, Veronica tried to quell the guilt and remorse that filled her chest.

Why didn't I find a way to help? I could have given a special report, or...

Hunter's next words interrupted her self-recrimination.

"The man who kidnapped and killed Astrid may still be in Willow Bay. He might know that Astrid sent you that comment."

Lifting a gentle hand, he brushed a strand of long, dark hair off her face, his fingers warm against her cold skin.

"You could be in danger," he said, his voice low. "He's already killed one woman. I doubt he'd hesitate to kill another."

"Skylar!" Veronica gasped, pushing his hand away and reaching for the handle to slide back the door. "He's still got Skylar."

*   *   *

Nessa was standing behind the crime scene tape talking to Detective Vanzinger when Veronica finally spotted her.

Ducking under the tape, Veronica hurried toward the chief of police, ignoring the surprised shout from Andy Ford. She reached Nessa's side just as a hand fell on her shoulder.

"It's okay, Andy, I've got this."

The young officer dropped his hand, and Nessa waited for him to return to his post before waving Veronica and Vanzinger to the side and out of the way of the crew working the scene.

"I guess Hunter didn't waste any time telling you who's in that tent," Nessa said with a scowl. "I told him it was off the record."

"What about Skylar?" Veronica asked, in no mood for a lecture. "If that is Astrid Peterson, then what about the other girl? What do we do to find Skylar before she turns up dead, too?"

Vanzinger spoke up before Nessa could reply.

"We couldn't find anything about a girl named Skylar who's gone missing," he admitted, a frown creasing his forehead. "There's nothing in any of the databases, national or local. Detective Jankowski and I looked everywhere we could think of."

"Keep your voices down." Nessa glanced over her shoulder. "None of this information has been released yet and you never know who might be listening."

Following Nessa's eyes toward the scene perimeter, Veronica saw Mackenzie Jensen. The journalist gave Veronica a hard stare, then bent her head to scribble on the notepad she was holding.

"If Mackenzie Jensen gets wind that you know the victim's identity before she does, she'll be screaming about preferential treatment and police corruption," Nessa moaned. "We'll be on the *Gazette*'s front page by tomorrow morning."

Veronica dismissed Nessa's worry about the journalist. She didn't have time to engage in a petty rivalry with Mackenzie Jensen. Not when the woman who had reached out to her was already dead, and another woman might still be in danger.

A tall man in a dark jacket approached the scene perimeter and ducked under the tape. When he removed his sunglasses and looked around, Veronica recognized Special Agent Clint Marlowe.

Marlow caught sight of Nessa and Vanzinger standing to the side. He began to walk toward them with an impassive, almost bored expression that irked Veronica.

He doesn't seem very concerned that a woman on the FBI's missing persons list has just been discovered dead in the middle of town.

She felt Nessa stiffen beside her. The police chief put a firm hand on Veronica's arm.

"He doesn't know it's Astrid Peterson over there," she murmured. "And it isn't your place to tell him. I'll handle this."

Veronica looked into Nessa's tired, blue eyes, suddenly noticing that the chief didn't look well. She nodded reluctantly.

"I thought the press was supposed to stay on that side of the tape, Chief Ainsley," Agent Marlow said, raising an eyebrow. "Or do things work differently in Willow Bay?"

"I was just leaving." Veronica's cheeks grew hot with anger at the condescending tone he'd used to speak to Nessa. "But now that you're here, Agent Marlowe, would you mind answering a few questions for viewers who are concerned about the increase in criminal activity in small towns throughout South Florida?"

Marlowe's eyes narrowed at Veronica's request.

"Yes, I'd mind," Marlowe said, his voice hard.

"Well, then would you mind telling me exactly what progress your trafficking task force has made thus far? Could the crime here today be related to the crimes your task force has been investigating?"

Prodding Veronica toward the perimeter, Nessa cleared her throat.

"I thought you were leaving, Veronica," Nessa said, lifting the tape so that Veronica could slip under. "I'll follow up with you on our discussion later."

Marlowe turned his back on Veronica, apparently done with her questioning, but he stopped when she called out again.

"Agent Marlowe, do you have any comment on the claims that an organized crime network is operating here in Willow Bay? Are you investigating an organization calling itself the Diablo Syndicate?"

Turning to Veronica, Marlowe pointed a big finger in her direction.

"Be careful, Ms. Lee. You don't want to run up against any of the organizations the Bureau is investigating. These groups are usually dangerous, and they don't like people who ask too many questions."

A deep voice spoke up behind her.

"The press has a right and an obligation to investigate and report on crimes that impact the community," Hunter called out, moving up to stand next to Veronica. "And from what I've seen today, the people in this town are in very real danger. They want answers."

Veronica saw Mackenzie Jensen walk up behind Hunter, her pen scribbling on her notepad as she listened.

"Agent Marlowe, the women I've been interviewing as part of Channel Ten's reports on trafficking are still living in fear," Veronica said, picturing Ruby's frightened eyes. "I'm sure our viewers would like to hear what the joint task force is doing about it."

Shooting an annoyed look at the crowd behind Veronica, Marlowe stepped closer and lowered his voice.

"Any woman who feels she's in danger should contact her local police department, not her local television station."

"These women are *scared*, Agent Marlowe."

Veronica's voice trembled with outrage.

"They've been threatened by the men who have abused them, and they're terrified they'll be arrested if they go to the police for help."

The crowd suddenly fell silent and began to part, making way for Wesley Knox. The brawny forensic technician appeared, pushing a metal gurney toward the tent. No one spoke as the wheels rattled against the rough concrete path, and then crunched through the leaves.

As the tent flap closed behind Wesley, Veronica realized they must be getting ready to take Astrid Peterson's body to the medical examiner's office for autopsy.

With any luck, the M.E. will find something during the autopsy to help them find the bastard who did this because the FBI doesn't have a clue.

Looking back to where Agent Marlowe had been standing, Veronica saw that he and Nessa were gone.

CHAPTER FIFTEEN

essa pulled on protective coveralls and booties, then held her breath, preparing to face the stench of decomposing flesh. But when she opened the tent flap and stepped inside, only the damp scent of dead leaves greeted her.

The dead woman's body was already on the gurney, her legs and arms slightly bent, and her strawberry blonde hair falling back to reveal the snow-white skin of her face, silent and frozen in a pose of eternal sleep.

Looking up as Nessa approached, Iris pulled a thin white sheet up to cover the pitiful figure. A frown settled between the medical examiner's kind brown eyes as she met Nessa's gaze.

"It'll take another twenty-four hours for her to thaw out enough for a proper autopsy," Iris said, her tone apologetic, knowing the delay would be an inconvenience. "I'm pretty sure we can get it done tomorrow, but I'll have to let you know a time once I get her back to our facilities and we see how long it takes."

The fleeting thought that she was going to have to miss Cole's Saturday afternoon flag football game came and went as Nessa and Iris waited for Wesley to back up the medical examiner's van as far as the gate.

Soon the gurney was being rolled back over the grass and onto the walkway. The crime scene crew had moved back the perimeter and cordoned off a wide path from the tent to the gate.

Within minutes the gurney had been loaded into the medical examiner's van, and the big vehicle pulled away from the curb.

Standing on the sidewalk, Nessa stared after the van until she felt her phone begin to vibrate in her coat pocket. She groaned, tempted to let the call roll to voicemail. She needed to get something to eat and wanted a few minutes to think about what to do next.

But the possibility that it might be Jerry calling prompted Nessa to pull out her phone and glance down at the display.

Where are you? Starting press conference now at City Hall.

The text from Tenley Frost started Nessa's feet moving along the pavement. She'd forgotten that, against her better judgment, she'd agreed to support the media relations officer at a press conference about the dead body discovered in Old Willow Square.

Why the hell did I say I'd talk to the press now? We haven't even gotten a chance to plan out a statement. What is Tenley going to say?

As Nessa approached City Hall, Tenley's sleek auburn bob was visible behind a cluster of reporters and their camera crews surrounding the podium. Vanzinger and Jankowski stood stiffly behind her. Neither man looked happy to be there.

Most of the bystanders who had flocked to the square at the report of a dead body had already wandered off now that the body had been taken away. Nessa saw that, other than the press corps, only a few dozen people had made the effort to walk the block to City Hall.

Must be too cold to wait for dull city officials to make a statement.

Circling the crowd, Nessa attempted to study the faces of the people who'd decided to stick around.

Is the man who killed Astrid Peterson here in the crowd?

She heard someone calling her name before she could get a good look at everyone. Vanzinger waved to her from the podium, his red crewcut covered by a white knit cap.

"We're about to start, Chief," he called to her, sounding nervous.

"There you are, Nessa," Tenley murmured in relief, grabbing Nessa's hand and tugging her toward the podium. "I'll introduce myself first, and then you and the detectives on the case. Which one of you can give a brief update on the investigation?"

Shaking her head at Tenley's wide-eyed question, Nessa tried to step back, but Tenley held on to her hand.

"We just got started on this investigation," Nessa whispered, turning her face away from the increasingly restless press corps. "We don't have any update to give at this time."

"They're all standing here now," Tenley whispered back with a pasted-on smile. "So, think of something...."

Before Nessa could protest further, Tenley turned to tap her long nails against the microphone. The reporters turned expectant eyes to the podium at the sound.

"Thank you for joining us today," Tenley said, adopting the upbeat tone she'd perfected back when she'd been Channel Ten's star reporter. "I'm Tenley Frost, Willow Bay's media relations officer, and joining me at the podium is chief of police Nessa Ainsley."

As Tenley continued with her standard introduction and greeting, Nessa again surveyed the faces staring up at the podium, expecting to see someone suspicious in the crowd.

"And now I'll turn the microphone over to Chief Ainsley to give a brief update on the investigation."

Inching toward the podium, Nessa tried to focus on the people she knew. Veronica Lee was there, grim and silent, as was a crew from Channel Six, and Mackenzie Jensen with the Willow Bay Gazette.

"The WBPD was called to Old Willow Square this morning after a body was discovered on a bench in the area. Officers responded within minutes, as did emergency services, but unfortunately, the woman was already deceased."

A wave of dizziness washed through Nessa as she spoke, and she had to grip the edge of the podium to steady herself.

"The woman's identity has not been confirmed at this time, and an autopsy will be conducted within the next twenty-four to forty-eight hours to determine cause and manner of death."

Nessa swayed slightly on her feet, and for one terrifying moment she thought she was going to pass out, then suddenly a strong hand closed around her arm.

"I got you, Chief," Vanzinger murmured, helping her back from the podium, his big arm holding her upright as she fought another wave of dizziness. "Jankowski can finish up."

Watching Jankowski take her place at the podium, Nessa sucked in a breath of chilly air, willing her legs to stop shaking.

"I'm Detective Simon Jankowski, and I'm leading the investigation with my partner, Detective Tucker Vanzinger."

Jankowski straightened his tie and adjusted the microphone. Nessa assumed he was stalling for time while he thought up something to say. She tried to step forward again, but Vanzinger held her arm and shook his head.

"Based on our initial investigation, we're treating the death in Old Willow Square as a homicide. We are in the process of interviewing potential witnesses and have no suspects in custody at this time."

A murmur of voices started up at his statement, but Jankowski ignored them, plowing ahead without pause.

"We will provide further updates to the press and the public as the investigation proceeds. The victim's identity will be released once an autopsy has been completed, and family members notified."

Raising his voice to be heard over the growing noise of the crowd, Jankowski leaned forward to speak directly into the microphone.

"We have no further information to share at this time."

His brusque tone suggested questions would not be welcome, but the reporters immediately began to shout.

"Is the killer still on the loose?"

"Was the victim a local resident?"

"Can you provide details on the age or ethnicity of the victim?"

"Are the people in the community in danger?"

Jankowski stepped back from the podium, and gestured toward Tenley Frost, leaving the media relations officer to field the barrage of questions.

Nessa's head had stopped spinning, and her legs felt steady enough to carry her back to her office. She looked up at Vanzinger and smiled weakly.

"Thanks for the support. I didn't stop for lunch and...well, I guess it all just caught up with me."

"I didn't want to say anything, but you were looking kind of sickly earlier at the scene," Vanzinger said, keeping his hand on her arm. "I think you better get yourself checked out, Chief."

Shaking her head at the idea, Nessa shrugged off his arm. Before she could tell him she'd be fine, Mackenzie Jensen blocked her path.

"Chief Ainsley, why is the FBI involved in the investigation?"

"The feds aren't involved, and we said no more questions." Vanzinger's voice was hard. "Now please clear the path."

"I saw an FBI agent at the crime scene," Mackenzie insisted. "Why were the feds at the scene of a local homicide?'

Nessa pushed past the journalist without a response. She hadn't had a chance to think about Marlowe's sudden appearance at the scene, but Mackenzie had a point.

Why was Agent Marlowe at my scene? What or who was he looking for?

First, she needed to eat lunch, and then she would seek the answer to Mackenzie Jensen's question.

* * *

Nessa had just taken another bite of her cheese and tomato sandwich when Marlowe knocked on the doorframe to her office.

"I got your text," he said, holding up his phone in one hand as his tall figure filled the doorway.

Swallowing the bite more quickly than she'd planned, Nessa coughed, then grabbed for her water bottle and took a few sips.

"Yes, thanks for coming," she said, clearing her throat. "I wanted to ask why you were at the scene in Old Willow Square."

She wiped her hands with a napkin and threw it in the trash, but her eyes never left Marlowe's face.

"Mayor Hadley's son came in while we were having a meeting," Marlowe said without hesitation. "Said a dead body had been found in the square, and that the woman was a possible trafficking victim. Naturally, I decided to see what was going on for myself."

Stunned that Hunter had shared the confidential information about Astrid Peterson with Mayor Hadley, Nessa took another long sip of water and sighed.

"Hunter Hadley had no right to share that information with his father...but he was telling the truth. The woman we found is most likely Astrid Peterson, the one who went missing in Montana."

Marlowe's expression didn't change.

"She's the one Veronica Lee asked you about," Nessa continued. "She sent a message saying she was being held against her will. She said she was like the women in Veronica's reports on trafficking."

"Yes, I remember the woman," Marlowe said, his eyes flicking to the phone he held in his hand. "I forwarded the information to the agent assigned to the case. I'll let him know she's been found."

Frowning at Marlowe's callous tone, Nessa leaned back in her chair and crossed her arms over her chest.

"What does it take to get a show of emotion out of you, Agent Marlowe?" Nessa asked, no longer bothering to tone down her southern accent. "You hear that a young woman who reached out to us for help was killed and left on a park bench, and all you can say is you'll update the agent in charge?"

Marlowe raised his eyebrows but didn't reply.

"Did you all even bother looking for Astrid Peterson?" Nessa demanded. "Did you even try to find out what happened to her?'

"Not me personally, Chief Ainsley," Marlowe said, a hint of sarcasm coloring his voice. "But I know the assigned agent, and I can guarantee he did everything humanly possible to find that woman."

Moving into the room, Marlowe positioned himself in front of her desk. She lifted her head to look up at him, suddenly feeling small and vulnerable.

"Just because I don't let my emotions get in the way of doing my job doesn't mean I don't care," Marlowe said calmly. "I don't have the luxury of falling apart every time we find a dead body."

"Have a seat, Agent Marlowe," Nessa said, pointing to the chair across from her, "I'm getting a neck ache here."

Finally flashing a smile, Marlowe lowered himself into the chair and leaned his elbows on the desk in front of him.

"Now, is there anything else you wanted to know?"

Nessa leaned back in her chair and shrugged.

"I'd love to get an update on Operation Stolen Angels," she said. "I'd be interested in knowing if the task force has made any progress finding the men that have been preying on this community."

Sticking his phone into the pocket of his jacket, Marlowe adjusted his position in the chair, as if settling in for an extended stay.

"I think we're pretty close to figuring out who's running the new organization," he said, sounding pleased. "We worked with Miami PD last year to take down a similar group, and it seems some of the same men are involved. Only now they work for a different boss."

"Let me guess," Nessa said dryly. "The guy calls himself Diablo."

Marlowe nodded.

"That's why we're calling the group the Diablo Syndicate. We know they've established connections with buyers and sellers through the darknet. It's just a matter of time until we find out who Diablo really is and what rock he's hiding under."

Thinking back to Ruby Chase's interview, Nessa wondered if the girl had been telling the truth about seeing Diablo. If so, would she be able to identify him? Could she be the key to stopping the guy once and for all?

"What would you say if I told you I know a girl who has seen this guy Diablo? That she may be able to identify him. Maybe even lead us to him.

Suddenly Marlowe's placid expression tightened with interest.

"I'd say I need to speak to her as soon as possible."

Nessa sipped again from her bottle, unsure she was doing the right thing. What if Ruby Chase had been making up a story to get herself out of trouble? What if she'd simply heard the rumors about Diablo and used the name to her advantage?

"Who is this girl that can identify Diablo?"

Marlowe's eyes narrowed.

"And more importantly, *where* is she?"

Staring into the agent's dark eyes, Nessa wondered again if she'd made a mistake telling Marlowe about Ruby Chase.

CHAPTER SIXTEEN

Ruby Chase stared out the window of Dr. Horn's office with red, achy eyes. She'd woken up that morning thinking of her father and of little Rory, imagining her little brother watching cartoons on the living room floor while her father tried to make pancakes in the kitchen.

Dad never was able to make them fluffy the way Mom used to.

Thoughts of her family back in Daytona had strengthened Ruby's cravings for the little pills that could take the edge off her guilt and her loneliness. The little pills had been at the heart of her downward spiral, but they now seemed like her only salvation.

Looking around as the door opened, Ruby saw the Hope House director bustle into the room carrying an armful of files and a mug of coffee.

"I hear you're not doing so good today, Ruby. What's going on?"

Ruby turned back to the window, surveying the parking lot beyond. The day she'd been in the office with Veronica Lee, she'd looked out that same window. She was sure she'd seen one of the men who'd been at Diablo's compound. A big man who had barked orders at the others.

"I need something to take the edge off, Dr. Horn," Ruby said, trying to keep her voice steady. "I'm feeling shaky, and I've been having these dreams..."

"I'm sorry to hear that, Ruby. And why don't you call me Reggie? Everyone else does, and I think we need to get to know each other better if I'm going to be able to help you."

Ruby nodded, looking down at her hands. She didn't like the idea of telling the counselor anything about herself. She didn't want anyone to know the kind of person she was or the things she'd done.

"Now, why don't you tell me about these dreams. Maybe if we can figure out why you're having them, we can make them go away without needing any medication."

"I don't want to think about the dreams," Ruby blurted out, clenching her hands into fists on her lap. "I just want something to make them go away. Please, just give me some pills and I won't bother you anymore."

Waiting until Ruby had finished with her outburst, Reggie shook her head and gave her a sad smile.

"It doesn't work that way, Ruby. You need to face your problems in order to overcome them. The pills will only make it all worse."

The counselor crossed the room to sit in the chair next to her.

"Now, tell me how you got here, Ruby. Tell me what it is that you can't face without the pills. Sometimes just saying the words out loud takes away their power to control you."

Ruby felt her shoulders slump under the weight of everything she'd been holding inside. But how could she tell this stranger what she'd done? She hadn't told anyone the whole story. She didn't even allow herself to think about it most of the time.

"I'm not here to judge you, Ruby. We've all made mistakes, but that's part of being human. It's what you do after you make a mistake that counts the most."

Turning back to the window, Ruby shook her head.

"What if you just keep making mistakes, again and again?"

Tears burned her eyes as she thought of all the stupid decisions she'd made. So many bad choices which had caused so much pain.

"I got hooked on prescription pills back home," Ruby found herself saying. "When I couldn't get any more, I tried to steal them, and I got busted."

She kept her eyes on the entrance to the parking lot as she spoke, half expecting to see Diablo's big SUV pull in at any minute.

"I'd just turned eighteen, so I decided to leave. I thought maybe if I got away from home, from all the mistakes I'd made, it'd be better for everyone."

Swallowing hard, Ruby couldn't force herself to tell the truth. At least not the whole truth. She couldn't relive the car crash that had taken her mother's life and had left her dad in both physical and emotional agony. She wasn't ready to shame herself even further by admitting she'd tried to treat her grief with her father's drugs.

Only she and her father knew just how low she'd fallen. The look on his face when he'd found his prescription bottle in her purse had seared itself into her heart. After everything he'd been through, she'd betrayed him and disappointed him.

She'd left home the next day, leaving behind only a note of apology. Assuring him she'd be all right, and that she'd come back when she'd fixed herself, and when she could be the kind of daughter and sister he and Rory deserved.

"I had enough money to take a Greyhound bus to Tampa," she said, finding her voice. "When I tried to buy pills from a girl at the bus station, she told me she knew someplace I could stay."

Reggie sat still, her deep brown eyes resting patiently on Ruby's face, as the memories came rushing back.

The glassy-eyed girl sat next to her on the concrete bench, her hands nervously fumbling with a small baggie of pills she'd pulled out of the pocket of her jean shorts.

"How much?" Ruby asked, looking at the pills, and thinking of the few crumpled bills remaining in the bottom of her backpack.

"You can have 'em for free if you want," the girl offered, swiping a hand under her nose and sniffing. "I know a place you can stay, too."

"Nah, I'm supposed to meet someone," she lied, not liking the vacant look in the girl's eyes. "But I'll give you a five for two pills."

Digging in her backpack, Ruby pulled out her last five-dollar bill and extended it toward the girl, who just stared at it in confusion.

"Don't you want a bag?"

"I'm kinda' short on cash," Ruby admitted, ready to walk away.

The girl hesitated, then motioned for Ruby to follow her.

"I can't open this here," she said, shaking the bag. "Follow me."

Ruby watched the girl walk to the edge of the platform and disappear around the side. After a minute, she walked over and looked around the corner after her, but a black SUV was blocking her view.

Straining to see past the big vehicle, Ruby didn't notice the man come up behind her until he'd put his massive hand on her arm, forcing her toward the idling SUV.

"What the fuck?" she'd sputtered, trying to wrench her arm away.

The man tightened his grip as he pushed her toward the back door, which swung open to reveal the glassy-eyed girl and another burly man wearing a black t-shirt and dark sunglasses.

"Shut up or I'll call my cop buddies and tell 'em about your little habit," the man grunted, barely opening his mouth. "And don't try anything stupid, like jumping out of the car. I know where you live, and I might have to pay a little visit to your family."

Ruby knew the man was bluffing. There was no way he knew about her father and little brother across the state in Daytona.

But she wasn't so sure about the threat of turning her into the cops.

She thought of the half-empty prescription bottle in the bottom of her backpack. Could she risk getting picked up and maybe causing her dad more worry? Hadn't she already done enough to hurt him?

"It's no big deal," the glassy-eyed girl said, still clutching the baggie in her hand. "And they'll give you all the pills you want."

Plucking her backpack from her hands, the man shoved her inside and slammed the door shut. Then the SUV was rolling away from the bus station, heading out of Tampa and onto the highway. Ruby watched the signs blur past until the vehicle finally veered off the exit ramp onto Highway 42.

They'd just passed a sign welcoming them to Willow Bay, when the SUV swung into a narrow turn-off, hidden by overhanging trees. Branches scraped along the side of the vehicle as it bumped along an unpaved road, finally exiting into a clearing. The driver stopped to wait as a big gate swung open, and then nosed the SUV through and jerked to a stop.

Climbing out of the SUV, the driver opened Ruby's door and motioned for her to get out. She stepped out onto hard-packed dirt and gazed around at the big fence topped with barbed-wire, suddenly scared that the men were actually cops and that she'd been taken to some kind of backwoods jail.

The fence surrounded a collection of long, low buildings, which appeared to have been faded by years of baking in the Florida sun. Thinking the place looked like it had once been some kind of prison or military compound, Ruby was led to a building near the back of the property.

A heavyset man sat next to the entrance in a wooden chair smoking a cigarette. He wore jeans and a black jacket; a shotgun was propped against the wall next to him.

"What's your name?" the man muttered, looking her up and down with greedy eyes. "You from around here?'

"We picked her up at the bus station on our way back," the driver of the SUV said before she could answer. "She was looking for pills."

The man held up her backpack and pulled out her wallet, removing her driver's license from the little plastic pocket in the front.

"Her name's Ruby Chase, and she's from Daytona."

Reaching for her bag, Ruby felt an iron fist grab her wrist.

"Whoa there, Ruby," the man said, amused. "No need to be rude. We're not going to hurt you. You treat us right and we'll treat you right."

The man in the chair rose and picked up the shotgun just as the door beside him opened. A girl appeared holding two thick bags of white powder.

Her eyes weren't as glassy as the girl at the bus station, but she looked at Ruby with disinterest as she slipped past, as if she were used to seeing women held at gunpoint.

"Go on in," the man with the gun said to Ruby. "I think it's time we all get better acquainted."

Her mind rebelled at the memories beyond that door. That was the stuff of her nightmares and the images that haunted her. She could never go home now, never face her father and her little brother again.

Forcing her thoughts back into Reggie's office, Ruby wrapped her arms around herself and shivered.

"The girl I met was working with a group of men. They used my pills to...to get me to work for them, too. They wouldn't let me leave."

Reggie nodded as if she understood.

"Do you know who these men were?"

"All I know is that they worked for a man called Diablo. His men used the women they picked up to sell drugs and make deliveries. They threatened me and said if I told anyone..."

A sudden movement in the parking lot caught Ruby's eye. A black car had pulled in. Could it be Diablo or one of his men? Had Reggie called them and told them she was there?

Her heart thudded in her chest as she stared out the window. But then an elderly woman stepped out of the black car and began to walk toward the building. It wasn't someone coming for her; she was safe.

"Are you okay, Ruby? Is there something out there?"

Reggie leaned forward to look out the window.

"No, there's nothing," Ruby said, swallowing back words about the man she'd seen before.

Maybe that had just been my imagination, too. Maybe the withdrawal is making me see things. Maybe I'm going crazy.

Trying to pay attention to Reggie's calm voice, Ruby forced herself to turn away from the window.

"I'm sorry you had to go through that," Reggie said softly. "But you're here now, and if you complete the program, you have a good chance of staying clean, and of going back home."

Ruby wished the words were true. But there was no way she could run back to her father. Not while Diablo and his men were still out there looking for her.

If they were to track her down and find out about her father and Rory, they'd used them to threaten her, as they did with the other girls. She'd known better than to let the men find her true weakness.

If they don't know about my family, they can't use them to control me.

"I need to make a phone call," Ruby said. "I want to call home."

"That's a wonderful idea." Reggie's face lit up. "We usually ask residents to use the phone in the rec room, but this time I'll let you use mine."

The counselor stood up and motioned to the phone on her desk.

"I'll give you some privacy," she said, heading toward the door.

Once the door had closed behind Reggie's small figure, Ruby took out the card Detective Bell gave her and picked up the handset. When the call went to voicemail, Ruby was tempted to hang up. She hesitated, then stuttered out a hurried message.

"Detective Bell, this is...this is Ruby. Ruby Chase. I just wanted to ask you something. I guess I'll try back later."

Dropping the handset back on the base, Ruby crossed to the door and stepped out into the hall. She felt too jumpy and nervous to go back to the solitude of her room. The sound of the television led her to the rec room, where several women were watching the local news.

Veronica Lee was on the screen. Ruby recognized the reporter's red coat; it was the same one she'd worn the other day. She stepped closer to hear what Veronica was saying.

"A woman's body has been discovered at Old Willow Square today," Veronica said, her eyes grave as she looked into the camera.

"The police are calling the death a homicide, but they have no suspects in custody at this time."

Ruby's pulse raced as she listened to the rest of the report.

A woman was dumped in the park and the cops have no clue who did it.

Her mind flashed back to the big man outside Reggie's window. What if Diablo's men knew she was there? Would they try to kill her?

Maybe I should call Detective Bell again. Maybe she can protect me.

But the girls at Diablo's compound swore that Diablo had connections everywhere, even in the police department.

What if she brings that nasty Detective Ingram with her?

Worries that the cops would lock her up, or maybe even turn her over to Diablo's men, began to take shape in her mind. Detective Bell knew where she was, and she and her partner could come for her at any minute. Once she was in custody, she'd be at their mercy with no one to help her. She could trust no one.

Then a face flashed through her mind.

The man with Detective Bell said he would help me, and I believed him.

A commercial interrupted the news report, and Ruby turned and hurried back to her room. She once again pulled out the card Detective Bell had given her. This time she turned it over and looked at the name she'd written across the back.

Frankie Dawson, Private Investigator.

Grabbing her jacket, Ruby headed toward the door.

CHAPTER SEVENTEEN

Pulling his hoodie tighter around him, Frankie sat back on Little Ray's sagging couch and watched the big man reach for another cigarette. The old double-wide trailer had no heater, and the chilly air from outside seeped under the door and through the cracked window.

"You do know smoking can kill you, right?"

Frankie glared at the cigarette in Ray's chubby hand.

"You're just mad cause you want one." Ray chuckled as he lit the cigarette and took a deep drag. "Now what the hell did you want to talk about? I gotta get to work."

Reaching into the pocket of his hoodie, Frankie felt around for a stick of gum. Pulling off the silver wrapper, he stuck it in his mouth and began to chew as Ray exhaled a thick cloud of smoke.

"I've been hearing talk on the street about some dude named Diablo," Frankie said, trying to sound casual. "You haven't heard anything, have you?"

Ray threw back his massive head and laughed, jiggling cigarette ashes onto the grayish carpet.

"Diablo?" Ray ran his fingers through his beard and shook his head. "Shit, I haven't heard that name in a while, man."

"But you have heard it?"

Nodding his head as he took another drag, Ray grinned.

"That's just some bullshit name people throw around to try to scare each other. And whenever the cops picked us up and asked if we knew who'd done something, we always said it was *Diablo*."

Ray wiggled his plump fingers in the air and widened his eyes.

"The dude was like some boogeyman or something."

His words echoed what Ingram had told Peyton earlier, and Frankie felt a shiver along his spine.

"So, you don't think this guy is real then?" Frankie narrowed his eyes. "You haven't heard a new group's running drugs around here?"

A frown replaced Ray's smile.

"You know I don't get involved with that shit anymore. I've been keeping my hands clean. Have been since I got out of the joint."

Raising his eyebrows, Frankie studied the big man's face.

"Just because you're clean, doesn't mean you don't know what's going on, man. You have friends. I'm sure they talk."

Ray hoisted himself off the couch and hitched up his pants. He looked down at Frankie, all hint of amusement gone.

"I don't want any trouble, Frankie," he said, hooking his keys off the counter. "I'm doing pretty good. I've only got twelve more payments on this place and it's mine. And my Chevy's all paid off."

He turned off the lights and opened the front door.

"Now, come on, I'll give you a ride back to town."

Climbing into the little Chevy pick-up truck, Frankie chewed nervously on his gum, wondering what the big man wasn't saying.

He'd met Little Ray in prison a decade earlier. Frankie had been wrongly convicted of armed robbery, and Ray had been caught with enough weed to start a small bonfire. Realizing they'd lived in the same small town, the men had started an unlikely friendship and had stayed in touch after Frankie's sentence had been overturned.

Frankie was sure Ray still had plenty of connections, even if he had gone straight years before. If somebody new was dealing drugs in or around Willow Bay, Little Ray would know about it.

They'd just pulled out onto Old Shepard Highway heading west when Ray spoke again.

"Why are you so interested in some lowlife pushers anyway?"

Keeping his eyes on the road ahead, Frankie shrugged.

"A friend of mine had a run-in with these scumbags. They seem like real bad news. I thought you'd point me in the right direction."

"And then what? You get your skinny ass killed?"

Little Ray's hands gripped the Chevy's steering wheel, and Frankie heard something in his voice he'd never heard before.

"You're scared of these guys, aren't you?"

"Fuck no, I'm not scared," Ray sputtered. "At least not for myself. But you're in no shape to go up against these guys."

He glanced in his rearview mirror, as if Diablo or his men might be tailing them, then looked over at Frankie.

"I thought that shit about him calling himself Diablo was a joke," Ray said. "But maybe that's just a way for him to stay under the radar. Whatever he's calling himself, I've heard the dude is crazy."

"Heard from who?"

Frankie saw the turnoff toward downtown coming up. He wanted an answer from Ray before it was too late.

"Come on, man, who told you about this guy?"

Stopping at a red light, Ray turned to Frankie and shook his head.

"I'm not a damn snitch, Frankie, you know that."

The light turned green and Ray floored the little pick-up. He took a right onto Waterside Drive, and then a left onto Bay Street, bringing the Chevy to a stop in front of Barker and Dawson Investigations.

"There was a group in Miami that got busted last year," Ray said, not looking at Frankie. "They ran drugs, women, maybe even guns. The feds took them down. The big shots got hard time, but some of the grunts are already back on the street."

"Our streets?" Frankie asked. "These grunts are around here?"

Ray shrugged.

"I ran into a buddy from the joint a few weeks back. Said he'd come here after the bust went down in Miami. He didn't mention the name Diablo. Just said he's still in the game and business is booming. Oh, and he said the guy he works for is a real psycho."

* * *

Frankie dropped into the chair in front of his desk just as his cell phone buzzed in his pocket. His heart sank when he saw the number.

"Hey, Reggie, what's up?"

"Ruby Chase is gone. She's not in her room, and we can't find her anywhere in the building. I just thought you'd want to know."

Reggie sounded upset.

"I don't have any other contact info for her, and since you were the one that arranged for her to come here…"

"Yeah, I'm glad you called me, Reggie," Frankie said, trying not to let her hear the disappointment in his voice. "Thanks for letting me know."

Ending the call, Frankie held the phone in his hand, tempted to call Peyton Bell. The detective would want to know that Ruby had left Hope House before finishing the program.

But the remembered sting of Peyton's words stopped him. She'd made it clear he wasn't welcome poking his nose into her investigation. She'd said the task force was working on it.

So, who am I to butt in and tell the task force anything now?

Switching on his computer, Frankie opened his time log and began entering in the hours he'd spent tailing Garth Bixby. The campaign manager had spent most of the day at City Hall, other than the hour or so he'd spent at Old Willow Square.

Unable to bear another afternoon twiddling his thumbs outside Bixby's office, Frankie had made an executive decision to visit Little Ray before Bixby left for the day.

Frankie checked his watch, calculating he should have another hour before Bixby left the office. He was sure he hadn't missed anything important and was in no hurry to return.

As long as I'm outside City Hall in time to tail the cheating bastard on the way home, no one else has to know a damn thing.

Closing out the spreadsheet, Frankie wondered where Ruby Chase could have gone. Did she have a family to go back to? Was there someone out there looking for her?

He opened a web browser, navigating to the usual missing person websites, and searched for someone meeting Ruby Chase's description. After ten minutes he had to admit there didn't appear to be anyone looking for Ruby Chase.

Once he closed the browser, Frankie stared at the desktop, wondering what to try next. His eyes fell on the Facebook icon, and he clicked on it, searching for the group page that posted notices from families desperate to find a missing child, or parent, or sibling.

I wish they'd had this when I was out looking for Franny.

Frankie had spent countless nights searching for Franny. Facebook hadn't been an option back then, and he remembered roaming the streets of Memphis looking for his little sister. That last night had been the worst night of his life.

Maybe someone out there is looking for Ruby. Maybe that person is just as desperate as I used to be when Franny would go missing.

Scrolling through the photos and messages on the page, Frankie didn't notice Barker until he was standing in front of him.

"Mrs. Bixby wanted to come by and pick up our invoice," Barker said between gritted teeth. "We didn't think you'd be here."

Barbie Bixby stared at Frankie's screen. He saw the sides of her mouth turn down, but her forehead didn't crease into a frown.

Looks like the Botox is working as promised.

Turning away from the screen, Frankie smiled up at Barbie, trying to think up a plausible excuse for his presence in the office rather than outside City Hall, but he drew a total blank.

"Aren't you supposed to be tailing my husband?"

Barbie put both hands on her narrow hips and raised one perfectly shaped eyebrow. Her disapproving stance reminded Frankie of his mother, but he decided against sharing that observation with her.

"Or am I paying you to surf the internet, now?"

Frankie thrust a nervous hand into the pocket of his hoodie, feeling around for a piece of gum, but came up empty. He stuck his other hand in his pants pocket, finding only his phone.

Pulling the phone out with a flourish, Frankie held it up in the air.

"I came back here to download the pics and video I'd taken. Got so much stuff my storage was full." He leaned back in the chair and smiled. "I figured I could be back outside City Hall by closing time."

He followed Barbie's skeptical gaze to his computer, the Facebook logo clearly visible on the big screen.

"I was just checking to see if your hubby has been posting anything online that we should be aware of. You'd be surprised how many people are caught cheating by something they post online."

"I've been married three times," Barbie replied with a sigh, tucking a glossy strand of honey blonde hair behind a delicate ear. "Nothing surprises me anymore when it comes to liars and cheats."

A flush of guilt colored Frankie's cheeks as he realized he was one of the liars Barbie was talking about. The poor woman might be a bit hard around the edges, but she hadn't gotten that way without help from men like Garth Bixby.

And like me.

Turning her back on Frankie, Barbie crossed to Barker's desk and waited while he printed out the latest invoice for their services. She didn't stop to review the charges, just stuck the paper into her designer handbag and headed toward the door.

"I'll give this to my accountant. He'll put a check in the mail."

As the door slammed shut behind their most lucrative client, Barker sank into his chair and let his head drop into his hands.

"I'm sorry, man," Frankie muttered, his eyes moving back to the computer screen. "It's just been a really crappy day and looking at all this isn't helping."

Barker raised his head and sighed.

"Okay, what have you really been doing?"

"I've been looking for a girl. She's in trouble and I thought..."

Staring at Frankie's bowed head, Barker sighed.

"Another one, huh? You're starting to make this a habit."

But his eyes softened as Frankie looked up, and he smiled.

"If Taylor ever gets in trouble again, and I can't be there, I'd want you to be the one looking out for her," Barker said, his eyes misting over at the thought of his daughter. "You helped bring her back to me, and I haven't forgotten that."

Frankie tried to smile, but the posts from families trying to find missing loved ones kept flashing through his head. He didn't have time now, but he promised himself he'd spend more time later trying to find out where Ruby came from, and who might be looking for her.

Maybe the only people looking for the poor girl are those thugs that roughed her up. Maybe she really is all alone in the world.

The possibility that yet another girl was lost to the darkness and doom of addiction made Frankie crave a hard drink. Maybe more than one. He stood and crossed to the door, knowing he had to keep busy or the craving might take over.

"Okay, back to my post."

He threw Barker a jaunty salute as he went out the door, but an ache had settled into his stomach, and it didn't fade as he walked the few blocks to City Hall. It was the same feeling he always got when he thought about his little sister.

The terrible certainty that he'd failed Franny surged through him all over again, along with the impulse to stop Ruby Chase from suffering the same, sad fate.

Why do I have to see Franny in every messed-up girl I meet?

Squeezing his eyes shut against the image of Franny's still, pale face, and the thinness of her bruised, ruined arms, Frankie wondered if his sister was up there somewhere, urging him on.

It would always be too late to save Franny, but it seemed that there was always another girl out there, just as lost and alone as his sister had been. Another girl that needed saving.

CHAPTER EIGHTEEN

Skylar figured the Professor had been gone for at least three days, but she'd slept fitfully off and on, and now had no idea what time it was, unsure if it was night or day, or if time really even mattered in the small, dark safe room that was, for the moment, her whole world.

Closing Astrid's now worn-out copy of *Pride and Prejudice*, Skylar whispered the words she'd read so many times in the last week.

"Think only of the past as its remembrance gives you pleasure."

She wished she could force her mind to follow that advice. If only she could stop herself from thinking of the things she'd seen and heard. Remembering her past gave her no pleasure, only pain.

Running her fingers over the spine of the book, Skylar wondered if it was time to move on to another book on the shelf. Although she'd already read each book in the safe room many times over, even the ones she didn't like, it was always satisfying to pick up a book and start from the beginning.

The very act of starting something created the illusion that there was something she needed to finish. A task to complete, and a purpose to keep her going. Losing herself in the pages of these books was the only way she could escape the cold silence of the little room that was her prison.

Skylar slid *Pride and Prejudice* back on the shelf, keeping it near the front, in a place of honor. She'd gotten the book from Astrid's book bag, along with a thick volume of Shakespeare's plays and sonnets.

The big book stirred thoughts of Astrid as she pulled it from the shelf, and Skylar squeezed her eyes shut, blocking the image of blood-stained snow that trembled at the edge of her memory.

Opening the book to *Hamlet*, Skylar flipped through pages until she found the words that she'd carefully underlined.

In this sleep of death what dreams may come...

She wondered what would happen if she were to let herself just sleep, and never wake up. Would the nightmares still come? Would the Professor haunt her even then?

Would the women that haunt my dreams be with me, too?

She closed the heavy book, shutting out the words and the thoughts that came with them, and put it back on the shelf, careful not to bend any of the pages.

With only two shelves full of books to last a lifetime, Skylar had to make do with what was available, and she fiercely protected the treasured books that she'd managed to scavenge from the discarded backpacks and bookbags left behind by the safe room's unwilling visitors.

Several books still bore the name of a college student that would never get a chance to find out if the story had a happy ending. Skylar tried not to look at the names too often.

Kneeling beside the little cot, Skylar carefully pulled out the small pile of paper she'd been saving. Most of the paper in the stack had already been filled with sketches.

She let her eyes linger over the scenes of winter beyond the big fence, vegetables blooming in the little garden, and the faces of women who had come and gone throughout the years.

She lifted a small finger and traced the outline of a woman's face on a slip of paper, wondering if she'd ever seen the lovely face, or if the woman it belonged to lived only in her dreams.

Something about the woman was familiar. Maybe it was the look of hopelessness in her eyes or the trace of a sad smile that turned up the corner of her mouth.

Standing to look at her own reflection in the small mirror above the sink, Skylar frowned, then picked up a pencil and began moving it through the air, imagining the lines she would need to draw to capture the forlorn expression on her own pale face.

But she couldn't afford to waste a piece of paper on a self-portrait, could she? She didn't know when she'd have the chance to filch more paper. Of course, if the Professor never came back, the drawing might be the only thing left to prove Skylar had ever existed.

A pang of hunger stopped her morbid thoughts, and she crossed to the storage shelves where the Professor had stacked enough boxed, canned, and packaged food to last a year.

Picking up a can of tomato soup, Skylar opened the can and poured the thick red liquid into a small saucepan, then placed the pan on the two-burner hotplate that was her only cooking appliance.

As she waited for the soup to heat up, Skylar imagined that the weather was growing colder outside, and pictured the snow piling up on the treetops on the other side of the fence.

She realized she missed watching the sky fade from blue to black outside the big windows as she cooked the Professor's dinner.

Skylar had been the only one the Professor allowed to roam freely around the big house while he spent countless hours at his computer, obsessed with the world outside the compound.

During the summer she'd been tasked with growing vegetables and fruit in the back garden, which was surrounded by a high concrete wall and equipped with a high-tech security system.

The relative freedom she'd been given had gone only as far as the compound's big fence. It had often been taken away without notice whenever the Professor decided it was safer for her to go underground.

But now that she'd been trapped in the safe room for days, reduced to moving around the small area with no natural light or air, the upstairs world seemed like an unattainable dream.

Standing under the hatch that provided the only way up and out of the safe room, Skylar wondered if she could find a way to reach it without the little ladder.

Could she stand the little cot on end? Or maybe take out the shelving and build her own ladder?

The ideas all seemed impossible, and the little voice in her head scoffed at the possibility she'd be able to concoct some kind of solution on her own.

Even if I did manage to get up there, the hatch is locked from the outside.

Skylar smelled the scent of bubbling soup, and turned away from the hatch, knowing she had to eat to keep up her strength.

But a disturbing thought had wormed its way into her mind as she'd looked up helplessly at the hatch.

What will happen if the Professor doesn't come back? Will I live out the rest of my life locked away down here? How long will I last?

Spooning the hot soup into her mouth, Skylar tried to clear her head of the troubling questions. She finished the soup without really tasting it and went back to her room to sit on the cot.

The sketches were still in a pile on the floor, and she picked up the paper on top, staring again at the face of the woman with the sad smile.

Holding the slip of paper against her chest, Skylar curled up on the cot and closed her eyes. Within minutes she was dreaming.

Skylar heard the woman's frantic voice shouting up at her. Looking down, she tried to make out the woman below, but her face was cloaked in darkness.

Staring upward, Skylar gazed at the circle of brilliant blue sky above her.
"Climb up, Skylar. We have to run and hide."

Skylar tried to move her legs, but she was too scared. Her legs were frozen with fear, and she felt her body start to wobble on the ladder.

Soft arms suddenly surrounded her.

"I've got you," the woman whispered. "Hold on tight."

Skylar felt the sweet warmth of the woman's breath on her face as she was carried up toward the light.

Gasping at the sting of icy air on her face, Skylar looked around, squinting in the brilliant sunshine, blinking against the wind that sent her hair whipping around her face, blocking her view.

"Now run, Skylar. Run for the woods and don't look back."

The ground was frozen solid under her little shoes, and she slipped and fell forward, her bare hands sinking into a clump of snow.

Scrambling to her feet, she saw the trees in the distance. The tops of the trees were covered in snow, and the sun glistened off the blinding whiteness as she ran forward, her breath puffing out in front of her.

Skylar jumped when a big hand fell on her shoulder.

Lifted high into the air, her hands flailed as she was carried back toward the dark opening in the earth.

"Skylar!"

The scream echoed in the air.

Kicking at the arm holding her, Skylar broke free from the iron grip.

Then she was falling and falling, until at last her head connected hard with the frozen ground and the sky blinked out and disappeared.

The burning odor roused Skylar from her sleep. She hadn't turned the hot plate off, and the remnants of the soup had blackened in the pan, filling the little room with an offensive smell.

She switched off the hot plate and dropped the pan in the sink, shaken by the intensity of the dream.

Was the woman in the drawing the same woman that had been in her dream? The woman that had told her to run and hide?

Something bad happened to that woman.

The words fluttered through her mind, but she pushed them away, not sure if she was unable or unwilling to remember.

Walking back to the hatch, she looked up and frowned. Had the dream been a memory or a warning?

In her dream, the ladder had led up to a bright blue sky.

This couldn't be it. This hatch leads to the bottom floor of the house.

Could there be another way out?

There are grey wolves and mountain lions out there, girl. They'd love nothing more than to have you for dinner.

The Professor's grim words echoed in her ears. What would happen if she did manage to get outside?

It's probably snowing again, and the wolves might be howling.

She wasn't sure what would be worse, the Professor finding her, or being hunted down by the other predators that roamed the forest.

Forcing the Professor's angry face out of her mind, Skylar picked up a pencil and found her last empty sheet of paper.

I'll draw Astrid before I forget what she looked like. Before it's too late and there's nothing to prove she was ever here. Before I disappear, too.

CHAPTER NINETEEN

Tucker's Truck Stop was quiet as the Professor pulled off the highway. The old gas station didn't see much traffic in the colder months when few people ventured off the interstate on their way to the coast. Steering the big rig into the lot, he noted the white Honda parked under a battered *Truck Repairs Here* sign.

The car had been left just as he'd been promised, and the Professor grunted in satisfaction as he maneuvered into an empty parking space reserved for semis and RVs.

Jumping down from the cab, the Professor jogged across the lot and circled the white car. It wasn't as new as the black Toyota he'd used the night before, but it would do. Looking around to make sure he wasn't being observed, he opened the driver's door and slipped behind the wheel.

He leaned forward to open the glovebox, picking up the key fob and eyeing the big Ruger inside. His contact had delivered everything to plan. Now he just had to wait for Diablo to arrive.

A drop of water splashed onto the windshield, and then another. Within minutes the rain was beating down on the little car.

Starting the Honda's engine, the Professor flipped on the heater. He was used to much colder weather, but he'd anticipated the Florida temperature to be almost warm, if not balmy, and was wearing only a thin jacket he wore on spring days back in the Bitterroot Valley.

The Professor adjusted his seat back and rested his hands on the steering wheel. Taking off his gloves, he stretched his bruised fingers as he replayed the events of the last twenty-four hours and planned his next move.

It had been relatively easy to transfer Astrid's frozen body from the big chest freezer into the backseat of the Toyota. She'd been stiff and, to his relief, hadn't started to smell of decomposition. It had almost been like moving an awkward piece of furniture.

But the trip into downtown Willow Bay had been nerve-wracking. The Professor had been sure someone would wonder why the black Toyota was circling around downtown in the pre-dawn hours. But the city had seemed deserted, and he'd encountered no one as he'd loaded Astrid onto the lightweight, folding wheelchair and rolled her into the old square.

Arranging her on the bench just as the sun started to rise in the east, the Professor had been prepared to greet any passersby calmly, as if he and his female companion were simply taking a rest before moving on about their day. But he'd been alone in the frigid square and had wheeled the chair back to the car without incident.

He'd been elated as he'd dropped off the Toyota and climbed back in his rig. Parking at a rest stop on the interstate, he'd slept like a baby most of the day, waking only to buy a sandwich and coffee from the rest stop café and check the local news on the mounted screens in the visitor's center.

Veronica Lee's report on the body found in Old Willow Square had set his heart pounding, and he imagined everyone in the little town was watching, including his ex-wife.

The traitorous bitch is about to learn that I always keep my promises.

A fist suddenly pounded on the passenger side window, and the Professor saw a man lean over and motion for him to unlock the door. Tempted to take out the Ruger just in case things went south, the Professor decided against it.

129

He doesn't have the balls to kill me outright, even if he wanted to.

Leaning over, the Professor unlocked the door, and Diablo dropped into the passenger seat, his black leather jacket dripping rainwater onto the console between them.

Diablo wore a dark hoodie under his leather jacket, with the hood covering his head, and dark glasses, though the sun had already dropped below the western horizon, and thick rain clouds obscured any daylight that remained.

The Professor gave the man a cursory look, quickly confirming that the man sitting next to him was in fact the man he'd expected.

There was no need to ask him to push back the hood or to take off his glasses. The Professor already knew what Diablo looked like, along with almost everything else about him.

If living in hiding all those years navigating the darknet had taught him anything, it was how to follow an online trail.

And the Professor had found many trails leading back to the man sitting next to him. The man who'd recently started calling himself Diablo hadn't exactly laid low his whole life, and he hadn't been savvy about using the darknet.

Assuming that no one on the illicit discussion boards would be able to track him down, Diablo hadn't counted on the cunning and persistence of the man who'd created the discussion board dedicated to trafficking drugs, weapons, and on occasion, even human cargo.

"Okay, I'm here," Diablo muttered, keeping one hand on the door handle as if prepared to jump out at any minute. "You said you had information for me. What is it?"

The Professor reached into his pocket. Diablo stiffened, then relaxed when he saw that the Professor held only a newspaper clipping from the *Willow Bay Gazette.*

"What's that, a help-wanted ad?"

Diablo's sarcastic grin evaporated as he saw the headline on the front page of the newspaper.

"You're big news around here, aren't you, Mr. *Diablo*?" The Professor drew out the name as if it tasted bitter on his tongue. "And you'd be even bigger news if your new career were to be exposed."

The dark glasses hid Diablo's expression, but the Professor could see the hand on the door handle ball into a fist. He spoke before Diablo could say something they would both regret. He now had the upper hand, and it was time to offer Diablo the bait.

"However, it seems we have mutual enemies, and I have information that will help us both get what we want."

"And what's that?" Diablo sounded suspicious.

"Revenge on those that have wronged us," the Professor replied.

Diablo started to speak, but the Professor held up his hand to silence him, realizing only then that he'd forgotten to put his glove back on. He wrapped his hand around the steering wheel, hoping Diablo hadn't noticed his two missing fingers.

"We don't have time to waste," he said, irritation over his error hardening his words. "If we come to an agreement tonight, I'll send you all the details on the message board. It'll be enough to blow the lid off this little town."

The Professor raised his other hand and smirked when he saw Diablo flinch as if he'd expected to see a gun. Diablo's shoulders relaxed when he saw that the Professor held another piece of paper.

He dropped a printout on the console between them and tapped a finger on the older woman in the image.

"I want *her* dead. I want you to kill her."

He didn't wait for Diablo's reaction before tapping the same finger on the younger woman in the picture.

"This one bring me alive. Make sure she's not harmed."

Pushing the paper in Diablo's direction, the Professor placed both hands on the steering wheel and looked through the windshield at the dark parking lot. A man carrying a cup of steaming coffee hurried past, his breath visible in the cold night air.

131

"Why don't you just take care of these two yourself?" Diablo muttered, gripping the paper in his fist. "You're the badass, right?"

Gritting his teeth, the Professor tried to keep his tone calm.

"Let's just say they may be expecting me. And as an outsider, I'd attract attention hanging around waiting for an opportunity. While you...well, you know the town. You can do what's necessary."

Diablo stared down at the image, then shook his head.

"How do you know I'd be interested?"

The professor produced a nasty smile.

"I know everything I need to know about you. Which is why you're sitting here. You have as much to gain, and as much to lose, as I do."

When Diablo didn't react, the Professor tried again.

"I don't trust anyone to do anything unless it's in their own self-interest. Which is why I'm willing to trust you'll find this little arrangement to your liking."

Drumming his fingers on the dashboard, Diablo looked over at the Professor, then out at the rain, which was starting to slow.

"If I do you this favor...what happens next?"

"Kill the mother and bring the daughter to me unharmed," the professor said, his voice cold. "After that, you'll never hear from her, or me, again."

Diablo held up a hand in protest.

"Wait just a minute, *Professor.*"

Removing his dark glasses, Diablo turned to stare into the Professor's cold green eyes.

"You know the state of Florida still has the death penalty, right? So, I'd be risking my life to take out this woman, and for what?"

His words didn't worry the Professor. They just signaled that negotiations had begun. He was suddenly curious as to what Diablo would want from him.

"What are you saying?"

"I'm saying this seems like a lopsided deal."

The Professor scratched at the rough skin on his chin, waiting for Diablo to make an offer, wondering what he was willing to do to get his ex-wife taken care of once and for all.

Maybe the question should be what won't I do?

Sitting back in his seat, Diablo reached into his jacket pocket and pulled out his phone. He scrolled through his photos and stopped on a picture, then held the display up to the Professor.

"If I fix your problem, it's only fair you fix mine."

Staring at the lovely woman in the picture, the Professor hesitated, surprised by the request. He'd expected the man to ask for money, or maybe drugs. Then again, who was he to judge? He looked at the woman on Diablo's display again and smiled.

This little favor might be just what I need to get back on track.

The Professor glanced up at Diablo and nodded his agreement, trying to hide his satisfaction with the arrangement. He was looking forward to getting hold of the woman. Although she was older than most of the women he dealt with, she was undeniably gorgeous. The right buyer would pay a pretty penny for her.

Thinking of the buyer who was waiting for Astrid, the Professor realized his problem might be solved. The man was getting impatient, and he was expecting to get his money's worth. Money that the Professor did not want to return.

A small smile lifted the corner of his mouth as they worked out the arrangement. The lovely replacement for Astrid Peterson would be an unexpected bonus, and his main objective was now in sight. Soon his ex-wife would be dead, and his daughter would be back where she belonged.

CHAPTER TWENTY

Veronica woke on Saturday morning to a persistent pounding on the front door. Sitting up in bed with a start, she saw that Winston had still been asleep, too, and that the big tabby cat now looked as tired and grumpy as she felt.

Pulling on her robe and stepping into her slippers, Veronica padded down the stairs and peered through the front window. Hunter Hadley stood on the front step. He lifted his fist again to pound on the door as Gracie sat calmly beside him on the welcome mat.

Fear mingled with irritation as she pulled back the deadbolt and opened the door, taking in his worried frown and the copy of the *Willow Bay Gazette* he held under his arm.

Hunter stepped past her into the hall before she could ask what had happened. She waited until Gracie had also trotted inside, shivering against the cool air that had slipped in along with the white Lab, then closed the door

"I tried to call, but you didn't answer your phone."

Holding the paper toward her, Hunter's expression was grim.

"You need to see this."

Staring down at the paper, Veronica saw that Hunter was holding the front page of the *Local News* section, and she was suddenly very sure that she didn't want to see whatever story or news article was in that paper.

"I'm sorry for doing this," Hunter said, stepping closer. "But I didn't want you to hear this from anyone else."

Drawing in a deep breath, she took the paper from his hand, her eyes widening when she saw the headline, and her chest tightening as she read the story.

Exclusive: Mayoral Candidate Ling Lee's Secret Identity Exposed

By Mackenzie Jensen

Willow Bay, Florida - As the mayoral election draws near, voters in Willow Bay will be startled to learn that the current principal of Willow Bay High School, and the city's first female candidate for mayor, has been living under an assumed identity for over two decades. Documents obtained exclusively by the Willow Bay Gazette show candidate Ling Lee was originally born as Lisa Li, a California resident who attended the University of California, and who was reported to have died in a car crash in San Francisco twenty-eight years ago.

Questions remain as to why Lisa Li changed her name to Ling Lee and moved to Willow Bay under an assumed identity. Calls to Ling Lee for comment on this story were not returned, but we assume Ms. Lee will have to answer the questions that will be in voters' minds about her true identity prior to the election, which is only two weeks away.

Veronica's gaze moved to the black and white photo next to the article. She walked to the living room and sank onto the sofa, her eyes still fixed on the image.

Her mother looked out of the photo from across the years. She'd been young and beautiful, and according to the name scrawled across the old photo, back then she'd been Lisa Li.

"Ronnie, what's going on? Is someone here?"

Her mother's voice sounded from the top of the stairs.

Veronica glanced up at Hunter, panic on her face.

"It's just me and Gracie," he called out. "I brought Veronica the Gazette. There's something in it that you both need to see."

"Is it another attack piece by that Mackenzie Jensen?" Ling asked, starting down the stairs. "I'm not sure why she's so against me."

Veronica pushed herself off the sofa as her mother stepped into the room. Unable to meet Ling's questioning gaze, Veronica handed her the newspaper and waited.

Wincing at the first soft gasp from her mother, Veronica moved closer and put her arm around Ling's narrow shoulders.

"This can't be...how did she...oh my goodness..."

Ling's voice faded as she struggled to find the words. Finally, she turned stunned eyes to Veronica.

"After all these years, it's finally happened."

Veronica had to strain to hear the shocked whisper.

"I thought it had been too long. I thought it was all over."

"Is this true then, Ma?" Veronica asked, gesturing to the paper. "Did you really change your name? Are you Lisa Li?"

Tears welled in her mother's eyes as she nodded.

"It seems it's pointless to deny it, now that this is in the paper."

Throwing the newspaper to the ground, Ling ran a small hand through her unbrushed hair and sighed. She turned to Veronica and put a trembling hand to her daughter's face, gently pushing back a lock of dark hair.

"The worst part is having you find out like this," she murmured, then turned to the sofa. "Let's sit down, so I can explain."

Hunter cleared his throat and motioned to the door.

"I can leave if–"

"No." Ling's tone was adamant. "Veronica is going to need you."

Her hand was ice cold as she led Veronica to the sofa and sat down next to her.

"You've always wanted to know about your father, but I was never able to tell you the whole truth. Now, I find I must tell you."

Dread settled in Veronica's chest at her mother's words.

She had all but given up on finding out the truth about her father. Although Ling had explained he'd been a bad man, and that he'd done terrible things, Veronica had decided she would leave him, along with the pain he'd caused her mother, in the past.

I guess the past didn't want him either.

Blinking back tears, Ling spoke in a voice trembling with emotion.

"My name was Lisa Li. I had to change my name when I went into the witness protection program, back when you were just a baby."

Veronica squeezed her mother's hand, holding back her own tears at the thought of Ling as a young mother giving up her name and her identity in order to save herself and her child.

"I met your father at the University of California, San Francisco," Ling continued. "I was very naïve, but I thought I knew everything."

Smiling sadly, Ling shook her head.

"He said he was a new professor in the Fine Arts department, and I believed him. In fact, I believed everything he told me without question, and we were married within a few months."

She gave Veronica's hand a tight squeeze.

"And you came along soon after. But by then I'd realized something was wrong. I'd caught my new husband in more than one lie, and he had become secretive and even violent."

Her face hardened at the memory.

"When you were still a newborn, I started thinking of leaving him. I could finally see him for what he really was, and it scared me. I overheard him talking to people about drugs, and about girls. I decided to follow him and find out what he was really doing."

Closing her eyes, Ling drew in a deep breath.

"What I found...what I saw...it was horrifying."

She swallowed hard and shook her head.

"I couldn't stay after that, but I couldn't leave knowing what he was doing to those women. I couldn't leave knowing what he would do to me if he ever found me."

"So, what did you do?" Veronica asked, holding her breath.

Ling squared her small shoulders as she met Veronica's gaze.

"I went to the police. I told them everything I'd seen, and I agreed to help them find out more. Eventually, I agreed to testify against him and his accomplices."

"And that's why you had to go into witness protection?"

Shaking her head, Ling grimaced at the memory.

"My testimony helped to convict him, but he'd been wounded in the takedown and lost two fingers on his right hand. When he was in the hospital, he managed to escape police custody. After that, he went on the run, and I knew he would come for me. I knew he'd try to kill me and take you away."

Ling got to her feet and walked to the window, staring out toward the street with haunted eyes.

"So, I agreed to go into the witness protection program. The team assigned to me believed me when I told them he would never stop looking for us. They made it look like you and I had been killed in a car crash, and they gave me a new identity."

"Why Ling Lee?" Veronica asked. "Why that name?"

Shrugging at the question, Ling turned back to her daughter.

"They suggested I use the same initials, just to make it easier to remember. Your initials were kept the same as well."

The words sent a jolt of shock through Veronica. Up until then, she'd only been thinking how her mother had been affected. Now she realized that her life, and her name, had been forever changed as well.

"What was my name?" she whispered. "Before…"

"I named you Vivian," Ling said wistfully. "I always thought the name was so glamorous."

Veronica looked to Hunter, who'd been standing quietly by the door, and managed a pained smile.

"I guess it's not too hard to imagine. Lisa Li becomes Ling Lee, and Vivian Li becomes Veronica Lee."

Ling shook her head and sighed.

"No, your name was not Vivian Li," she said, biting her lip. "You had been given your father's last name."

Rising from the sofa, Veronica went to stand beside her mother.

"What was my name, Ma?"

Her voice cracked on the words.

"Locke," Ling said gently. "Your given name was Vivian Locke."

"And my father's name?"

The expression on Ling's face hardened.

"His name is Donovan Locke. He used to call himself *Professor* Locke, but he never was a real professor. I think it was a title he used to impress and trick young women."

She looked into Veronica's eyes and sighed.

"This news in the paper, it could be very bad. If your father is still alive, and if he were to see it."

"You think you could still be in danger?" Hunter asked.

Veronica heard the worry in his voice, and she suspected she knew the answer to his question.

If her mother had been in the witness protection program, she must have been in serious danger. Now that her new identity had been revealed, she could be in danger again.

"Veronica's father is a very dangerous man," Ling said, her tears replaced by a glint of anger. "He promised me back then that he would kill me if I ever left him. If he finds out I'm still alive, I have no doubt he will try to fulfill that promise."

"Are you still in contact with the witness protection program?" Hunter asked. "Is there someone there you can call for help?"

Nodding up at him, Ling pointed toward the stairs.

"Yes, I have a number saved. It's in my phone upstairs."

Minutes later Veronica watched as her mother tapped on a contact in her list and waited. Almost immediately she heard a brusque voice on the other end.

"U.S. Marshal Service, witness security program, how can I help?"

Listening in numb disbelief as her mother explained who she was and what had happened, Veronica felt Gracie come up beside her and nuzzle at her hand.

The Lab suffered from PTSD, having survived a brutal tour of duty in the Middle East with the US Army, and after years of receiving treatment for the condition, she now had a knack for offering comfort in times of stress.

When Ling finally put down her phone, she turned to Veronica and took a deep breath.

"They're sending someone here," she said, swallowing hard. "They said to just sit tight and wait."

CHAPTER TWENTY-ONE

Nessa dragged herself into the kitchen and automatically poured herself a cup of coffee, even though she wasn't sure she would be able to stomach anything this morning. She never did look forward to an autopsy, but the thought of Astrid Peterson's pending autopsy seemed to be causing her more upset than most.

Carrying the mug to the little kitchen table, she sank into a chair next to Jerry and rifled through the newspaper sections, looking for anything in the news about the body found in Old Willow Square the day before. She was worried there might be an unflattering picture of her from the press conference when she'd almost collapsed at the podium.

Nessa hadn't mentioned her little wobble to Jerry, and she didn't want him finding out on the front page of the newspaper. But when she picked up the local news section, she was surprised to see that the death in Old Willow Square hadn't garnered the main headline.

"Mayoral Candidate Ling Lee's Secret Identity Exposed," she read aloud to Jerry, who had his face buried in the sports section.

"What?"

He lifted his head and stared over the paper in his hand as Nessa skimmed the article with growing incredulity.

"The *Gazette* is saying that Ling Lee has been using an assumed identity. They claim her real name is Lisa Li, a woman from California who supposedly died twenty-eight years ago."

Studying the picture of Ling Lee next to the article, Nessa tried to make sense of what she was seeing. Could the story be true? Glancing at the byline, she saw Mackenzie Jensen had written the story, and she frowned over at Jerry, who had folded the sports section and put it back in the pile.

"You think this could be Mayor Hadley's doing?" she asked. "Some kind of ploy to discredit Ling Lee right before the election?"

Jerry shrugged, but his expression was thoughtful as he stood and carried his cup to the sink.

"I doubt the editor of the *Gazette* would greenlight the story unless she had something to back it up," he said with reluctance. "But it is hard to believe. I mean, she's taught half the folks in this town."

"If it is true, Ling Lee's campaign for mayor is likely over."

Staring down into her mug, Nessa contemplated another term of Mayor Hadley and his buddies on the city council.

"Well, I wouldn't give up hope so fast," Jerry soothed, seeing her glum expression. "Find out all the facts before you pass judgment."

"What I want to know is how Mackenzie Jensen got this information," she said, shaking her head. "It just seems like very convenient timing, considering Mackenzie's been writing disparaging articles about Ling's campaign from the beginning."

Nessa tipped the untouched contents of her mug into the sink and decided she might as well head into work. She wanted to be there for Astrid Peterson's autopsy, even though it was a Saturday.

"Looks like I'll have to miss Cole's game today."

Jerry pulled her into a hug as she was heading for the door.

"You feeling okay?" he asked, leaning back to look into her face. "I know you're stressed, but you don't seem like yourself."

"Maybe I'm an imposter, like Ling Lee."

Her attempt to lighten the mood fell flat. Jerry just stared at her with the worried frown she knew so well.

"I'm fine," she insisted, wriggling out of his arms. "But I need to get downtown. Iris is going to perform the autopsy on the woman we found some time today, and I don't want to miss it. "

"You're the chief now, Nessa," Jerry said, stopping her in her tracks. "You should let the detectives stand in on the autopsy. Get some rest today, come with me and the boys to the game, and let them do their jobs."

Spinning to face him, Nessa felt the room around her sway. She gripped the doorframe for support.

"That's not my style," she said, trying to steady herself. "I can't sit around at a flag football game while there's a killer leaving dead bodies in the middle of my town."

Jerry stepped forward and gripped her arm.

"Hey, you really aren't okay, are you? What's going on?"

"I said I'm fine." Nessa turned toward the door before he could see the fear in her eyes. "I'll come home once the autopsy's through. Now, I've got to go."

* * *

The downtown streets were quiet as Nessa walked the few blocks from the police station to the medical examiner's office. Passing a sleek black SUV parked by the curb, she was surprised to see Tenley Frost climb down from the passenger seat and head toward City Hall.

Nessa stared after the SUV as it pulled away.

Is that Garth Bixby's car?

The city's media relations officer had every right to talk to Mayor Hadley's campaign manager, but Nessa wondered why they'd met up on a Saturday. Were they planning something related to the mayor's campaign or the upcoming election?

Looking after the SUV, Nessa couldn't be sure who was driving. The vehicle's dark tinted windows shielded anyone inside from view.

Who knows, Mayor Hadley could be in there, too. Maybe they've been holding secret strategy sessions in Bixby's SUV. Nothing would surprise me with that man.

Tenley looked up as Nessa approached, and the police chief wondered if guilt had put the pretty pink flush on her cheeks.

"Oh, Nessa, I didn't see you there," Tenley said, smoothing back her hair and straightening the lapels of her navy-blue coat.

"I'm on my way to the ME's office," Nessa said, looking pointedly at her watch. "The autopsy of the woman we found at Old Willow Square is scheduled for later today."

Tenley was too worked up to respond to Nessa's comment.

"Can you believe this morning's story in the *Gazette* about Lee Ling?" she said, her eyes wide. "Mayor Hadley has already called me twice. He wants to issue a statement as soon as possible."

Nessa frowned and crossed her arms over her chest.

"A statement about what? What does Ling Lee's past have to do with official city business?" she demanded. "The mayor shouldn't be using the media relations office to make statements against his political opponent."

Shrugging her slim shoulders, Tenley sighed.

"I know, and I pushed back saying it was inappropriate, but he insists he needs to assure parents of students at Willow Bay High that the city is looking into the matter. He claims he's already gotten calls from parents asking for an explanation."

The words deflated Nessa's outrage. She knew Mayor Hadley's intention was to destroy Ling's reputation, but he had a point.

144

If the story in the *Gazette* proved to be true, Ling would need to explain herself and verify her teaching credentials and qualifications were in fact still valid.

"Well, I'll leave it to you and the mayor to figure out," Nessa said, starting forward. "I need to get going."

As she left Tenley behind on the sidewalk, Nessa found herself questioning the woman's motives. The media relations officer had professed to support Ling Lee's bid for mayor, but the sight of her getting out of Bixby's car raised doubts in Nessa's mind.

All thoughts of Ling Lee and the upcoming election vanished when Nessa saw Agent Marlowe standing with Jankowski and Vanzinger outside the medical examiner's office.

The three men turned to Nessa as she approached. She saw Vanzinger frown, but he didn't say anything until they were all walking into the big building.

"What are you doing here, Chief?" he murmured, as he held open the door for her to pass through. "We got this, and you weren't doing so good yesterday. Why don't you get some rest?"

Glaring at him in annoyance, Nessa shook her head.

"I'm perfectly fine," she muttered under her breath. "And I want to know what's going on in this town if that's okay with you."

Wesley Knox greeted them in the reception area, leading the group down the hall and into a room where protective gear was waiting.

Once they'd all pulled on masks, coveralls, and booties, the forensics technician showed them to the autopsy suite. The dead woman's body was already waiting, her small figure covered with a white sheet.

Decomposition had begun its destruction of the body; the sickly-sweet smell of decay hit Nessa as soon as she walked in, causing her to gag behind her face mask.

Vanzinger looked over at her with concern, but Nessa ignored him as she took her place around the metal gurney, willing her stomach to settle down.

"I'm Iris Nguyen, the chief medical examiner for Willow Bay," Iris said when she saw Agent Marlowe suited up beside Nessa.

"Sorry, Iris." Vanzinger gestured toward Marlowe. "I brought along Special Agent Clint Marlowe with the FBI. He's working with us on a task force that might have an interest in this case."

"That's fine," Iris said. "Let's get started then."

Motioning to the body on the table, Iris positioned herself at the head of the metal gurney facing the detectives.

"We've been waiting for her to thaw out for the last twenty-four hours," Iris explained. "We've already done what we could to prep the body and take preliminary photos and measurements."

Iris pulled back the white sheet, eliciting a gasp from Nessa at the sight of the woman's small body on the table, a gaping gunshot wound in the center of her chest.

"Is that...the exit wound?" Nessa asked, trying to speak without breathing in the cloying odor that wafted up.

"Yes, as we observed yesterday, the deceased incurred a fatal gunshot wound in the left back region," Iris confirmed. "As you'll see when we turn her over, no soot, stippling, or muzzle stamp is visible on the skin around the entrance wound."

She motioned to the reddish-brown wound on the woman's chest.

"And based on the size and shape of the exit wound, I've concluded she was shot from a distance, probably with a high-velocity rifle."

The three tall men around the table listened with rapt attention to Iris, and Nessa tried to gauge their reactions, thinking they looked like a band of giants next to the petite medical examiner.

"So, no bullet, then?" Jankowski abruptly asked, his deep voice muffled behind his mask.

Shaking her head, Iris looked up to meet the detective's eyes.

"No, the bullet went through clean. We've already x-rayed the body for fragments and came up with nothing."

Iris moved to the bottom of the table and lifted the sheet to expose the woman's stiff, discolored feet.

"The body appears to have been frozen almost immediately after death, but I suspect she might have been exposed to freezing temperatures before death, as well."

Iris sounded unsure as she pointed to the dead woman's toes.

"See, here? The redness and swelling could very well be signs of frostbite. But I can't be sure."

"And time of death?" Vanzinger asked hopefully. "You have any idea when she died?"

Nessa wasn't surprised when Iris shook her head.

"When a body's frozen like this it's hard to say," the medical examiner admitted. "I think we can assume she'd been dead at least twenty-four hours before her body was found."

"And what about an identification?" Marlowe asked. "Have you been able to positively identify her yet?"

This time Iris nodded.

"We have had luck there."

Crossing to a long metal counter against the wall, Iris used a gloved hand to pick up a see-through evidence bag. Nessa saw an ID card of some kind in the bag.

"A University of Montana ID was in her pocket."

Iris sounded sad as she held the bag up to the light.

"Astrid Peterson was a first-year student. We managed to contact her parents already. They live in Sweden and they were willing to make identification via a remote video call."

"Shit," Vanzinger said. "Part of me was hoping I was wrong."

Swallowing back her own disappointment, Nessa put a hand on Vanzinger's thick shoulder and sighed.

"At least now her parents know," Marlowe murmured, and Nessa was surprised to see something like sadness in his dark eyes.

Iris cleared her throat and seemed to hesitate.

"What is it, Iris?" Nessa asked, sensing the medical examiner had something else she needed to say.

"We also found something quite unexpected." Iris cast a questioning glance at Wesley. "Why don't you show them, Wesley."

The young forensic technician crossed to the counter and picked up another evidence bag. He held it out in front of him so they could all see the laminated ID card inside.

"We also found something else in Astrid Peterson's pocket," Wesley said, raising his eyebrows. "It didn't make a lot of sense until I saw the *Willow Bay Gazette* this morning."

Nessa stared at the University of California student ID. She leaned closer, squinting to read the student's name.

"Who's Lisa Li?' Marlowe asked from behind her as Nessa gaped at the card, her mind whirring. "And what does she have to do with Astrid Peterson's homicide?"

"That's a good question," Nessa said, not sure she knew how to explain. "And I think we're gonna need to find the answer if we hope to catch Astrid Peterson's killer."

CHAPTER TWENTY-TWO

Peyton arrived at the WBPD later than she'd planned, having stopped by Hope House on the off chance that Ruby Chase may have returned to the rehab facility, but no one there had seen the girl since she'd taken off the day before.

Pushing through the station's front door, Peyton wished she hadn't agreed to meet Ingram. It was Saturday after all, and this had been her scheduled weekend off after working the last few weekends in a row.

But her partner wanted to stop by the convenience store where Ruby Chase had been picked up. The manager who had been working the day she'd been arrested was scheduled to work the day shift, and Ingram was determined to question him.

"Detective Bell?"

Peyton paused and looked toward the desk sergeant, who appeared flustered as he waved her over.

"Sorry to bother you, Detective, but do you know if the chief's coming in today? I've been trying her cell phone with no luck."

Before Peyton could answer, the man standing in front of the desk turned to her and nodded, sticking out a hand.

"I'm Deputy Marshal Vic Santino, a criminal investigator with the U.S. Marshals Service."

He flashed a set of even white teeth along with his identification.

"I knew finding the chief here on the weekend was a long shot, but it's an urgent matter that can't wait. Anything you can do to get me in touch with Chief Ainsley would be appreciated."

"Nice to meet you, Deputy Santino. I'm Detective Peyton Bell."

Giving his hand a quick shake, Peyton returned his smile, curious as to what the U.S. Marshals Service wanted with Nessa.

"I'll give Chief Ainsley another call," she said, resisting the urge to ask what case had brought him to Willow Bay. "After the day we had yesterday, I'm pretty sure she'll be in today."

Just as she tapped on Nessa's name in her contact list, Santino's phone buzzed in his pocket. He pulled out the phone and motioned to the door.

"I'll take this outside. Be right back."

Peyton kept her eyes on Santino's lean frame pacing back and forth on the sidewalk outside as she listened to Nessa's phone ring. She was startled when a familiar voice sounded behind her.

"You looking for me?"

Spinning around, Peyton saw Nessa standing in the lobby, her phone vibrating in her hand.

"The U.S. Marshals are looking for you," Peyton blurted.

"All of them?" Nessa asked, raising an eyebrow.

Peyton grinned and pointed out the window.

"I think it's just that one for now," she said, looking back at Santino. "He says he's a criminal investigator with the U.S. Marshal Service, and he needs to see you urgently."

"Well, we better get him in here then."

Nessa walked to the door and flung it open just as Santino shoved his phone back in his pocket. He looked up and nodded at Nessa.

"Chief Ainsley?"

"You got me," Nessa said. "Now, what do you want with me?"

* * *

Peyton sat in the briefing room with Nessa and Santino, hoping Ingram wouldn't find out where she was. She knew Nessa would never let her partner sit in on the discussion with the deputy marshal, and she was more than eager to hear what he had to say.

"I'm sure you know the U.S. Marshals Service is responsible for apprehending federal fugitives," Santino said, sitting forward in his chair as if he might get up and go at any minute. "But you may not be aware that we also operate the witness security program."

"I'm aware," Nessa said. "And I'm guessing we must have a fugitive or a witness here in our little town."

Santino nodded, and Peyton could see stress on his face for the first time. The deputy marshal was in a hurry.

"Maybe both," he said. "Ling Lee is a resident in your community. She's been in the witness security program for many years. It seems her real identity was revealed in your local newspaper. She alerted us this morning, and I'm the lucky investigator who got the case."

Unable to stop herself, Peyton asked the next question before Nessa could.

"So, who's the fugitive?"

"Donovan Locke."

Santino's voice hardened as he said the name.

"He was convicted of multiple felonies involving human trafficking, drug distribution, and possession of illegal firearms. His ex-wife testified against him, but he ended up escaping federal custody. He's been on the run for twenty-eight years."

Widening her eyes, Peyton couldn't hide her shock.

"And you've never been able to track this loser down?"

"I wasn't on the investigation team back then," Santino countered, but he didn't sound offended. "From what I can see in the files, the trail went cold, and this is the first time Locke has shown up on the radar in years."

"And you have reason to believe this man, this Donovan Locke, may be here?" Nessa asked. "Why would he come to Willow Bay?"

"Lisa Li is his ex-wife," Santino explained. "She testified against him. After Locke escaped, she went into witness protection. Based on our records, the protection team tried to make it appear as if she and their child died in an automobile accident."

Nessa stared at Santino as the pieces started to fall into place.

"And now he knows she's alive and in Willow Bay," Nessa murmured. "Which explains a lot."

"What do you mean?" Santino asked.

"I mean I think Locke's already here," Nessa said slowly. "And I think he's left us a calling card."

Pulling out her phone, Nessa scrolled to the photos she'd snapped of the school IDs that had been in Astrid Peterson's pocket.

"This ID was in the pocket of a homicide victim we found in Old Willow square yesterday morning. We think the victim was kidnapped and being held against her will. Maybe even intended for trafficking based on what we know."

Nessa passed the phone to Peyton, who passed it on to Santino.

"Then Locke is already here," Santino said, staring down at the phone. "And based on what you've just told me, it looks like he's still running the same type of operation he was convicted of before."

"So, what's the plan to catch this guy?" Peyton asked.

Santino stood and walked to the door.

"First, I need to meet with Ling Lee to update her on the situation," he said. "Once we get her somewhere safe, we can pull a task force together and hunt the bastard down."

He turned to Nessa.

"I prefer to coordinate efforts with local law enforcement whenever possible. Is there someone on your team that can accompany me to the Lee residence?"

Refusing to get her hopes up, Peyton kept her eyes on the table in front of her as she waited for Nessa's response. She was eager to work on the case but doubted Nessa would trust her with such an important, potentially high-profile assignment.

"Detective Bell can go with you." Nessa turned to Peyton. "I'll let Ingram know you've been re-assigned until further notice."

Peyton felt a pang of worry for Ruby Chase.

"Wouldn't Jankowski or Vanzinger make more sense?" she asked.

"They're already on the trafficking task force, and actively working the Astrid Peterson homicide," Nessa reminded her.

"Besides, Ling Lee knows you," she added. "And she told me how much she appreciated your work on the Greyson case. She thought your response likely saved her life. I think she'll feel more comfortable if you join Deputy Marshal Santino."

Before Peyton could get up to join Santino at the door, Nessa leaned forward and grabbed her hand.

"This assignment is strictly confidential, Detective Bell," she said, holding Peyton's gaze. "You tell no one what you've heard here without my explicit permission. And that goes double for telling Ingram."

Blinking at Nessa in surprise, Peyton nodded.

"Let's go, then," Santino said, opening the door for Peyton. "I want to get to Ling Lee before anyone else does."

CHAPTER TWENTY-THREE

The damp chill in the morning air didn't bother Ling Lee as she sat on the little patio. She had wrapped a fuzzy wool shawl around her shoulders before going into the back garden to get some fresh air, and the sun was already starting to warm up the winter day. A few birds had even ventured down to peck at the feeder.

It'll be back in the eighties next week. We'll all be wearing shorts again.

But optimistic thoughts of the future were hard to sustain with everything going on, and images from the past kept pushing forward, demanding Ling's attention.

The aging faces of her mother and father hovered at the edge of her memory. They were her biggest regret. She'd had to give them up to save herself and her child, sacrificing her connection with the previous generation to secure the survival of the next.

If only I'd listened to my mother. If only I'd followed her advice.

Those pointless words had echoed in her head for the last twenty-eight years, and they still managed to sting.

She'd been so young and sure of herself when she'd left home, headed for college and the secrets of the world outside her family's modest home. Her parents had been worried, and yet, so proud of their little girl, unaware they were sending her into the path of a predator who would take her away from them forever.

Gripping the arm of her chair in remembered agony, Ling replayed the last phone call she'd made to her parents after realizing her only hope of escape was to disappear into the witness protection program.

She'd known then if Locke had the chance, he would try to use them against her, and she couldn't let them suffer for her mistakes. She'd decided it was safest for them all to let her parents live out the rest of their lives without looking over their shoulders.

"If anything were to happen to me, remember I love you, and that I had a good life. You were great parents. You did everything right."

She'd wanted to be brave, but her voice had trembled as she realized she might never speak to them again.

Many times during her first few years in Willow Bay she had been tempted to call them. To tell them she was alive, and that they still had a beautiful, smart granddaughter who was safe and healthy.

But she'd known that would be too dangerous. If Locke remotely suspected she was still alive, he would be listening and watching for any sign of her. She would be putting them in danger, along with herself and her young daughter. No, it was best if they knew nothing.

And then suddenly they'd been gone, dying within months of each other. Ling hadn't found out until long after any funeral services had been held. She couldn't have gone even if she had known.

Feeling then that the remaining ties to her previous life had been irrevocably cut, Ling had gone on, hiding the truth from everyone around her, even her own daughter.

Now it's time to face the past. I have to make sure Veronica understands just how dangerous her father is. She has to know the truth.

After the article in the *Gazette*, Ling figured that everyone in town would eventually learn the truth whether she liked it or not. The ability to keep her secret any longer had been taken away from her.

What she couldn't understand was how Mackenzie Jensen had found out about her past. How had the journalist gotten hold of the pictures and details of a life she'd buried under decades of time?

"Ma?" Veronica's strained voice called from the back door. "There are people here to see you."

Pushing herself up and off the chair, Ling drew the shawl closer around her small body, a chill that had nothing to do with the weather coursing through her.

A handsome man stood next to Detective Peyton Bell in the foyer. Not much taller than the detective, the man was lean and fit. His dark hair brushed the collar of his shirt, giving him a casual air, although his strong jaw was clean-shaven.

"Ms. Lee? I'm Deputy Marshal Vic Santino, a criminal investigator with the U.S. Marshal Service." He held Ling's eyes as he spoke as if he wanted to make sure she understood what he was saying. "I've asked the local police to partner with the USMS on this situation, and they've assigned Detective Bell to the case."

Ling looked over at Peyton and nodded, relieved to see Nessa had assigned the same detective who had helped save her from Zander Greyson. Peyton had been sharp and persistent, as well as kind.

Nothing like that oaf of a partner she's been saddled with.

Opening the front door, Hunter Hadley let Gracie trot inside first, then removed the jacket he'd put on to take the Lab out for a walk. He turned to shake hands with Santino and Peyton.

"Ms. Lee, we really need to talk about the situation right away," Santino said, giving Hunter an uncomfortable glance. "It's a sensitive matter, so if we could speak alone..."

"This is Hunter Hadley," Ling said, moving across the hall to rest a proprietary hand on Hunter's arm. "He's like family to me, and I'd like him and my daughter to stay. They need to hear this as well."

Santino hesitated, then turned to Hunter and Veronica, who stood together in the hall beside Gracie.

"The information I'm about to share must be kept completely confidential," Santino said, his voice taking on a serious tone that sent a shiver down Ling's back. "It could very well be the difference between life and death."

The fear in Veronica's bright green eyes told Ling that her daughter knew just how dangerous the situation was, but the stubborn tilt to her chin said she was ready to do anything necessary to protect her mother.

"Do you both understand?" Santino asked, searching their faces. "Can you take that risk and make that kind of commitment?"

"I'm an investigative reporter," Hunter said, then nodded at Veronica. "We both are, actually, and we're used to protecting our sources at any cost."

Santino raised an eyebrow.

"Reporters? I'm supposed to brief two reporters?"

He looked over at Peyton, who shrugged.

"I trust them both with my life," Ling said, stepping in front of Veronica and Hunter. "They've already saved it once, and I'm sure they would do anything humanly possible to do so again."

"We're putting the lives of anyone involved in the case on the line as well," Santino said, still skeptical despite Ling's words. "If the case is compromised, the fugitive we're after wouldn't hesitate to kill anyone who gets in his way."

Walking toward the living room, Ling motioned for Santino and the others to follow.

"Let's get started, Deputy Santino. We don't have much time."

She was relieved to see the deputy exhale deeply and nod to Peyton. There was no way she could keep her daughter in the dark any longer, and she couldn't let Veronica go through this without Hunter's support.

Ling settled onto the sofa, reassured to see Winston nestled into his favorite spot on the windowsill. Some things hadn't changed.

"So, do you think my ex-husband will find out I'm still alive, now that the information has been published in the newspaper?"

Her question brought a troubled grimace to Santino's face. He rubbed his hands together, as if trying to figure out how to tackle a particularly difficult problem.

"Ms. Lee, your ex-husband already knows you're alive," Santino finally said. "I suspect he provided the photos and information used in the news article. And there's reason to believe he is already here in Willow Bay."

Gasping at his words, Ling tried to speak, but her throat constricted in fear. After all these years of hiding, Locke had finally come for her.

"What reasons?" Veronica asked, sitting next to Ling and taking her mother's hand. "How can you know?"

"The body that was found yesterday in Old Willow Square had two IDs on it," Peyton said, stepping forward. "One ID belonged to the victim, and the other...the other was an old University of California ID issued in the name of Lisa Li."

Clutching Veronica's hand, Ling stared up into Peyton's face.

"He's killed someone already?" she whispered, wondering if this was all just a bad dream. "Someone from Willow Bay?"

Dread wormed its way into her stomach.

"Who is it?" she moaned. "Who did Locke kill?"

"Astrid Peterson," Veronica muttered in a dazed voice. "He killed a young college student named Astrid Peterson."

Ling turned to Veronica in confusion.

"How do you know?"

"She was a woman that tried to ask me for help," Veronica said, swallowing back a sob. "I didn't know it was my....my *father* that she was trying to escape. I tried to help her, but..."

Pulling Veronica into a hug, Ling attempted to comfort her, even though she knew this was just the beginning. More pain was sure to come. Locke would see to that.

"Your ex-husband put that ID on the victim's body for a reason, just like he dumped the body in the middle of town for a reason."

Santino spoke directly to Ling, his voice hard.

"He meant it to be a message. He's telling you, and everyone helping you, that he's coming for you, and that he'll kill anyone who gets in his way."

"So, what's the plan then?" Hunter asked. "Have you arranged for her to go into hiding?"

Jumping to her feet at the words, Veronica shook her head.

"Why should my mother have to give up her life again because of that man?" Her voice shook with fury as she turned to Santino. "She's been living in fear all this time. Why can't you all just find him and...and kill him?"

Ling stood and gathered Veronica into her arms.

"It's okay, Ronnie," she soothed. "I don't mind. As long as I know you're safe, and I'm not risking anyone else, I'll be fine."

Santino cleared his throat.

"I'm working on bringing together a task force, as well as arranging for a temporary safe house. In the meantime, we've positioned a patrol outside, and we'll keep an officer assigned to Ms. Lee's protection."

Catching Hunter's eye, Ling tried to smile.

"I'll take Ronnie in the kitchen and make some coffee," she said, trying to keep her voice light. "It may be a long day."

Hunter's eyes fell on the copy of the *Willow Bay Gazette* discarded on the floor and clenched his hand into a fist.

"And I'm going to find out how Mackenzie Jensen got hold of that photo." His voice vibrated with anger. "She must have a source. Maybe if we find the source, we'll find Locke."

CHAPTER TWENTY-FOUR

The Willow Bay Gazette's main office was located in the heart of downtown on the corner of Central and Park Avenue, but the front doors were locked, and the lights were out inside the lobby when Hunter arrived.

Pulling on the big glass doors in frustration, he stared into the dark interior, and then circled around the building, looking for the employee entrance. He knew the lobby might be closed to the public on the weekend, but there had to be some staff inside hard at work.

They've got to be in there getting the Sunday edition ready.

A metal door flung open just as he turned the corner, and a group of women stepped outside, their voices raised in lunchtime chatter.

"Excuse me," called Hunter, holding up a hand.

The conversation abruptly stopped as the women turned to stare at Hunter. He didn't see the woman he was looking for in the group.

"Do any of you know if Mackenzie Jensen's working today?"

Giving Hunter an appreciative smile, a tall woman in a bright pink blazer and knee-high boots stepped forward with a nod.

"Mackenzie's *always* working," she said, arching an eyebrow. "But I think she already went out for lunch."

A giggle erupted behind her, but the woman ignored the other women as Hunter turned to survey the area with impatient eyes.

"Why does Mackenzie always get the cute ones?"

Realizing the woman in the boots and pink blazer had spoken and was still staring at him, Hunter shook his head.

"Oh, no, I'm not a...a friend of hers," he explained. "I need to speak to Ms. Jensen about one of her stories."

The woman gave him a knowing smile and a wink. A young woman in a yellow sweater and high ponytail stepped out of the group and pointed toward the Starbucks across the street.

"I think Mackenzie went to get a coffee with a friend."

"She has lots of *friends*," the woman in the pink blazer said with a trace of envy. "Mackenzie's a lucky girl."

But Hunter didn't hear her wistful remark. He was already jogging across the pavement toward the Starbucks.

Waiting impatiently for a black SUV to roll by, Hunter crossed the street and hurried to the door of the coffee shop. The warm, rich smell of coffee enveloped him as he stepped inside, his eyes immediately searching for Mackenzie Jensen among the little tables scattered around the cozy shop.

He'd almost given up and turned for the door when he saw her slim figure standing by the counter in the back. She was talking to a man who had his back to the room, and it wasn't until Hunter was halfway across the room that he realized who the man was.

Garth Bixby must have sensed Hunter come up behind him. He turned around, already wearing a wide smile. Hunter tried to think if he'd ever seen the man without one.

The guy must sleep with a smile on his face.

Bixby was oblivious to Hunter's scowl. He threw an arm around Hunter's shoulders and raised his cup of coffee as if making a toast.

"Congratulations are in order, Mr. Hadley!"

Shaking off the man's arm, Hunter stared at Bixby in confusion.

"What are you talking about?"

"Your father's re-election is in the bag, now, thanks to Ms. Jensen's brilliant reporting," Bixby gushed, throwing a broad wink at Mackenzie. "There's no way the citizens of Willow Bay will vote for a woman who's lied about her own name and background."

A shrill ring sounded in Bixby's pocket and he dug out his phone.

"I gotta take this," he said, heading toward the exit with a distracted wave. "The boss is calling."

"That could be Mayor Hadley, or it could be his wife," Mackenzie said in a dry voice after Bixby was gone. "She's got him on a tight leash."

Looking up at him with a smile that didn't quite reach her eyes, Mackenzie took a long sip from her cup, then sighed.

"Do you have a problem with me, Mr. Hadley?" she asked, raising her eyebrows. "Did my little story make your girlfriend mad?"

"Was that your intention?"

Hunter tried to keep his voice calm. He suspected Mackenzie would enjoy knowing she'd gotten to him.

"I'm just doing my job and informing the public," she said, sipping again from her cup. "I couldn't let our voters elect someone with a shady past, could I? Someone who isn't who she claims to be."

Hunter wasn't about to take her bait and start arguing.

She'd love to get an angry quote from me to use in tomorrow's edition.

He had to remember that nothing mattered now except finding Donovan Locke and ensuring he could no longer be a threat to Veronica, her mother, or any other woman who might fall into his clutches.

"Where'd you get your information, Mackenzie?"

"My source has requested to remain anonymous, and I can't reveal anything about the individual." The journalist's eyes widened in mock outrage behind her glasses. "That would be unethical."

Shaking his head in frustration, Hunter tried again. She obviously didn't understand the gravity of the situation.

"Listen, Mackenzie," he said, stepping closer. "For your own safety, you need to tell me who gave you this information."

"Sorry, Mr. Hadley," she responded, looking up with a satisfied gleam in her eyes. "But I never reveal a source. It's bad for business."

Hunter shook his head, trying to keep his cool.

"Unless..."

He narrowed his eyes at the word.

"Unless what?"

"Well, I do loosen up after a few drinks," she said, swaying closer so that she was only inches away. "You could take me to dinner tonight and we can...see what happens."

Taking a step back, Hunter crossed his arms over his chest.

"That's never going to happen."

Mackenzie shrugged.

"Okay, then how about we cut to the chase and you offer me a special correspondent gig over at Channel Ten. I'd look great on camera, and I could boost your ratings."

"If you're looking for a new opportunity, contact Spencer Nash, the station manager," Hunter said, growing tired of her games. "I'm just an investigative reporter trying to do my job. Now, who's your source?"

Loud buzzing erupted from Mackenzie's purse before she could respond. She dug out her phone, scanned the text message across the display, and looked past Hunter toward the door with worried eyes.

He turned to follow her gaze, but couldn't see anyone coming in.

"Sorry, I gotta run."

Looking around as if someone might be watching her, Mackenzie shoved her phone back in her purse and bolted for the door.

Hunter reached for her arm, but she jerked away.

"Leave me alone, Mr. Hadley," she snapped. "And if you're such a great reporter, you can go find your own sources."

He followed her out the door, reluctant to let her walk away before he'd gotten the information he needed.

"If you don't want to tell me who your source is, then tell the U.S. Marshal that's in town. I have a feeling he'll be getting in touch with you very soon. I recommend you tell him everything you know."

Mackenzie stopped to glare at him.

"Are you trying to intimidate me, Mr. Hadley?" she snapped, her eyes narrowing behind her glasses. "I thought that was more your father's style."

Spinning on her heel, Mackenzie started down the sidewalk, and Hunter found himself racing after her, not knowing what he could say that hadn't already been said.

"You could be in real danger, Mackenzie!" he called.

Mackenzie didn't look around. As she neared the corner, a big man stepped out of a doorway, bumping into Hunter with a loud grunt.

The papers the man had been carrying fluttered to the pavement, and Hunter stopped to scoop them up, thrusting them toward the man with a hurried apology.

"You missed one," the man said, sticking out a massive arm to stop Hunter as he pointed to a sheet of paper next to the curb. "Those are important papers."

Hunter looked toward the corner, but Mackenzie was gone. He picked up the paper and handed it to the big man, getting a good look at his face for the first time.

The man looked familiar, but Hunter couldn't put a name to the face, or remember where he might have seen him before.

"Watch where you're going next time," the man grumbled before turning to proceed down the sidewalk with his papers under his arm.

Still brooding over his failure to persuade Mackenzie to reveal her source, Hunter decided to stop by the Channel Ten station before heading back to Veronica's house. He needed to let Finn and Spencer know he'd be out of commission for a while.

Pulling into the lot, Hunter noticed the big Channel Ten News Van was still parked in the space where Jack Carson had left it the night before. Staring at the van, Hunter felt an idea take shape.

I think I may know where Ling Lee can stay while they hunt down Locke. And once we get Ling somewhere safe, I'll find Mackenzie and try again.

CHAPTER TWENTY-FIVE

Mackenzie Jensen squinted as she stepped into the parking garage, her eyes slowly adjusting to the dim light and shadows as she made her way to the stairwell. Pushing through the heavy door, she peered up the stairs, suddenly remembering the warning Hunter Hadley had called out after her.

"You could be in real danger, Mackenzie!"

Dismissing the words with a toss of her hair, Mackenzie hurried up the concrete stairs and out onto the second floor of the garage, making a beeline for her new Volkswagen Jetta.

She reached in her purse, fumbling to find the little key fob that always seemed to find its way to the bottom. When she finally managed to push the button to unlock the doors, she jumped at the jarring *beep-beep* that followed.

Finally, with a sigh of relief, she sank into the driver's seat, her heart thumping. Before she could start the engine, her phone buzzed with another text.

Looking down at the display, she saw he'd sent another message, even though she still hadn't responded to the first one.

What did you tell Hunter Hadley?

She looked up just in time to catch movement in her rearview mirror. Then a fist rapped twice on the passenger side window. Mackenzie stifled a scream, realizing she hadn't reengaged the locks.

A man's face appeared in the window, and then the door opened, and he was climbing inside.

"You scared me."

She tried to calm her breathing as he dropped into the passenger seat and slammed the door shut.

"Why didn't you answer my text?"

His voice was clipped.

"There was nothing to say. I didn't tell Hunter Hadley anything."

She wasn't sure why she felt so defensive. She'd done exactly what he'd told her to do. And she'd put her job on the line for him. But his accusing tone made her feel guilty.

"Actually, I did tell him something. I told him I'd gotten the information from an *anonymous source.*"

She looked over to gauge his reaction, surprised to see the angry set to his jaw. He certainly wasn't in the same flirty, teasing mood he usually adopted when they were together.

An unwelcome suspicion entered her mind. One she'd had before but hadn't wanted to entertain; she'd been enjoying all the sneaking around and secret hook-ups too much.

But maybe he's not really into me. Maybe it's all just an act.

The possibility that he'd pursued her with the intention to get his stories in the *Gazette* wasn't farfetched. She'd used the same tactic before to get a story. But the idea that the man had played her at her own game prickled Mackenzie's pride.

It's my own fault. I've been an easy target.

Gripping the steering wheel, she gave him a sideways glance.

"So, I guess the honeymoon's over now that I put the story into the morning edition as you wanted?"

He didn't respond to her sulky accusation, and she sat for a minute in silence, stung by his indifference.

I've risked my reputation, and this is the thanks I get?

Hunter Hadley's warnings replayed in Mackenzie's mind, and her hurt and anger began to morph into an idea. Maybe she could still get something out of the situation after all.

"I'm not sure I can keep my part of the bargain." She figured the threat would get a reaction. "You weren't straight with me."

"What do you mean?"

It was his turn to look over in alarm.

"Hunter Hadley told me that the story is way bigger than you implied. I'm all for breaking a story under Veronica Lee's own nose, and in her own family, but you never said the story would bring the U.S. Marshals down on me."

She saw surprise in the man's dark eyes, then doubt.

"Who told you that? Hadley?"

"Yeah, he was really worked up," she said, remembering the intensity in Hunter's eyes. "I don't think he's going to just let it drop. Looks like you really opened a can of worms with this one."

The man ran a hand through his hair as he stared at her.

"I can't sit on this forever, you know," Mackenzie said, unable to resist turning the screw. "This is too big, and now the U.S. Marshals might be involved. I'm going to have to say something."

"Okay, whatever."

His voice softened, and he sat back against the seat.

"As long as you keep my name out of it, I'll give you my source."

Surprised at his sudden surrender, Mackenzie's eyes narrowed. She studied his profile, unsure if he was serious.

"Really? Why would you do that? What would *you* get out of it?"

He chuckled and looked over at her with a wicked grin, his bad mood gone as quickly as it had appeared.

"You know me too well."

Lifting a hand, he caught a long strand of her silky hair and twisted it around his fingers, studying her face.

"How about this. Let's go back to your place. I'll write down the details on my source, and then you can do something for me."

The man tugged on the hair in his hand and pulled her closer.

"You know exactly what I like."

Turning her face away before he could lean in for a kiss, she resisted the temptation he presented. She wasn't sure he was worth the risk anymore.

"I thought you had a thing for bad boys."

His voice deepened, causing her to swallow hard.

"You know I do, but..."

"Then come on, let's go."

She hesitated, still feeling that something wasn't right.

"Don't you want to get your car?" she finally asked.

"I don't think I can wait that long. I'll ride with you, and you can drop me off...after."

Mackenzie nodded and started the engine, suppressing a smile.

He might think he's playing me, but I'm the one about to get a scoop.

She'd get the information about his source before he changed his mind. There could be another big story in it for her. And if the U.S. Marshals did come calling, she'd have something to give them.

Mackenzie didn't intend to go to jail to protect her sources.

I'm not the type to be anyone's sacrificial lamb.

And a story big enough to draw the attention of the U.S. Marshals could get her national attention. She was already imagining the recognition and awards she was sure to get as she pulled out onto Park Avenue and headed east.

Veronica Lee may be the golden girl on local news, but Mackenzie Jensen will be the biggest name in investigative journalism this town has ever seen.

* * *

Mackenzie's plan had fallen into place by the time they'd arrived at her little house on Hawthorne Road. She'd use her mini recorder to get everything the man said on the record. Once she found out who his source was, she'd make an excuse for him to leave.

Parking the Jetta in the garage, she led him into the kitchen, reaching into her purse to press the record button before dropping the purse on the counter. Now she just had to get him to talk.

"Okay, so who's your source," she said, spinning around to face him. "Who told you about Ling Lee's past?"

Her eyes widened as she saw the little gun in his hand.

"I don't think that matters anymore," the man said, lifting the gun and aiming at her chest. "No one is ever going to hear about it."

Frozen in fear, Mackenzie stared at the gun, unable to move.

"And if you were any kind of investigative journalist, you would be asking a different question," he sneered. "But you've been too blind to see that you had the best scoop in town in bed with you all along."

Trying to make sense of his words, Mackenzie lifted her eyes to his, shaking her head in confusion.

"What are you saying?"

"I'm saying you've been sleeping with the man the FBI, the WBPD, and now the U.S. Marshals Service have been looking for, and you never suspected a thing."

Still not sure what he was talking about, she tried to stall for time, hoping if he meant to shoot her, he'd have already done so.

"Why would they have to look for you?" she managed to say between trembling lips. "Everyone in town knows you. You're not that hard to find."

"Few people know who I really am," he muttered. "I haven't been Diablo for very long, but I have enjoyed it. The cops and the feds are as clueless as you've been all this time."

170

Mackenzie inched backward. Was he joking, or had he gone mad? Did he really think he'd become the boss of a crime syndicate?

Gauging how quickly she could make it to the door, she forced herself to go along with him, pretending she accepted his story.

"I won't tell anyone," she said, sucking in a deep breath. "I think that's...that's exciting. I'm mean, you know I like bad boys, right?"

She lifted a hand toward him, but he shoved the gun closer.

"I know you like getting your story," he growled. "And you'd love nothing more than to expose me as Diablo."

Shaking her head in denial, Mackenzie felt panic rise in her chest.

"No, I wouldn't do that. I was just trying to find out who'd told you about Ling Lee. I wasn't going to give them your name."

"If I told you my source, I'd be signing my own death warrant," the man scoffed. "The man who gave me that information would kill me as soon as look at me. Besides, he and I have a deal. And if I let you live, you could cause trouble for both of us."

Lunging for the door, Mackenzie tried to grasp the handle, but the man was too fast. Grabbing a handful of long hair, he yanked her back against him, silencing her scream with a big hand.

"I'm sorry it had to...come to this," he grunted, dragging her into the living room. "We had fun, but...looks like I'm...going to have to...kill your big...story."

Mackenzie struggled against the man's steel grip as he dropped her onto the sofa. She tried to sit up, but he forced her back down, covering her face with a throw pillow she'd bought at a second-hand shop only months before.

Issuing a silent scream, Mackenzie didn't feel the barrel of the gun nestle into the pillow, and she didn't hear the muffled shot as the man pulled the trigger.

CHAPTER TWENTY-SIX

Veronica looked out the front window again, hoping Hunter would be coming up the walk, but the only thing of interest was a WBPD patrol car parked by the curb. Scratching Winston behind the ears, she smiled down at the purring tabby cat, glad to see the day's events hadn't interrupted his routine.

Turning at the sound of voices and footsteps in the hall, she saw Peyton preparing to leave. Deputy Santino stood at the door beside her, talking to Ling Lee.

"Take another fifteen minutes to finish packing, and then we'll head out," Santino said, checking his watch. "We've managed to find a secure location. You'll stay there temporarily while we come up with a more permanent arrangement."

Ling nodded her agreement as Veronica stepped into the hall.

"Deputy Santino?"

Veronica's mouth felt dry and cottony as Santino turned toward her, but she knew she had to tell him what she'd been thinking before he left. She might not get another chance.

"When you find Locke, can you try to bring him in without killing him?" She glanced at her mother before continuing. "It's just that the woman he killed, Astrid Peterson, she mentioned another girl named Skylar was with her."

A frown creased Santino's forehead, and he looked to Peyton.

"I'm not completely familiar with the situation, yet," Peyton admitted. "But I'll touch base with Vanzinger and Jankowski right away to make sure we get all the details."

Feeling a sudden chill, Veronica wrapped her arms around herself as she tried to explain.

"I know it's unlikely, but Skylar may still be alive. If Locke is killed before he can tell us where she is, we may never find her."

Veronica had spent the last few hours wondering who Skylar was, and where she could be. As much as she'd thought she wanted her father dead so that he could never threaten her mother or anyone else again, she knew now that would be a mistake.

There could still be a chance to save Skylar if they find Locke in time.

Santino met Veronica's worried eyes with a reassuring nod.

"A possible hostage or captive will make things harder, but it's better to know going in than finding out later. I can promise you we'll do everything we can."

Peyton nodded in agreement, then turned to Ling.

"You better get packed, Ms. Lee." She motioned to the stairs. "We need to get you out of here as soon as possible."

Ling's calm demeanor suddenly cracked, and she reached out for Veronica, looking up at her with frightened eyes.

"Come with me, Ronnie," she pleaded. "I don't want you to get hurt. There's no telling what Locke will do."

Knowing there was no way she could give her mother what she wanted, Veronica shook her head.

"I told you, Ma. I can't go into hiding while my father is still out there hurting people. I have to help end this...once and for all."

Ling held Veronica's gaze.

"You have his eyes, you know," Ling finally said. "And it seems you also have his perseverance."

Veronica stiffened at the comparison, but Ling reached up to cup her daughter's chin in her hand and shook her head.

173

"But that's where the likeness ends, Ronnie," she murmured. "You have a kind heart, where he has none. And you persevere for good, while he works for evil. You're all light, and he's full of darkness. That's what makes me so scared."

Dropping her hand, Ling turned away.

"If Locke has to work to find me, maybe he'll leave Ronnie alone for the time being." She looked at Peyton and Santino with a resigned sigh. "Maybe it will buy more time for us both."

"Sometimes the hardest thing to do is to walk away," Santino said in a quiet voice as if the matter had been settled.

A hush fell over the hall, and then Ling crossed to the stairs.

"I'll get my suitcase," she said, her voice now firm.

Santino nodded and turned to the door.

"Detective Bell and I will be waiting outside."

Once Ling had gone upstairs and the hall was empty, Veronica headed back into the living room and crossed to the window, where Winston still stood watch.

Tears stung her eyes as she lifted the big tabby cat and held him against her. She needed to be strong for her mother, but Winston would understand.

A black SUV with dark tinted windows pulled up to the curb behind the patrol car, followed by Hunter in his Audi. Veronica watched as Hunter stepped out and greeted Santino. The two men began talking in a close huddle, as Peyton appeared to give directions to the men in the SUV.

"What are they up to, Winston?" Veronica whispered. "And how long will it take them to find my father?"

* * *

A deafening silence filled the house after Ling had been driven away in the black SUV. Veronica sat at the kitchen table nursing a cooling cup of tea with Gracie curled up by her feet.

The white Lab had stayed close to her most of the day, and Gracie's quiet presence had proven to be more soothing than Veronica could have imagined. She'd always been a bit skeptical about the concept of emotional support animals, but Gracie had turned her into a believer.

Taking another sip of the lukewarm tea, Veronica wondered when Hunter would be back. He'd told her he had an errand to run, and that he'd return shortly. Thinking she may have missed his call, she walked to the charging station on the counter, but it was empty.

"Now, where did I leave my phone?"

Gracie looked up at Veronica's muttered words and watched as Veronica scoured the kitchen before heading into the living room. In the effort to get her mother packed and out of the house she must have put the phone down and left it somewhere.

Finally finding the phone on her bedside table, Veronica was alarmed to see she'd missed six calls, and that there were several unread text messages. Deputy Santino had advised her that Ling would not use her phone while she was at the safe house, but perhaps her mother had tried to call from another number?

Veronica scanned the missed calls, seeing only one number she didn't recognize. The caller had left a message, and Veronica felt her throat constrict as she tapped on the voicemail icon.

The small voice was hard to hear, but she knew right away that it wasn't her mother. From the noise in the background, it sounded like the call was being made from a mall or a busy restaurant.

Listening carefully, Veronica tried to make out the words.

"Um, Veronica? This is Ruby Chase. I'm not at Hope House anymore. I, um...I was scared because I saw one of Diablo's men there. But now I don't have anywhere else to go. Hello?"

175

The recording ended abruptly, leaving Veronica staring at the phone. She tapped on the callback option, but no one picked up. She let it ring a dozen times, then hung up.

Guilt flooded her. She'd completely forgotten about the poor girl who'd been a victim of men just like her father. Men who would abuse and exploit innocent women without remorse.

Recalling how scared and alone Ruby had seemed, Veronica knew she had to try to find her. She sat on her bed and tried to think.

Where is there to hide in Willow Bay? Where would Ruby feel safe?

The sound of footsteps on the stairs caused Veronica's heart to thump in her chest. Reaching into the drawer of her bedside table, she pulled out her Glock and crept quietly to the open door.

Hunter's tall figure appeared on the landing. He stopped short when he saw Veronica standing in the bedroom doorway, the big gun in her hand.

"I guess you didn't hear me come in."

Letting out her pent-up breath, Veronica started to rush forward but Hunter held up a hand.

"Put that thing away first," he said, giving the Glock a dirty look. "You could have killed me. Then who would be here to protect you?"

"That's not funny," Veronica said, spinning around and returning the gun to its place in the drawer. "I thought you were my father come to take me home."

Hunter followed her into the room and looked around.

"I always wanted to get you in here alone," he said, pulling her close. "But I never wanted it to happen this way."

Resting her head on his chest, Veronica sighed.

"The house already seems so empty without Ma."

She closed her eyes against the pain, wishing they could forget everything outside the house, but Ruby's pale face hovered in her mind, unwilling to let her rest.

"Ruby Chase called and left a message. I think she needs help."

Hunter looked down in confusion, and Veronica was surprised he didn't seem to remember.

"Remember, the girl that called me from Hope House?" Veronica said. "The one that said she was held by men who worked for Diablo. She also said she knows what he looks like."

"Where is she now?"

Veronica shrugged and crossed to the window, looking down onto the police cruiser still parked outside.

"That's the problem. She didn't say."

"Then, I'm not sure what we can do," Hunter said, coming up behind her. "It isn't safe for you to go looking for her."

Staring out the window, Veronica nodded her agreement.

"You're right. It's not safe for *me* to go, but what about *you*?"

Hunter shook his head.

"I'm not leaving you alone."

"I'm not alone," Veronica protested. "I've got Officer Ford right outside my window, and Nessa on speed dial."

She pointed to her bedside table.

"And if they fail me, I've always got my Glock."

CHAPTER TWENTY-SEVEN

Nessa had just sat down at her desk when Riley Odell appeared in the doorway. The state prosecutor had recently announced her engagement to Tucker Vanzinger, so Nessa wasn't surprised to see her carrying a take-out bag from Bay Subs and Grub.

"Is that Vanzinger's lunch?" she asked, wrinkling her nose at the pungent smell of onions and peppers wafting from the bag. "I didn't know you offered delivery services."

"Right now, that sounds a whole lot better than what I've been doing," Riley fumed, leaning on the doorjamb.

Raising an eyebrow, Nessa waited for Riley to explain.

"I know you must be busy with the homicide in Old Willow Square and the task force and everything," Riley said, shaking her head. "But when you have a little free time, remind me to tell you what Judge Eldredge has done now."

"Oh, no, you can't leave me hanging like that," Nessa said with an eager grin. "You know how much I *love* old man Eldredge."

Riley stepped into the room and lowered her voice.

"He actually granted Nick Sargent a *six-month delay* so he can find a new lawyer. And you can bet his new lawyer's first motion will be to have the case moved to another venue."

Shifting the sandwich bag to her other hand, the state prosecutor tucked a strand of dark, shiny hair behind her ear.

"And I'm sure Eldredge will grant the request," she said, rolling her eyes. "It's just a matter of time before I'll be driving down to Miami or up to Jacksonville for the trial."

Nessa scowled at the thought of Nick Sargent whining to Judge Eldredge about unfair treatment. The ex-reporter hadn't been worried about the unfair treatment of the people he'd extorted.

"Well, don't go too far. Very soon you may have bigger fish to fry than Nick Sargent," Nessa said with a grimace. "I attended an autopsy this morning and the man who killed that woman has a very long history. Once we bring him in, you're gonna be a busy bee."

The memory of Astrid Peterson's cold body on the metal autopsy table turned Nessa's stomach, and the smell from Vanzinger's lunch wasn't helping.

"Do you have a suspect yet?" Riley asked, her delivery duties forgotten as she inched closer. "I know Tucker was all worked up last night, but he didn't want to talk about it."

"It's a strange case." Nessa wasn't sure how to explain without going into too much detail. "But yes, we think we know who killed the woman in Old Willow Square, and the U.S. Marshals are already here to help us track him down."

Riley's eyes widened in surprise.

"Wow, that's a first," she said. "I've never had the USMS involved in a case I've been working on before. I'm guessing this guy must already be a fugitive?"

"Yep, his name is Donovan Locke, and he's been on the run from the U.S. Marshals for decades, so there's no guarantee they're gonna catch him now."

Opening her mouth to tell Riley about Donovan Locke's connection to Ling Lee, she closed it again when she saw Tenley Frost standing behind Riley in the doorway.

Nessa wondered how long the media relations officer had been standing there, and how much she'd heard.

"Tenley, I didn't expect to see you here on the weekend," Nessa called out. "Mayor Hadley must be bugging you for a statement."

"I better get this sandwich over to Tucker," Riley said, slipping past Tenley to make a quick getaway.

Once Riley had fled down the hall, Tenley stepped into the room and wrinkled her nose.

"I can't stand onions."

She waved a delicate hand in front of her face.

"When I was pregnant with Avery Lynn, just the smell would make me sick. I've never been able to eat them since."

Flashing an impatient smile, Nessa looked at her watch.

"I'm kind of busy, Tenley. What can I help you with?

"As you guessed, Mayor Hadley would like to issue a statement in time to make the morning edition of the *Gazette*."

She opened her bag and took out a notepad and pen.

"Now, I understand from Iris Nguyen that you've identified the body and that the next of kin has been notified, is that correct?"

"Yep, if that's what Iris said, that's correct."

Making a note on her pad, Tenley looked up.

"And, Iris said the victim's name is Astrid Peterson, a twenty-three-year-old college student who was originally from Sweden."

"That sounds about right."

Nessa knew what the next question would be, but she wasn't sure how to answer. She couldn't tell Tenley the truth about Ling Lee's connection to the man who'd killed Astrid Peterson. Not yet at least. Although it would all have to come out in the end.

"So, what has your investigation revealed so far? Do you know who committed the homicide? Do you have a suspect we can name?"

Picturing Tenley climbing out of Bixby's SUV that morning, Nessa shook her head. She didn't know if she could trust the woman with confidential information. Especially information that Mayor Hadley and his campaign manager would use against Ling Lee.

"Chief Ainsley?"

Dave Eddings knocked on the doorframe.

"What's up, Dave?" Nessa asked, sensing a possible way out of her predicament.

"I'm looking for Special Agent Marlowe," the officer said, studiously keeping his eyes off Tenley's striking figure as he hovered in the doorway. "Hunter Hadley's out here asking to speak to him."

Jumping up from her desk, Nessa summoned an apologetic smile for Tenley as she crossed the room.

"I really need to see what's going on out there, but I'll write up a summary of our findings so far and email it over as soon as possible."

Tenley shrugged in helpless agreement as Nessa swept past her into the hall and out into the lobby, where Hunter paced in front of the big glass windows, his handsome face a mask of impatience.

"Mr. Hadley, I hear you're looking for Special Agent Marlowe."

"I have information about a possible trafficking victim who may be in trouble." Hunter's voice was strained. "She called Veronica to ask for help. I'm here to pass on the information to Agent Marlowe."

Guiding Hunter down the hall, Nessa stopped outside the briefing room where the joint task force had set up operations. She knocked twice on the door, then pushed it open. Vanzinger and Jankowski sat at a long table with several other men in shirtsleeves and ties.

"Sorry to bother you guys, but I'm looking for Agent Marlowe."

Jankowski stood and joined Hunter and Nessa by the door.

"Agent Marlowe had to step out for a meeting."

He eyed Hunter with suspicion.

"Is there something I can do to help you?"

"A girl named Ruby Chase needs your help," Hunter said. "She was held by men who were dealing drugs and forcing women to work for them. She says she saw the boss. His men called him Diablo."

A gleam entered Jankowski's eyes at the name.

"Where is this girl?" the big detective asked. "If she knows where Diablo is, we need to speak to her."

"Ruby was in rehab over at Hope House, but she got spooked. Now she's back on the street, and she's scared."

The door to the briefing room opened again, and Agent Marlowe stepped inside. He didn't look happy to see Hunter and Nessa.

"What's going on?"

Jankowski spoke up before Hunter could.

"A victim's been in touch with Channel Ten. The girl escaped from the Diablo Syndicate. She may be able to lead us to him."

"Where is she?" Marlowe asked, turning to Hunter.

Meeting Marlowe's eyes, Hunter shrugged.

"We don't know where she is. That's why I'm here."

There was an edge to Hunter's voice Nessa hadn't heard before.

"I was hoping your task force would be able to find her. You guys are supposed to be stopping traffickers, and saving victims, right?"

Looking toward Nessa, Marlowe raised an eyebrow.

"If I remember correctly, you assigned detectives to the Ruby Chase case. Any update on where she is?"

The image of Ingram's scowling face flashed through Nessa's mind. Now that Peyton was working with Santino to protect Ling Lee, the Ruby Chase case was all Ingram's.

"I can check with Detective Ingram," Nessa said with reluctance.

Marlowe nodded, then reached into the pocket of his jacket. He pulled out a card and handed it to Hunter.

"If you hear from Ruby Chase again, call me right away."

He turned back to Nessa.

"In the meantime, let's get with Detective Ingram and see what progress he's made. I'm sure if we work together, we can find this girl. Then we can find out what she knows about Diablo."

CHAPTER TWENTY-EIGHT

Frankie's walk into downtown Willow Bay took longer than usual. He'd had the day off from the all-consuming Bixby case, but had woken up restless, thinking about Peyton; thoughts about the pretty detective brought back his worries about Ruby Chase. He couldn't help wondering where she was, and if Diablo's men had gotten hold of her again.

After he'd spent the morning pacing around the house, his mother had finally told him to go outside and find something to do. It reminded him of when he was a kid in Memphis, and she'd forced him to go outside and play whenever he complained of being bored.

In no hurry to get to the office, Frankie had taken his time, stopping to buy a new pack of gum, and watching a flag football game in the park. He finally arrived at Barker and Dawson's Investigations just as a cluster of clouds moved over the sun, throwing the street into chilly shade.

Unwrapping a stick of gum, Frankie popped it in his mouth and sank into his chair. He'd decided another search through social media might help him uncover something about Ruby that could help him track her down. Someone out there must be looking for her.

Everyone has someone who cares, right?

He turned on the computer, but before it had time to boot up, he heard a rustling sound in the back room. He paused and was just about to dismiss the noise as his imagination, when he heard the rustling sound again, followed by a thud.

That was definitely not my imagination.

Picking up the baseball bat he kept propped beside his desk, Frankie stood and crossed to the flimsy wooden door that separated the two rooms. Another thud from behind the door started his pulse racing. He put a hand on the handle and applied gentle pressure.

The door swung in to reveal the darkened supply room. The little cot he often used, much to Barker's displeasure, was hidden in shadows, but he thought he could see a figure on top.

Shifting the bat to his other hand, Frankie flipped the switch on the wall, flooding the little room in fluorescent light.

The figure on the cot snuggled under Frankie's Miami Dolphins blanket and a small foot in a dirty sneaker thudded against the wall.

"What the...Ruby?"

Frankie moved into the room, his shock turning into relief.

"Ruby, wake up."

Staring down at the girl's sleeping face, he could see how young she really was. Just a teenager. About the same age, Franny had been the last time he'd seen her.

He considered letting Ruby sleep, but then her eyes fluttered open, and she looked up at him with sleepy bewilderment.

"Rory?"

Frankie shook his head and smiled down at her.

"No, my name's Frankie. This is my office...and my cot."

Ruby's eyes widened; she pulled the Miami Dolphins blanket tighter around her, scooching back against the wall.

"Um...sorry," she said, rubbing the sleep from her eyes. "I knocked but nobody answered. The door was unlocked."

"Yeah, sure it was," he said. "I always leave my door open for anyone walking by. Just in case they want to take a nap on my cot."

Walking back to the doorway, Frankie leaned against the doorjamb and crossed his arms over his skinny chest.

"So, how about you tell me what's going on?"

A shadow fell over her face, and Frankie thought he could see the gears spinning in her head as she tried to think up a lie that would sound plausible.

"And before you waste time thinking up some bullshit story, do us both a favor and tell me the truth. Otherwise, I can't help you."

"Why should you want to help me?"

Frankie shrugged.

"That's a long story," he muttered. "And maybe it doesn't matter, since you must already believe that I want to help you. If you didn't, you wouldn't be here. You wouldn't have come here looking for me."

Turning her face away, Ruby spoke in a stiff voice.

"I didn't have anywhere else to go. I got through a few days of detox, but I'm still...well, I still need something to get me by."

"Is that why you left Hope House? To get a fix?"

Ruby shook her head.

"No, I was scared," she protested. "I saw one of Diablo's men at that place. I think he was looking for me."

The possibility that a trafficker was trolling rehab facilities for new victims wasn't hard for Frankie to believe. He knew from experience just how hard it was to stay clean once addiction had gotten you in its iron grip, and the men who wanted to exploit young addicts would know as well.

It's the perfect place for these scumbags to find new victims. Half the work of breaking them down has already been done.

But the idea that Diablo would send one of his men to hunt down one runaway girl seemed less likely. Unless she had information that could bring him down.

"Ruby, did you get a good look at Diablo? I mean, could you pick him out of a line-up, or maybe even lead the cops to his hideout?"

"Oh no, I'm not talking to the cops again," she said in alarm. "They wouldn't believe anything I said. Just wanted to lock me up."

He couldn't argue with her bitter words. Based on the conversation he'd overheard between Peyton and Ingram, Ruby was right; Ingram didn't believe her, and he was determined to prove she'd made up her story.

And I'm not so sure even Peyton is willing to fight for the girl.

Frankie's spirits sank at the thought that Peyton might side with Ingram. He'd been so sure she had changed. That she was one of the good ones now. That was why he'd let himself fall for her.

Maybe I miscalculated. Maybe I let myself believe she was different now because I wanted it to be true. Maybe I'm still just a damn fool.

But the image of Peyton's wide amber eyes lingered in his mind. And if he couldn't believe that people were capable of changing, then what did that say about his own chances?

"You try calling Detective Bell," he heard himself say. "She got you out of jail and into Hope House, so she must want to help."

"Or maybe she just wanted to get me somewhere Diablo's men could get hold of me," Ruby muttered.

Frankie frowned.

"What are you saying?"

"The girls at the place I was being held...they said Diablo had connections in Willow Bay. That he even had cops working for him."

Scratching the stubble on his chin, Frankie considered the words. Could Peyton be that cunning? Would she have used him to get Ruby into a vulnerable place where Diablo's men could find her?

It just didn't add up. If she was working with the traffickers, why would she have driven Ruby to Hope House instead of taking her straight back to the hideout? And why would she have stood up to Ingram when he wanted to disprove Ruby's story?

"Detective Bell is on your side," Frankie finally said, dismissing any notion that Peyton was Diablo's pawn. "She tried to help you once, and I'm sure she'd do it again if you gave her a chance."

Ruby didn't look convinced.

"If the cops don't find Diablo and take him down, you'll never feel safe," Frankie tried again. "And other girls are gonna end up in the same situation. He'll keep hurting people until someone stops him."

"And you think I can do that?" Ruby was incredulous. "I can't even stop myself from screwing up my own life. You think I have a hope in hell of stopping this guy?"

Throwing the blanket to the floor, Ruby jumped off the bed, but Frankie put out a big hand to stop her before she could make it to the door. The look on her face reminded him of all the times Franny had stormed out in a huff.

"Don't leave, Ruby," he said, his voice low. "If you do, I have a bad feeling you'll never come back."

She stopped and stared at him, confused by the sudden shift in his tone. He stepped aside, giving her room to pass through if she still wanted to go. Whatever she decided, it had to be her decision.

"Okay."

The word was small. Frankie raised an eyebrow.

"Okay, what?"

"Okay, you can call Detective Bell."

Pulling out his phone before she could change her mind, Frankie tapped on Peyton's number. He hadn't called her since the last time he'd seen her at Hope House. His heart beat faster as the phone rang.

After several rings, he heard a click, and then another few rings. Finally, Peyton's voicemail picked up.

"You've reached the desk of Detective Peyton Bell. I'm unable to take your call, but if you leave your name and number, I'll return your call as soon as possible. If this is an emergency, please hang up and dial 911."

"Peyton, this is Frankie Dawson. I need you to call me as soon as you get this message. Ruby Chase is in my office and wants to talk."

He disconnected the call and looked up at Ruby.

"You rest here until she calls back. I'll give you some privacy."

Closing the door behind him, Frankie shuffled back to his desk and sat down. He took out his phone, double-checked to make sure the ringer's volume was on high and set it on the desk in front of him where he could watch it.

Minutes later the front door swung open and Barker swept inside, bringing a burst of cool air with him.

"Guess what I found out?" Barker's deep voice filled the quiet office. "I had lunch with an old friend who works at City Hall and-"

He paused, sensing something was off.

"Why are you sitting there like that? What's wrong?"

"Nothing's wrong," Frankie said, unsure how to explain Ruby's presence on the cot in the back. "What did your friend tell you?"

"Apparently an office cleaner walked in on Bixby and a woman in a compromising position after hours. I figured it was Mackenzie Jensen, but my buddy claims the woman was a city employee."

Raising his eyebrows, Frankie tried to look interested as Barker crossed to his desk. When the older detective continued on toward the backroom, Frankie jumped up, but he was too late.

Barker was halfway into the room when he noticed Ruby huddled on the cot. She jumped up when she saw the big man, and Barker jerked back in surprise.

Retreating into the outer office with a glare toward Frankie, Barker put a hand over his chest, then motioned to Ruby, who hovered in the doorway.

"Okay, Frankie. Who is she, and what's she doing here?"

The front door swung open as Barker spoke. Two men stepped into the office. Frankie didn't know the bigger man, but he recognized Marc Ingram's thin, pinched face.

Ingram's eyes fell on Ruby with a satisfied gleam.

"Ruby Chase, I need you to come with me."

Frankie bolted out of his chair and stepped between the two men and Ruby, who seemed frozen in shock at their sudden appearance.

"Go with you where?" Frankie clenched his hands into fists. "She's no criminal. She needs somebody to help her, not arrest her."

The tall man with Ingram stepped forward.

"No one's being arrested. We just need to talk to Miss Chase in relation to an ongoing investigation."

Clearing his throat, Barker joined Frankie in the middle of the room. His solid presence blocked the men from approaching Ruby.

"Who's we?" Barker asked. "You with the feds?"

The man stared at Barker, then flashed an ID badge.

"I'm Special Agent Clint Marlowe with the FBI. I'm working with the WBPD on a case that Miss Chase might be able to help us with."

"Does Chief Ainsley know you're here?"

Ingram snorted, his face turning pink with indignation.

"I don't need Nessa's permission to do my job," he muttered between clenched teeth. "But maybe you've been retired too long to remember how things work in a *real* investigation."

Ignoring Ingram, Barker kept his eyes on Marlowe.

"Chief Ainsley informed me that Ruby Chase may have information vital to our case," Marlowe conceded. "When we got the message that she was here, we decided it would be prudent to detain her for questioning while we had the chance."

"Got a message from who?" Frankie asked, confused.

"From you, Mr. Dawson," Marlowe said. "You called and left a message for Ingram's partner that Miss Chase was here."

Frankie was dumbfounded. Had Peyton really passed on his message to Ingram? She knew what kind of a man Ingram was, and that helping Ruby was not on his agenda.

How could Peyton have done that to Ruby, or to me?

"Come with us, Miss Chase." Agent Marlowe gestured to Ruby. "We just need to ask you a few questions."

Walking toward the door, Ruby turned angry eyes to Frankie.

"You told me Detective Bell would help. Guess you were wrong."

Frankie watched until Ruby's small figure had disappeared through the door. Barker came up and put a big hand on his shoulder, but Frankie shrugged it off.

He didn't want to be comforted. He didn't deserve it. Not after he'd just failed another girl that needed help.

CHAPTER TWENTY-NINE

Sleep had been Skylar's only refuge since the Professor had gone away, but even that had now become a place of recurring nightmares and endless terror. Her mind was trapped in the foggy state between memories and dreams and couldn't break free.

Sitting up in her little bed, Skylar tried to recall a time of happiness or even hope. Had she ever had the chance to experience such emotions outside the pages of the books on her shelf?

Now, even her beloved books no longer lifted her depression.

Is this what death feels like? No sunlight, no air, no movement?

Fear was the only thing that assured Skylar she was still alive. Constant, relentless fear coursed through her body, pulsing like blood through veins. Dread of the Professor's return was eclipsed in her mind only by the terror that he never would.

In the meantime, she was forced to suffer the agony of waiting to find out which it would be. Until then, her ordeal would continue.

Unless I end it now. I could go to sleep and never wake up, never dream.

The Professor's cruel voice echoed in her memory, warning her not to touch any of the levers in the safe room.

"If you end up shutting off the air filtration system, you'll likely be dead before I even know what happened. Don't say I didn't warn you."

Slipping off the bed, Skylar shuffled into the adjoining room. She felt for the chain hanging from the ceiling and pulled.

Artificial light illuminated the shelves of supplies and food next to a big water tank. She leaned against the tank, using the full weight of her body to shift it several inches to the side to reveal the heavy lever the Professor had warned her about.

Skylar studied the lever and ran a small finger down its length, breathless at the thought that it offered her a way to end her suffering. It would all be over within minutes.

Looking around the little room, she took a deep breath and again reached for the chain and pulled, plunging the room back into darkness. She closed her eyes and steadied her breath, accepting the tomb-like room as her final resting place.

Her hand was steady as she positioned it on the lever, and her voice didn't falter as she whispered the words she'd memorized from Astrid's book of Shakespeare's plays.

Never from this palace of dim night depart again...here will I remain.

Her favorite play in the big book had been *Romeo and Juliet*, and she felt a small kernel of satisfaction that she would end her life in an underground tomb like the star-crossed lovers.

Giving a hard pull, Astrid felt the lever shift, then stick. She yanked with all her might and felt the lever snap down into place, before hearing a metallic click above.

A thin strip of light had appeared on the ceiling. Squinting up into the darkness, she saw a glint of metal. Using the shelves as a step ladder, Skylar climbed toward the light.

When she reached the top, she saw the lever had released a hidden latch on a small trap door concealed in the ceiling. Heart pounding, Skylar pushed the door up and stuck her head through.

She gasped as she recognized the narrow tunnel; she'd seen it many times in her dreams. A trickle of daylight from the end of the tunnel called to her, and she pulled herself up and through the trap door before she had a chance to think about what she'd do next.

Following the light, just as she'd done in her dream, Skylar found herself standing under an iron grate. Flecks of snow and debris littered the floor under the grate, and she saw that the small ladder she remembered was still affixed to the wall of the tunnel.

Skylar hesitated, suddenly scared of what she would find, or what would find her, if she went through the opening above her. Her dream had quickly turned into a nightmare once she'd gone up and into the light.

Will it be the same as in my dream? Only this time, will I be the one whose blood will be left in the snow?

Putting her foot on the ladder, Skylar thought again of the beautiful, frightened face that had beckoned to her in the dream. She heard the woman calling to her again, urging her on.

Climb, Skylar. Then run and hide.

The grate lifted easily in her hand, and she stuck her head up and over the side of the opening, realizing she was still inside the compound, just past the side of the house.

She crawled out into the waning daylight, the snowy ground stinging her bare hands as she pushed herself to her feet. Grateful to have her slippers on, she scurried toward the side of the house, aware that the Professor had cameras set up at almost every angle.

If he sees me, no telling how quickly he could get back here with his gun.

Scampering further along the yard, she leaned against the trunk of a gnarled maple tree, its branches bare of leaves but tipped with snow. She surveyed the yard spread out before her, gauging the distance to the big wall that encircled the property.

The possibility she could get over the wall was small, and the terrain she would encounter if she did was harsh. Her eyes moved to the big barn, but the terrifying memory of blood-soaked snow made her quickly look away.

I won't go into the barn, and I can't go over the fence.

She knew the only possibility to survive would be to get into the house. Maybe once she was inside, she could call for help.

But the doors would be deadbolted, and there were bars on all the windows. Even if she could make it past the cameras, Skylar doubted she'd ever be able to get inside.

She shivered as a light flurry of snow began to fall. Huddling closer to the barren tree, she looked up to see the remnants of daylight fading in the western sky.

It'll be night soon, and the wolves will come out.

Skylar wondered if wolves could jump over walls, or maybe even dig a way in under them, but the growing numbness in her now-soaking wet slippers turned her thoughts to finding shelter from the unforgiving winter weather.

Maybe I should just go back down to the safe room. I could stay in there until I figure out a plan.

But she couldn't make her feet move toward the grate.

If I go down that hole again, I might never come out.

Looking toward the corner of the house, she saw the small white camera mounted on the wall. She'd often seen the camera feeds on the Professor's computer when she'd bring him his lunch. There had been six little windows showing the doors, yard, and fence.

She assumed that meant there would be six cameras mounted around the exterior of the house. If she could somehow get to the back porch without one of the cameras picking her up, she may be able to find a way inside without alerting the Professor she'd escaped the safe room.

An owl hooted in the distance, and Skylar looked again to the west. Another thirty minutes and it would be dusk. Another hour and it would be full dark. She had to make her move now if she didn't want to be outside in the dark with the temperature dropping fast.

Edging along the house, she thought of the tools she'd used for gardening before the winter weather closed in. If the Professor hadn't moved them, her collection of spades, shears, and buckets should still be stored in the big crate by the back porch.

Skylar ignored her aching feet as she moved toward the porch, keeping low and staying close to the wall. When she reached the corner of the house, she pulled off her sweater and tossed it up and over the camera mounted overhead.

Moving quickly, she hooked an arm through a lightweight bucket and picked up a small spade. She slipped through the railings on the porch and lifted the bucket up and over the camera positioned above the back door.

Without stopping to think, Skylar smashed the sharp end of the spade against the glass windowpane in the back door, sending a shower of glass falling all around her feet. Ignoring the crunch of glass under her slippers, she leaned forward and stuck her head through the spot where the glass had been.

The air in the kitchen was incredibly warm compared to the freezing snow outside as Skylar looked around, seeing everything in place just as she remembered it.

Wedging her shoulders through the window after her head, she put her hands on the bottom of the frame and propelled herself through. A searing pain shot up her arm as a thick shard of glass sliced a long gash in one hand.

Hitting the floor with a sickening thud, Skylar lay motionless, watching the blood dribble from her hand onto the kitchen floor.

She'd made it inside and out of the cold, and she didn't think she'd made an appearance on any of the cameras. But as the icy wind whipped in through the broken window, she realized there would be no going back.

The shattered glass was proof that she'd broken the Professor's rules. She'd committed the ultimate sin of trying to run away.

If I'm still here when the Professor comes back, he'll kill me for sure.

CHAPTER THIRTY

A light rain had begun to fall by the time Tenley Frost left City Hall. It had taken some time to persuade Mayor Hadley that they would have to wait another day to release an official statement in response to the *Willow Bay Gazette* article on Ling Lee.

The mayor was insistent that the revelation of Ling's assumed identity required her to be placed on administrative leave from her duties as principal of Willow Bay High. However, he didn't have the direct authority to take such an action, and Brock Chandler, the school superintendent, hadn't returned his call.

Tenley hadn't been surprised. The two men were no longer on speaking terms after falling out over Channel Ten's recent report on city corruption. The report had included a recorded conversation between the mayor and the school superintendent that implicated them in a plot to exchange political favors for key endorsements.

Hurrying toward the parking garage, Tenley couldn't help marveling over Mayor Hadley's persistent denial of reality.

The mayor's delusional if he thinks Brock Chandler's going to do anything for him. Hadley threw him under the bus. What does he expect?

Her white Lexus was parked on the second floor, and Tenley tied the belt of her coat tighter around her slim waist as she made her way up the stairs and through the dark garage, eager to get to her sitter's house.

She'd asked Nora Fletcher to watch little Avery Lynn just for the afternoon, and it was already dark outside. The older woman would be too polite to complain, but Tenley didn't want to take advantage of the sitter's sweet nature.

Speeding through the city's almost empty streets, she noticed that a light rain had begun to fall. Raindrops dotted the windshield in front of her, and she switched on the wipers as she stopped at the light on Waterside Drive.

A bright set of headlights appeared behind the Lexus, causing Tenley to squint against the harsh glare. She adjusted her rearview mirror with an exasperated sigh.

Why do some people insist on driving with their high beams on?

Then the light turned green and she forgot about the inconsiderate driver as she continued down Waterside Drive, intent on getting to her little daughter.

She was trying to get the baby on a more regular sleep schedule, and she'd need to be home soon to begin their bedtime routine. It didn't matter that it was Saturday and that most single women like her would be out socializing. Tenley didn't like to brood on the limitations of dating a married man.

The wife always gets Saturdays. That's just the way it is.

Besides, if Tenley was honest with herself, she didn't really mind staying home alone with her daughter. She sometimes suspected that was the reason she'd picked someone so obviously inappropriate.

I don't want anyone invading the peaceful life I have with Avery Lynn.

Most men she knew were too arrogant or self-centered for her liking, and you never knew what you were going to get until it was too late. In her previous job as a reporter, and in her current role as the city's media relations officer, she'd reported on plenty of bad men who'd pretended to be heroes.

Like that horrible man Nessa had been telling Riley about today.

Tenley had overheard the police chief mention fugitive Donovan Locke to the state prosecutor earlier in the day. Her curiosity had been piqued when Nessa had kept the information from her, and Tenley's past as an investigative reporter had kicked in.

She'd quickly been able to link Donovan Locke's name to the U.S. Marshal's most wanted website, and she'd read all the gory details about the man who had been convicted of terrible crimes, including witness intimidation against his ex-wife, Lisa Li.

It hadn't taken her long to put two and two together; she now understood why Lisa Li had taken on a new identity as Ling Lee. Tenley felt empathy for any mother trying to raise a daughter on her own, but Ling's struggle had obviously been much more difficult than most.

The poor woman had to give up everything to escape her crazy ex.

Finally coming up to Surrey Way, Tenley turned left and pulled the Lexus into the driveway beside Nora's minivan.

The older woman lived in a quiet subdivision, and the dimly lit streets were empty. It seemed no one was willing to brave the chilly rain to walk their dog or get some weekend exercise.

Shutting off the engine, Tenley sat in the car, trying to figure out how she could get to Nora's door and back to the car with little Avery without them both getting soaked. She had an umbrella, but holding it while juggling a ten-month-old, a hefty baby bag, and a car seat wouldn't be easy.

She opened the door and prepared to run, deciding to forgo the umbrella; she'd cover Avery with a blanket on the way back. Sticking one foot outside the car, she groaned as her boot sank into a frigid puddle, then she climbed out and took a giant step over the water.

A gloved hand settled roughly over her mouth, stopping the panicked scream that filled her throat. Clawing at the arm that held her, she lifted her boot and kicked back hard against the man behind her. The kick elicited a grunt, but the man's arms only tightened around her as he dragged her to the back of a white Honda waiting at the curb, its engine running and the trunk already open.

Thrashing with all her strength, Tenley managed to turn around to face her attacker, but he wore a black ski mask that revealed only the cold glint of his eyes.

"Stop fighting or I'll go in there and get your brat, too."

His words knifed through her, stunning her into momentary silence as she thought of her baby daughter. Taking her silence as consent, the man shoved her into the trunk.

Tenley reached out and grabbed at his arm, terrified that once she was locked in the trunk, he'd go after Avery despite his words. Digging her nails in, she felt his glove come off in her hand as the man wrenched his arm away and slammed the trunk shut.

Gasping in horror, Tenley screamed into the confines of the little space, still holding the cold leather of the glove in her hand. Then the car jerked into motion, throwing her against the wall of the trunk and prompting another scream of terror.

She dropped the glove beside her, not wanting to be close to anything that had touched the skin of the evil man that now had her in his possession.

Picturing the last image she'd seen as the trunk closed, Tenley squeezed her eyes shut and began to cry. The man had been missing two fingers. She'd seen the pale hand as he'd raised it to slam the trunk shut, and had immediately recalled the description she'd read on the U.S. Marshals website only hours before.

As the Honda barreled down the highway, Tenley knew screaming or pleading would do no good. Not with a man who had already hurt so many women. Not with a desperate fugitive like Donovan Locke.

CHAPTER THIRTY-ONE

The Professor sped past Tucker's Truck Stop in the white Honda, slowing only when he saw the faded sign for Willow Bay Citrus. Turning the car onto a two-lane road just past the sign, he kept an eye out for other cars or unexpected pedestrians. But it seemed no one else was interested in visiting the abandoned processing factory on such a dark and rainy winter night.

The big rig was parked right where he'd left it. He'd been pleased to find a location that offered room to park a semi, as well as needed privacy to unload unwilling cargo away from prying eyes.

The Professor stepped out and surveyed the area. The ruined plant lay in silent darkness as he crossed to the back of the trailer. Moving quickly, he unbolted the lock, swung open one of the trailer doors, and unfolded a retractable step ladder.

He switched on the lights inside the trailer; nothing inside had been disturbed. The door to the hidden compartment at the rear of the trailer, undetectable if you didn't know what to look for, was still safely sealed.

Throwing back the latch, he opened the little door and stuck his head inside the eight-foot by four-foot room, nodding in satisfaction. Everything was prepared for the two women he would be transporting all the way to the Bitterroot Valley.

Next, he crossed to the corner of the trailer. Kneeling, he pried open a thin lockbox recessed into one of the wooded floorboards and took out a bag of blue pills. He'd need to make sure his passengers were quiet on the trip, and the Fentanyl would help.

He took out his pocketknife, then picked a pill out of the bag. One pill was sometimes enough to kill, but half a pill might not be enough to get the woman back to the ranch without a fuss.

Deciding to take a chance, he crushed the pill into powder and tipped the powder into a Styrofoam cup full of water. He set the cup to the side, before returning the bag to its rightful place.

He then grabbed a coil of rope off a hook and used the knife to cut off two sections, before sticking the knife back in his pocket.

Time to show my new guest her travel accommodations.

Hopping down from the trailer, the Professor positioned himself outside the Honda's trunk and drew in a deep breath. Flinging open the lid, he saw the woman's pretty face twisted in fear as he grabbed for her. He managed to hold her wrists together and wrap a segment of rope around them before she knew what was happening.

A high-pitched scream pierced the air and a boot kicked out, connecting with his stomach, forcing the wind out of him. He ignored the scream and the pain, concentrating on securing the other length of rope around the woman's ankles.

Hefting the trussed figure up and over the side of the trunk, the Professor dragged her toward the trailer, his sore hand aching along with his stomach.

"I'm too old for this shit," he muttered as he hauled her up the ladder and dumped her on the trailer's wooden floor.

Looking down at his throbbing hand, he realized his glove must be in the car.

The Honda's trunk was still open, and the Professor retrieved his glove before shutting it. Checking that he hadn't left anything in the car, he put the keys back in the glovebox where he'd found them. He'd let his contact know where to pick up the car once he and his cargo were safely away.

Going back to the trailer, he saw that the woman had managed to shift herself to the edge. Another few inches and she'd have fallen over the side and into the dirt below.

"Watch out now, girl. You'll end up damaging the merchandise."

"I'm a woman, not a girl," she hissed up at him. "And I have a name...and a daughter. Please, let me go, my daughter needs me."

Anger blossomed in the Professor's chest as he stared down at the woman's tortured expression.

"I've heard it all before, lady," he growled, resisting the urge to add emphasis to his words with a kick. "In fact, my ex-wife tried the same tactic. But it didn't work then, and it won't work now."

Ignoring her further protests, he dragged her to the back and bundled her into the hidden compartment.

"You stay in here, and you stay quiet," he ordered, then turned to pick up the Styrofoam cup. "This is all the water you're gonna get, and it's a long ride, so I suggest you drink it without a fuss."

He grabbed a handful of her thick auburn hair and pulled her head back, tilting the cup over her mouth. She coughed as the stream of water hit her dry throat but managed to choke it down.

The Professor took a long, assessing look at the woman, then closed the compartment door and latched it. He jiggled the door, double-checking that it was securely closed, but confident it would hold. The hidden room had proven invaluable when transporting human cargo in the past.

Switching off the trailer lights, he closed the door and bolted it, then made his way around to the cab. Once he was settled into the driver's seat, he allowed himself a minute to relax.

It's all going to plan. As soon as I have my daughter, I can head home.

The ringer on his phone had been set to silent while he'd taken care of his clandestine business, and he now dug it out of his pocket. He'd send Diablo a message, and then get himself something to eat while he waited for the Fentanyl to take effect.

His jaw tightened as he saw the notifications on his phone.

Motion detected in the backyard. Motion detected on the back porch.

Opening on the security app, he tapped on each camera, activating a live view of the compound. His forehead creased into a frown as he saw the cameras on the side of the house and the back porch were black. The other cameras showed snow falling on a darkened lawn and an empty front porch.

Has something happened? Could someone have broken in?

But the alarms on the front gate and both doors were still engaged. He couldn't think how anyone could have gotten through. Maybe the motion detector was triggered by heavy snow, and the snow blocked the lens or a gust of wind loosened a cable.

Or maybe Skylar's managed to get out of the safe room. Maybe she's running to alert the neighbors right now.

The disturbing thought rose unbidden in his mind, and he pushed it away. Even if the girl could get out, the closest neighbors were miles away, through forests frozen solid, and past iced-over streams.

The compound's remote location was the main reason the Professor had been able to stay hidden so long. And the people in the area respected privacy. They weren't the kind to snoop around or stop by uninvited for a chat.

Most people in the area didn't even know there was a house down the long road with the big gate and the no trespassing signs. And the big wall kept out any hikers or busybodies who might wander by.

But an uneasy feeling that something was wrong remained, and he suddenly wished he'd installed cameras inside the house and the safe room as he'd originally intended.

Worries that someone might be able to hack into the cameras had stopped him. After all, he'd been able to hack into similar systems many times himself, and he didn't like the idea of anyone else watching him or his girls.

Suddenly desperate to get back to the compound, he tapped on the number he'd saved his in contacts for Diablo. The call was answered on the second ring. The Professor didn't waste time with pleasantries.

"I've taken care of my part of the bargain," he said, impatience hardening his voice. "Have you made progress with yours?"

"So, you got rid of her?" Diablo asked as if he couldn't believe what he was hearing. "She's already...gone?"

The Professor tried to curb his irritation.

"Yes, she's gone. Now, have you gotten hold of the girl? Have you made arrangements to take out her mother?"

Diablo hesitated.

"Tell me you have a plan," the Professor said, ready to erupt.

"Calm down, the plan is in motion," Diablo assured him. "I've got everything in place. I've already taken out the only person who can identify me as the source of the article in the *Willow Bay Gazette*."

"Good," the Professor said, not too concerned about Diablo being outed for giving the journalist information on his ex-wife.

He didn't care what happened to Diablo, but he was glad he'd managed to smear her name and tear apart her reputation. The Professor wanted his ex-wife to suffer the same indignity he had suffered all those years ago.

And he wanted her to feel the pain of knowing that her daughter was lost to her forever, just as he had felt pain when she'd taken their child and deserted him.

"If all goes well, I should be able to deliver the girl to you in the next few hours," Diablo said. "Then I'll take care of her mother."

"Then I'll be heading out of state before midnight," the Professor said, already calculating driving time. "You have four hours."

CHAPTER THIRTY-TWO

The Channel Ten News station was buzzing with activity as Veronica sat at her desk and tried not to worry about her mother. She'd planned to stay locked away at home all evening, but Hunter had wanted to work with the news crew to produce a special report on Donovan Locke, and he didn't feel comfortable leaving her alone, even with the patrol car outside and the Glock by her bed.

But Veronica wasn't in the mood to be around people and pretend everything was okay. Her mother was out there somewhere in hiding, and her father had already killed one woman and was still on the loose. She hadn't even been able to help Ruby Chase.

"You still doing okay?"

Hunter stood by her desk looking down with worried eyes.

"I'm fine," she lied, looking over his shoulder to where Finn Jordan stood talking to one of the producers. "Looks like you and Finn are mobilizing all the forces, although I'm surprised Jack's not here. Didn't you ask him to help out?"

Hunter dropped his eyes and shrugged.

"Jack took the weekend off, but we'll get it done one way or the other," he said, sounding down. "I just hope if we put Locke's face out there, someone might see him and call it in. Besides, we need to warn the community; he could still be out there."

Veronica put a hand on his arm and squeezed.

"You aren't still upset about Mackenzie Jensen, are you?" she asked. "I would have been shocked if she'd just rolled over and gave you her source. That's not her style."

"I know, but it is frustrating that she has information that could help us find Locke, and won't share it," he admitted. "The good news is, I talked to Deputy Santino and he's agreed to go interview her tonight."

Hunter looked at his watch and produced a grim smile.

"He might even be over there now."

Veronica had little hope that Santino would get the journalist to share her source, but she didn't want to be negative, so she kept her opinion to herself. Hunter was feeling bad enough as it was.

Suddenly Finn was by her desk, his face tense.

"We can't put this report on at eleven without Spencer's approval," Finn said, shaking his head. "Last time we adjusted a Saturday night segment he had a fit. Said he can't be responsible for getting advertisers if he's not involved in programming changes."

Not wanting to add to Hunter's problems, Veronica hesitated, then decided it couldn't be helped.

"I also think you need to get Deputy Santino's advice about posting up details on the situation," she said. "He may not want Locke knowing that they are on to him and that the Marshals are hunting him down."

Hunter's face fell, but he nodded.

"Okay, you guys win. I'll put in a call to Deputy Santino and see what he thinks we can share with the public at this stage."

"What about Spencer?" Finn asked. "You want me to try to track him down? I could go over to his house and see if he's home."

The videographer looked over and smiled at Gracie, who'd settled in beside her desk.

"I'm sure Gracie wouldn't mind a little drive."

"That'd be great," Hunter said, but the expression on his face didn't match his words. "I just hope he'll listen to you."

Veronica scratched Gracie behind the ears and smiled.

"Why don't you go with him, Hunter?" she suggested. "You'll have a better chance at convincing Spencer, and it'll be good for both you and Gracie to get out of here for a bit."

Before he could protest that he didn't want to leave her alone, she gestured toward the crew and raised an eyebrow.

"And don't worry about me," she insisted. "I'm not going to be alone in here, am I? Now, you need to get going if you have any hope of having the report ready by eleven o'clock."

Veronica smiled as she watched Hunter follow Finn and Gracie through the door, glad to see Hunter doing what he loved again. He'd been miserable running the station instead of being a reporter. He was meant to be out in the world chasing down stories, not locked up in a newsroom chasing down advertisers.

She leaned back in her chair, suddenly grateful that Hunter had found his way back to his true calling after his struggle with the PTSD he'd incurred as a foreign correspondent in the Middle East. He'd made a good decision by teaming up with Finn to buy Channel Ten. Together they'd saved the station from financial ruin.

And it had all fallen into place when Spencer Nash had joined the team as station manager, freeing up Hunter and Finn to focus on what they loved to do. Although she disagreed with Spencer on many things, she knew Hunter respected him and counted on him.

I just hope Spencer will back him up with this report on Locke.

The possibility that Spencer may not be at home with his wife flitted through her mind. Rumors that the married station manager was seeing Tenley Frost had begun to circulate months ago, and there had even been speculation that he was the father of Tenley's baby girl. But Spencer had vehemently denied it, and the rumors had eventually dried up.

And Tenley hasn't come by to see Spencer at the station lately, so the rumors likely weren't true...or maybe they'd finally reached Spencer's wife.

Scolding herself for listening to idle gossip, Veronica went back to worrying about her mother, anxious to know she was safe and well. When her phone buzzed, she jumped and looked down at the text message with eager eyes, surprised to see Mackenzie Jensen's name.

Just wanted to say sorry about the story on your mom. It wasn't my idea.

Veronica stared at the message as if it had been written in hieroglyphics, trying to make sense of Mackenzie's words. How could an article under her byline not be her idea?

Tapping in a response, Veronica tried to phrase her message carefully. She didn't want to scare the journalist away.

Okay, whose idea was it? Can you tell me who your source is?

She held her breath, hoping she was about to learn who had revealed her mother's secret to the *Willow Bay Gazette.*

Sorry, but if my editor knows I've contacted you, he'll kill me.

It sounded to Veronica as if Mackenzie wanted to tell her but was scared. Maybe the editor really had pressured her. If she could convince the journalist she'd keep her secret, she may agree.

What if I didn't tell anyone that you gave me the source?

Mackenzie didn't respond to the message right away, and Veronica figured she'd blown it. Then her phone buzzed.

Maybe, but it's risky. I don't know. Not via text or over the phone.

Sucking in a breath of excitement, Veronica tapped in a response.

How about I come by your house now? No one else will know.

A minute passed and no text. When Mackenzie's response did come through, disappointment surged through Veronica.

No, I can't do that. Sorry.

Veronica knew she couldn't give up now. Not when she'd been so close. And if Santino showed up demanding Mackenzie's source, the journalist would likely refuse to give an official statement. Determined not to let the opportunity pass, she typed in a response.

I promise I won't let anyone else know it was you. Please, it's important.
An endless second ticked by, then her phone buzzed.
You'll come alone? No one else? And you'll keep it secret?
Veronica tapped a quick reply, her heart pounding.
Yes, I'll come alone, and I promise not to tell.
She felt a surge of victory at Mackenzie's final response.
Okay, but hurry. I'm going out soon. I have a date tonight.

Dropping her phone into her purse, Veronica stood up, ready to hurry out the door, then hesitated. Hunter would be back soon, and he'd likely panic if she were gone when he returned. But the bigger problem was she didn't have a car. She'd left her Jeep at the house, having ridden over with Hunter in his Audi.

She pulled her phone back out and tapped on the Uber app. The driver was nearby. A red Camry would pick her up in five minutes. That would give her enough time to write Hunter a quick note.

> *Hunter,*
> *I went to Mackenzie Jensen's house. She said she'll*
> *give me her source if I keep her name out of it. Will*
> *be back soon. Don't worry!*
> *Veronica*

Propping the note on her desk, Veronica added a notepad and freshly sharpened pencil to her bag, startled to see the Glock nestled at the bottom. She'd almost forgotten she'd brought it with her.

Pulling on her red coat, she dropped her phone into the pocket and headed outside. A WBPD patrol car sat in the lot, and she wondered if Officer Ford was still keeping tabs on her, but the red Camry pulled into the lot before she could make out who was inside.

Veronica waved the driver over, anxious to get to Mackenzie's house before the journalist left for her date. Sliding into the backseat, she snapped on her seatbelt and leaned back against the headrest, trying to plan out what she would say to Mackenzie. She couldn't risk spooking the journalist before she got the information she needed.

Ten minutes later the Uber driver pulled up to the curb outside the address Mackenzie had texted to her. Veronica stepped out and turned up the collar of her coat against the icy rain.

She scurried up the walkway and stuck out a cold finger to ring the doorbell. Listening, she heard no noise from inside. Panic set in as she wondered if Mackenzie had already left on her date. Looking back to the curb, she saw that the red Camry was gone.

She knocked on the door with little hope of getting a response, but to her surprise, the door swung slowly open, as if it hadn't been closed all the way.

Warm air drifted through the open door, along with an unpleasant odor. Wrinkling her nose, Veronica called out, her voice sharp with sudden fear. She reached in her purse and put her hand on the Glock.

"Hello? Mackenzie?"

A dim light was on in the foyer, and Veronica strained to see into the darkened room beyond. She thought she could see a shape on the floor. Was someone on the ground?

Stepping inside, she pulled the Glock out and held it in front of her as she moved into the house, her eyes beginning to adjust to the dim lighting. Finally, she was close enough to make out a high-heeled shoe, and then the leg attached to it.

"Mackenzie?"

She stopped in mid-step, gasping in shock as she saw the journalist splayed out on the floor by the couch, a shredded pillow over her head. A sudden movement behind Veronica made her spin around; no one was there.

Trembling with fear, she ran toward the front door, but it slammed closed just as she reached it, knocking the Glock from her hand. The man who had been standing behind the door stepped out and kicked the gun across the floor.

A strong arm wrapped around her throat before she could scream, and she felt the cold muzzle of a gun on her cheek.

"Fight me and I'll blow your head off," the man hissed, dragging her backward into the house.

He pushed her toward a door off the hall, and she stepped into the cold darkness of the garage. Keeping the gun pressed against her head, the man prodded her toward the car parked within. He opened the back door and shoved her into the backseat, throwing a blanket over her before wrapping some kind of cord around her to hold the blanket in place.

She struggled to get free, but the man jabbed the gun against the blanket and tightened the cords.

"You try anything stupid, and I'll kill you. It'd be a pleasure."

The man's voice sounded familiar, but she was too scared to think as the car backed out of the garage and then accelerated forward. Shaking with fear, Veronica shifted her hand to her pocket, attempting to get her hand on her phone.

"Stop moving around back there," the man muttered.

Inching her hand out of her pocket, she held her phone, trying to activate it but unable to see the display. As the car came to a sudden stop, Veronica used her thumb to switch the ringer off, then twisted forward and shifted her hand down so she could slide her phone into the top of her boot.

Maybe he won't think to look for it there. Maybe I'll get a chance to call someone for help.

The only thing keeping Veronica going was the feeling that if the man had wanted to kill her, he would have already done so back at Mackenzie's house.

He has plans for me. If I stay alive long enough, I might be able to escape.

CHAPTER THIRTY-THREE

Hunter held his phone to his ear, desperate to hear Veronica's voice on the other end. But the unanswered call rolled to voicemail again. Jabbing a thumb at the display, he ended the call. He'd already left two messages begging her to call him back.

Either she's deep in conversation with Mackenzie, or she's in trouble.

Gripping the Audi's steering wheel with both hands, he raced down Channel Drive, trying not to panic or overreact.

"It should be the next street on your right," Finn said, navigating from the passenger seat. "There it is, Hawthorne Road."

Hunter steered the Audi onto a street lined with neat houses cheerfully illuminated by porch lights and glowing windows. Finn pointed to a house with an ornate lamppost lighting up the walkway.

"According to Google, it should be that one."

Inhaling deeply, Hunter jumped out and hurried up the stone walkway. He rang the doorbell, then knocked loudly.

"I don't hear anything," he said, as Finn joined him on the porch, followed by Gracie. "It doesn't look like anyone's home."

The white Lab suddenly barked, causing both men to flinch and look down at her. Gracie began scratching at the bottom of the door, her paws frantic in her distress as she barked again.

"That's not good," Finn said, his eyes meeting Hunter's. "She's signaling again. She thinks there's a body in there."

Reaching out to grab the doorknob, Hunter was surprised to find it turning smoothly in his hand. He pushed the door open and stepped into the dark interior.

"Mackenzie? It's Hunter Hadley, are you home?"

Gracie barked and pushed past him, her paws scrabbling against the hard floor. She disappeared into the room beyond, and Hunter felt along the wall, searching for a light switch.

He finally found the panel on the wall and flipped the switch. A soft light flooded the room, allowing him to see the big, white Lab anxiously scratching at the floor in front of what appeared to be a woman's leg.

"Oh, no, Veronica!"

Finn's terrified yell shook Hunter out of his state of shock, and both men dashed forward, stopping short when they saw the body sprawled on the floor.

"It's not her," Hunter said, his voice cracking. "It's Mackenzie."

He knelt by the motionless figure, already knowing from the smell that it was too late to do anything to save the journalist, but he felt compelled to check her pulse just to be sure.

Glancing up, he shook his head at Finn, who immediately pulled out his phone and tapped in 911.

Hunter stood and looked around the room, scared of what he might find. If Veronica had come to meet with Mackenzie, she might have left when no one answered the door, but then again, she could have been attacked as well. She could still be in the house.

His eyes fell on a door leading off the hall. It was ajar, and he could see scratches along the wood as if something sharp had been dragged along it. Walking forward with quiet steps, he peered through the door into the pitch-black room beyond.

The smell of gas and oil told him he was staring into the garage, and as he flipped on the light switch, he prepared himself to see Veronica's body collapsed on the floor.

But the garage was empty. Whatever car Mackenzie had driven was gone, and there was no sign of a struggle.

"The police are on the way," Finn said, coming up behind him. "They said to be safe we should get out of the house and wait in the car until they arrive."

Hunter shook his head.

"I'm not leaving until I know Veronica's not in here."

As he stepped back inside the hall, his eyes fell on something half-hidden behind the door. Crossing the room in long strides, he bent and stared down at a gun. The engraved initials *VL* were visible on the grip. It was Veronica's Glock.

Just then soft footsteps sounded outside the door, and Hunter motioned to Finn to be quiet.

"Someone's on the porch," he whispered.

Bending to scoop up the gun, Hunter held it out in front of him and put his hand on the doorknob.

Finn hissed at him not to open the door, but Hunter had already flung it back and was holding the gun toward the dimly lit porch.

"Whoa there, big guy! Don't shoot!"

Frankie Dawson stood on the porch, his skinny arms raised in the air as he stared into the barrel of the Glock.

"What the hell are you doing here, Frankie?" Hunter asked, not lowering the weapon. "We've got a dead body inside, and the police are on the way, so you better talk fast."

"We're on a surveillance gig." Frankie's eyes widened as Hunter's words sank in. "Who's the body?"

Hunter ignored the question.

"Who's we?" he countered. "You got somebody with you?"

"Just me, Mr. Hadley."

Pete Barker stepped onto the porch, his hands lifted slightly as if showing Hunter he wasn't armed.

"We've been tailing Garth Bixby as part of a case we're working on."

"Yeah, he and Mackenzie Jensen have been going at it like rabbits for the last few weeks," Frankie added. "So, when Bixby's wife said he never came home tonight, we decided to swing by here. See if we could catch him making a booty call on camera."

Barker shot Frankie a sour glance.

"I think he gets the idea, Frankie. Now, what's happened here, Mr. Hadley? You said there's a dead body? Is it Bixby?"

"No, it's Mackenzie Jensen."

Hunter watched as a police cruiser sped around the corner, its lights flashing. As the officers jumped out and ran toward the house, Hunter lowered the gun and placed it on the porch.

He stared at the initials on the Glock's grip, his mind reeling at the likelihood Veronica had been abducted by Mackenzie's killer.

Who's taken you, Veronica? And where are you now?

CHAPTER THIRTY-FOUR

The cruiser's flashing lights startled Peyton as she turned the Dodge Charger onto Hawthorne Road. She glanced over at Deputy Santino, who was riding shotgun. He appeared to be as shocked as she was to see a patrol car parked in front of the same house they were planning to visit.

Pulling up behind the cruiser, Peyton and Santino climbed out and approached the house with caution. Dave Eddings frowned at Peyton as he waved her over.

"Detective Bell. I wasn't expecting you. The dispatcher said Detectives Vanzinger and Jankowski were coming."

The young officer nodded as Santino flashed his badge, then gestured toward the house.

"The scene still needs to be secured," he advised. "So far, we have reports of a dead body, and a gun's been found on the porch, but we haven't performed a thorough search inside yet."

A man stepped out of the shadows, and Peyton was shocked to see Hunter Hadley walking toward them.

"Mr. Hadley? What are you doing here?"

Santino glanced up at her words, immediately on alert as he saw the stricken expression on Hunter's face.

"What exactly is going on, Mr. Hadley?"

"Veronica left me a note saying she was coming here," Hunter said, speaking fast. "Apparently, Mackenzie Jensen agreed to reveal the source of her story on Ling Lee."

He cleared his throat, his voice raw.

"When I got here the door was open and Mackenzie was dead. She'd been shot, and Veronica's gun...I found it on the floor."

"Where's Veronica now?" Santino asked.

"I don't know," Hunter murmured. "I think he's got her."

His words sent a shiver down Peyton's spine.

"Who's got her?" she asked, stepping closer.

"Her father," Hunter said, turning to Santino. "I think Donovan Locke killed Mackenzie, and he's taken Veronica with him."

Eddings pointed toward the shadows.

"You might want to question the other witnesses that were here when we arrived," he said. "They haven't been inside, but they say they were watching the house."

A tall, thin figure emerged from the darkness, and Peyton suppressed a gasp as she recognized Frankie Dawson. Pete Barker's stockier figure joined him on the driveway.

"It sounds like we pulled up just a few minutes after Hunter arrived," Barker said, nodding a greeting at Peyton and Santino. "We're private investigators; a job we're working on led us here tonight. Mr. Hadley's car was parked outside when we pulled up."

Just then another cruiser roared around the corner and screeched to a halt in the road. Andy Ford jumped out of the car and jogged toward Eddings. Hunter intercepted the young officer before he made it across the yard.

"Where's Veronica?" Hunter demanded. "You were watching her, right? Did you see where she went?"

Andy's freckled face reddened, and he looked toward Eddings.

"I was getting a coffee when I got the call from Eddings that she'd been here," Andy admitted. "I didn't know she left the station. I didn't see her leave."

Putting a hand on Andy's arm, Peyton guided him toward the house, waving for Eddings to follow her.

"You two set up a perimeter," she instructed. "We need to search the house and call the crime scene techs out here."

"Looks like you've got a party going on here, *partner*."

Peyton turned around to see that Marc Ingram had arrived. Her partner's face was twisted into his usual scowl.

"I heard a homicide had been called in and thought I'd see if I can help. I figured Vanzinger and Jankowski might be busy with their little task force, and Nessa told me you've been reassigned."

He shot a dirty look at Santino, then caught sight of the other men.

"Is the WBPD so desperate for help we call on amateurs now?" he said, glaring at Frankie and Barker. "And why is there a reporter at the scene before it's been secured?"

Peyton stepped between Ingram and Hunter.

"Ingram, this isn't your case."

Her voice was firm as she met Ingram's angry gaze.

"Says who?" Ingram asked, frowning as he moved closer.

"Says Chief Ainsley," Santino said, stepping up beside Peyton and pulling out his USMS credentials. "She assigned Detective Bell to work with *me* and this scene is now under our control."

For a minute Peyton thought Ingram was going to argue with Santino, but then he huffed and turned on his heel, stomping away into the dark.

Feeling Frankie's eyes on her, Peyton looked over and met his gaze. He raised a hand to his forehead in a mock salute as Santino spoke beside her.

"Okay, then," he said, rubbing his hands together. "Let's go see what's inside."

Peyton stared down at Mackenzie Jensen, her chest tightening at the thought of the poor woman's last terrifying moments.

"The ME should be here soon," Alma Garcia said, pausing to take several photographs of the journalist's body. "In the meantime, you may want to get a look at what we found in the kitchen."

The senior crime scene technician moved away, but her heavy perfume stayed behind to mingle with the odor of decomposition. Peyton guessed Alma had been enjoying a night out on the town when she'd been called to the crime scene.

Moving into the kitchen, Peyton saw Vanzinger and Jankowski huddled around the kitchen table. A small recorder sat on the table between the big men.

"What's that?" Peyton asked.

Vanzinger put a finger to his mouth, signaling for her to be quiet, as Jankowski lowered his head toward the recorder.

"I can't make out all the words," Jankowski muttered, scratching absently at his impressive five o'clock shadow.

The big detective stuck out a finger to rewind the recording, as Peyton watched in confusion.

"Where'd you find that recorder?"

"It was in Mackenzie Jensen's purse," Vanzinger said, pressing the play button. "And it was still recording when we found it. This thing can keep going for like twenty hours."

Straining to listen, Peyton made out the sound of muffled voices.

"What's that?" she asked.

"That's the last few minutes of Mackenzie Jensen's life," Santino said from the doorway. "She recorded her own homicide."

The grim look on Santino's face worried Peyton.

"You've listened to this already?" Vanzinger asked, turning his blue eyes to Santino. "Could you hear what they're saying?"

"I heard enough to know that the fugitive I'm looking for has hooked up with someone named Diablo."

Jankowski and Vanzinger gaped at him.

"You're kidding, right?"

Santino walked to the table and picked up the recorder. He adjusted the volume as high as it would go and pressed play. A muffled woman's voice sounded.

"Okay, so who's your source? Who told you about Ling Lee's past?"

A man's voice responded. Peyton was able to make out most of the words as the conversation played out.

"I don't think that matters ...you've been too blind to see... you've been sleeping with the man the FBI, the WBPD, and now the U.S. Marshals Service have been looking for, and you never suspected a thing."

Peyton's eyes widened at Mackenzie's next statement.

"Everyone in town knows you. You're not that hard to find."

No one around the table moved as Mackenzie admitted she had been trying to find the source of the information about Ling Lee. The man's next words chilled Peyton to the bone.

"The man who gave me that information would kill me as soon as look at me. Besides, he and I have a deal. And if I let you live, you could cause trouble for both of us."

Wincing in horror, Peyton listened to Mackenzie's final moments.

"I'm sorry it had to...come to this. We had fun, but...looks like I'm...going to have to...kill your big...story."

The sound of the muffled gunshot echoed through the kitchen.

Santino reached over and shut off the recording. He looked around at the detectives, his face hard.

"Whoever this Diablo is, he killed Mackenzie Jensen, and he most likely has abducted Veronica Lee."

Meeting Peyton's eyes, Santino voiced what she'd been thinking.

"And if he really has hooked up with Donovan Locke, we'll probably have more victims on our hands before all this is over."

CHAPTER THIRTY-FIVE

Nessa greeted Cole and Cooper's whoops and shouts with her usual smile, trying hard not to show how much Peyton's call had shaken her as she hugged the boys and followed them into the kitchen. Jerry looked around from the stove wearing an apron and a smile. The smile faded as he saw Nessa's ashen face.

"Go wash up and brush your teeth," he called out to the boys, shooing them out of the room before turning concerned eyes on Nessa. "You missed dinner, but I saved you a plate."

"I just got a call that means I need to head back to the station," she said, deciding not to mention she would also be going out to the scene of a new homicide. "We got a mess going on if you haven't figured that out."

Taking her purse off her shoulder, Jerry tugged her toward the table and pulled out a chair.

"I'm not letting you leave unless you eat dinner first," he said, picking up a plate off the stove. "Voila! Jerry's famous spaghetti."

The garlic aroma of the sauce was overwhelming, but Nessa only smiled and picked up her fork. If she didn't at least try to eat something before she headed out, Jerry would worry, and at this point, she was ready to admit to herself that he might have a point.

As soon as things slow down at work, I need to make a doctor's appointment. It's been ages since I went in and had a check-up.

Twenty minutes later Nessa was back in her Charger heading toward Hawthorne Road. She'd insisted that Peyton play her the recording from the Mackenzie Jensen scene, and she couldn't get the man's muffled voice out of her head.

I know that voice from somewhere. Who is it?

She also couldn't get over Mackenzie's statement that the man called Diablo, the man they'd all been looking for, was someone well known in their town.

Hopefully, Alma will find fingerprints or some kind of evidence at Mackenzie's house to point us in the right direction.

Traveling south on Channel Drive, Nessa prepared to turn onto Hawthorne Road just as her phone vibrated on the dashboard.

Mayor Hadley's picture popped up on the display. She hesitated, tempted to let the call roll to voicemail, then reluctantly tapped to answer the call. Rustling noises sounded through the hands-free speaker, and then Mayor Hadley's voice was in the car with her.

"Chief Ainsley? Where are you?"

"I'm just pulling up to a scene," she replied, bringing the Charger to a stop alongside the curb in front of Mackenzie Jensen's house. "We've got another homicide if you can believe it."

Expecting the Mayor to ask for details about the new homicide, or maybe demand an update on the Old Willow Square homicide, Nessa wasn't prepared for his next statement.

"Tenley Frost is missing."

His voice was unusually subdued, and Nessa frowned as she turned off the engine and picked up her phone.

"What do you mean by *missing?*"

"Nora Fletcher called our office a few minutes ago. She's Tenley's sitter, and she's saying Tenley never showed up to get her daughter."

Nessa frowned at the phone.

"Could she just be running late? Maybe her car broke down?"

"That's not possible," Mayor Hadley replied testily. "Tenley's car is in Mrs. Fletcher's driveway, and her purse and phone are inside, but Tenley isn't."

Refusing to believe Tenley could really be missing, Nessa tried to think of plausible explanations, but none came to her.

"Chief Ainsley? Are you still there?"

"I'm here, Mayor," Nessa murmured, staring out at the flashing lights and crime scene van visible through her windshield. "And I'll get right on it. In fact, I'll take care of this one myself."

* * *

Nora Fletcher opened the front door as Nessa stepped onto the porch. The older woman held Avery Lynn on her ample hip, and the small girl peered at Nessa through sleepy blue eyes.

"Thanks for coming so quickly, Chief Ainsley," Nora said, ushering Nessa into a cozy sitting room. "I hated to bother the Mayor, but when I saw Tenley's car, I didn't know what else to do."

The older woman sank onto a chair and Nessa sat next to her.

"First of all, please call me Nessa," she said, taking a small notepad from the pocket of her jacket. "And now, tell me what happened. When did you see that Tenley's car had been left here?"

"Tenley's rarely late," Nora said, brushing back a strand of silvery hair that had escaped her bun. "So, I was surprised when she didn't show up by eight. I thought maybe with everything going on..."

A guarded look fell over Nora's face, and she looked away.

"Anyway, I went outside to put the trashcans by the curb, and I saw her car there. I was shocked to see it was empty."

"What did you do then?"

Nora shrugged and sighed.

"Well, I saw that the doors were unlocked, and I could see her purse sitting right there on the passenger's seat. I was worried someone might take it, so I brought it inside and waited."

Glancing up at Nessa with a look of remorse, Nora shook her head.

"I shouldn't have waited, I guess," she stammered. "But I was confused. I thought maybe she'd come back. That maybe she'd gone for a walk around the block, or...something."

Avery Lynn began to struggle in Nora's arms, and the sitter moved the baby girl to her other leg, bouncing her gently up and down.

"I tried to call her phone, but I could hear it ringing in her purse," Nora explained. "That's when I decided to call the mayor's office and see if she was there. They said she'd left hours before, and that she'd been in a hurry to get her daughter."

Hugging Avery Lynn against her chest, Nora looked up at Nessa.

"Something terrible has happened, hasn't it?"

"Let's not jump to any conclusions," Nessa said, trying not to reveal her growing concern. "But tell me, do have any idea where Tenley could be? Did she tell you anything that would make you suspect someone might want to harm her?"

Nora's eyes widened, and she shook her head, then hesitated.

"Well, I hate to say anything. I promised Tenley I wouldn't..."

"Anything you say will be kept confidential," Nessa assured her. "And if you know something that could help her, I'm sure Tenley would want you to tell me."

Looking down at Avery Lynn, as if the little girl might be able to understand what she was saying, Nora lowered her voice.

"Tenley was seeing a married man," she said, dropping her eyes in embarrassment. "She wanted to break it off, but she said there aren't many *eligible* men in Willow Bay..."

Her voice faded away as Nessa made a note on her pad.

"Okay, so who is this married man?" she asked. "Could Tenley possibly be with him now?"

A look of hope entered Nora's eyes, but she still hesitated.

"I promise to be as discreet as possible," Nessa said, starting to get impatient. "But I need to know who this man is so that I can make sure Tenley's not with him."

After another pause, Nora nodded.

"She's been seeing Garth Bixby," she whispered. "He's Mayor Hadley's campaign manager."

"Yes, I know who Mr. Bixby is."

Thinking of Tenley stepping out of the black SUV that morning, Nessa wasn't surprised as she wrote Bixby's name on her pad.

"Thank you, Mrs. Fletcher," Nessa said as she stood up.

"Oh, please call me Nora."

The older woman stood, positioning Avery Lynn on her hip again. "What are you going to do now?"

"First, I'm going to make a few calls," Nessa said. "I'll see if I can track down Garth Bixby. And I'll have a look at Tenley's car. If that doesn't turn up anything...well, we'll go from there."

Nessa made her way back to the front door, but before she could step out onto the porch, Nora put a hand on her arm.

"What about little Avery Lynn?" the older woman said, her voice strained. "Should I put her down to sleep here?"

Smiling at the sleeping baby in Nora's arms, Nessa nodded.

"Looks like she beat you to it," she said, reaching out a gentle finger to stroke the little girl's cheek. "She's already gone."

The rain had started up again, and Nessa pulled the hood of her jacket up and over her head as she walked to Tenley's Lexus.

She took out her phone and tapped on the flashlight icon, shining the stream of light on the car and studying the driver's side door. She was just about to reach out and open it when she saw the footprints in the mud beneath the door.

Two small footprints were visible around a shallow puddle of rainwater. A flurry of bigger, deeper boot prints surrounded the smaller prints. Nessa moved the beam of the flashlight along a series of footprints and drag marks on the ground.

Following the marks out to the road, Nessa stared down at the tire tracks leading away from the house. She drew in a deep breath and then ran to her Charger. Slipping behind the wheel, she tapped on Vanzinger's name in her contact list.

The detective answered on the second ring.

"Tenley Frost is missing, and it looks like she may have been abducted," Nessa said before Vanzinger could speak. "I'm wondering if the man who killed Mackenzie and took Veronica could have come after Tenley, too."

Vanzinger didn't seem to be surprised by her words. Perhaps it was becoming clear to them all that they had a madman lose in Willow Bay, and that more victims were to be expected.

"What time did she go missing?" he asked, his voice brisk. "And from where?"

"About eight o'clock according to the sitter. On the upper east side of town. A little subdivision near the corner of Elm and Surrey."

It took only seconds for Vanzinger to do the calculations.

"Then it's unlikely the man who killed Mackenzie could have abducted Tenley, as well. The two events happened about the same time, and across town from each other."

Nessa tried to think. They knew from the recording that the man calling himself Diablo had killed Mackenzie and that he was most likely working with Donovan Locke. Could Ling Lee's crazy ex-husband have taken Tenley Frost?

She looked down at the now soggy notepad in her lap. Raindrops had smeared her notes, but she could still read Garth Bixby's name.

"The sitter said Tenley's been seeing Garth Bixby," Nessa said. "I was planning to check in with him, to see if Tenley could be with him but now I'm-"

"Hold on, Chief," Vanzinger said, sounding excited. "Mackenzie Jensen was also sleeping with Garth Bixby. At least that's what your old partner Pete Barker told us."

Nessa shook her head, staring out at the rain as she tried to put the pieces together in her mind.

"You talked to Barker about the case?"

"He and Frankie Dawson were at the scene when we arrived. They'd been tailing Bixby. Some kind of surveillance gig. They said Bixby and Mackenzie had been sleeping together for weeks."

Shaking her head in disbelief, Nessa looked again at the blurry name she'd written.

"Garth Bixby's been fooling around with Mackenzie Jensen and Tenley Frost," she said slowly, not sure if she was talking to Vanzinger or herself. "One woman's dead and the other is missing."

"Yep, that's what it looks like," Vanzinger agreed, his voice vibrating over the connection.

"Right," Nessa said. "I think it's time to find Mr. Bixby."

CHAPTER THIRTY-SIX

Diablo turned the big black SUV onto the narrow, unpaved road, bumping past the overhanging trees that blocked the view of the place he now thought of as his base camp. He stopped outside the big gate, waiting for it to swing open, then drove through, happy to see the truck for the evening's shipment was already being loaded.

Men stomped back and forth over the muddy terrain, lugging boxes out from one of the long buildings hidden behind the thick walls and the barbed wire. A stocky man with a rifle slung over one massive shoulder waved at Diablo, then turned back to guard duty.

It was almost noon, and the sun was high in the cloudless sky, but the cold front was expected to last another few days, and most of the men wore hoodies or lightweight jackets as they worked. Diablo stepped out of the SUV and adjusted his expensive leather jacket.

Hoping his shoes wouldn't be ruined by the mud left behind after last night's rain, he cursed the State of Florida for not paving the road and courtyard of the old facility.

The place had opened up as a girl's reformatory in the early seventies and had operated for several decades before falling into disuse at the turn of the century.

Diablo had used a holding company to purchase the property and buildings at auction at a ridiculously low cost, and the deal had allowed him to set up clandestine operations just outside of town, resulting in a satisfying profit.

Making his way into the office that had previously belonged to the detention center's superintendent, Diablo crossed to the safe under the desk and entered in his secret code.

He surveyed the towering stack of hundred-dollar bills alongside bulging bags of white powder as he put away his new toy. The Sig Sauer handgun had replaced his old Berretta. He'd decided to treat himself after hearing the Navy Seals used the same model, and the previous night's events had provided Diablo with his first opportunity to use it.

Eliminating Mackenzie Jensen as a possible witness against him and delivering Veronica Lee to the Professor had completed the first part of the plan. The evening had gone as well as could be expected.

And it was satisfying to know that Tenley Frost was now out of his life for good and that his daughter would soon be with him. The cruel decision not to include him in his daughter's life had ended up costing Tenley her own life, and Diablo felt no remorse.

She got what she deserved, and now I'll get what I deserve: my daughter.

Closing the safe, Diablo paced over to the window and looked out at the men loading the truck. The shipment would net him another stack of cash, and it would be the first step in establishing the Diablo Syndicate as a key player in the South Florida gun trafficking scene.

Of course, he knew that wouldn't matter if his cover was blown. After a year of hard work, his new enterprise could be destroyed with one phone call or the testimony of one teenage addict.

Ruby Chase was at the police station right now. If she were able to provide a good description of him, it might be enough for a sketch artist to create a composite that would be recognizable to most of the people in town. His face could end up on the nightly news.

And it was even possible that Ruby could lead the task force back to his base camp. He still wasn't sure how she'd managed to escape, and he didn't know if she'd be able to find the way back to the overgrown road outside town.

Looking out of the office window, he stared at the big gate, imagining a SWAT team suddenly arriving to swarm over his base camp. But Diablo's biggest worry wasn't the runaway street kid. He had a much bigger problem than that. He still needed to fulfill the second part of his bargain with the Professor.

Or should I start calling him Donovan Locke?

He knew it had taken him longer than it should have to figure out the man he'd made a deal with was a dangerous fugitive. Donovan Locke had been in the trafficking business for three decades, and he'd been on the run from the U.S. Marshals Service for almost as long.

Reading about Locke's past and the array of crimes he'd committed, Diablo had been impressed with the man's ability to evade capture. He'd also realized just how dangerous Locke was, and that breaking his bargain with the killer wouldn't be a wise idea.

Although Locke had already left town as far as Diablo knew, the fugitive's darknet persona, better known as the Professor, would enact his revenge if Diablo failed to deliver.

I agreed to kill Ling Lee, and if I don't, I'll incur the Professor's wrath.

One email sent to the Operation Stolen Angels task force would be enough to open an investigation on him. From there, it would be a downward spiral of news stories, court appearances, and jail time. In the end, once the truth came out about Mackenzie Jensen's murder, he could even end up riding Old Sparky up in Raiford.

So, I've got to find Ling Lee and finish her off. But where the hell is she?

Diablo's men had been looking for Ling Lee for the last forty-eight hours, but no one had seen her, and none of Diablo's usual contacts knew where she had gone.

All Diablo knew was that the U.S. marshal who came to town had been tasked with protecting Ling and that he was hell-bent on hunting down her ex-husband, Donovan Locke.

Diablo figured if Locke was captured, the trail might eventually lead back to him, but he couldn't afford to worry about that now. His focus had to be finding Ling Lee and finishing her off.

Otherwise, his life in Willow Bay would be over for good, and he'd end up spending the rest of his life in prison or on the run.

But how do I find a woman who has vanished off the face of the earth?

Sitting down at the little desk in the corner, he opened his laptop and reviewed the news stories about Ling Lee, looking for any clue that might reveal where she could be. Most of the stories centered on her run for mayor, or the Zander Greyson case.

One of the photos showed Ling Lee standing with her daughter and Hunter Hadley in the Channel Ten station. Diablo studied the reporter's face, wondering where she was, and what her father had done with her. He imagined Hunter Hadley would be going mad about now, not knowing where his little girlfriend was.

That's it. Hunter Hadley's bound to know where his girlfriend's mother is hiding, and he'll want to tell her that her daughter is missing.

Opening the door to the office, Diablo waved over the only man he trusted to do such an important job. Leading the big man into his office, he explained what he needed him to do. With any luck, he'd know Ling Lee's whereabouts by the end of the day.

* * *

The man's call came sooner than Diablo expected.

"You found her?" he asked before the man could speak.

"Hadley and his marshal buddy are headed toward the interstate now," he said. "But they did make one stop."

231

The man rattled off an address as Diablo listened eagerly.

"It looks like there's a plainclothes guy outside the house," the man continued. "I'd say the woman they're hiding must be inside."

"Okay, keep watching the house. I want to know who goes in and who comes out," Diablo ordered. "And if the guy out front takes a break, you go in and take her out."

The man laughed.

"Yeah, right," he snorted, laughing again. "You think I'm going to off some broad under the nose of the U.S. Marshals? I'm not crazy, and you aren't paying me enough to kill anyone. Why don't you leave the lady alone? We got a big shipment to handle and–"

"Enough!" Diablo barked, irritated by the man's laughter. "Just tell me when the coast is clear, and I'll take care of it myself."

He thought of the shiny new gun in the safe and decided he might as well keep it with him. He'd need it if he got the call that Ling Lee had been left unprotected. And it could come in useful during his next errand. He would finally be taking back what was rightfully his.

Donovan Locke now has his daughter, and it's time for me to go get mine.

CHAPTER THIRTY-SEVEN

The semi-truck rumbled on and on without end as Veronica sat in the trailer's hidden compartment, her back against the wall, her knees raised, and her head resting on her folded arms. She lifted her head to glare up at the little camera mounted on the wall, then dropped it again, trying to push back the anger and fear so she could think more clearly.

She knew the camera allowed her father to watch her and Tenley on his phone as he drove the big rig. Most likely he wanted to make sure they weren't trying to escape, although Veronica suspected he might also be worried about Tenley's condition.

The media relations officer was slumped beside Veronica, her auburn hair spilling out over the floor, and her face pale and motionless in the dim overhead light.

Reaching out to put her finger on the woman's delicate wrist, Veronica could feel a slow, erratic pulse. Whatever her father had given Tenley had knocked her out, and she showed no sign of waking.

Veronica's eyes kept returning to the cup of water on the floor next to her, but she resisted the impulse to drink from it, even though her mouth was dry and her throat tight.

If she allowed herself to be drugged, she would be as helpless as Tenley now was, and she'd never be able to figure out a way for them to escape.

The urge to close her eyes grew stronger as the monotonous hum and vibration of the tires on the road lulled her into a state of sleepy despair. It would be so easy just to close her eyes and forget about everything that had happened.

But the fear that she would wake up in a locked room somewhere, and never again have a chance to see the light of day, kept Veronica from giving in to the release that sleep would offer.

Turning her head so that her long, dark hair fell over her left boot, Veronica slowly moved her hand down, slipping it inside the boot and feeling the hard edge of her phone.

The last time she'd dared to check her phone, she'd been devastated to see that it had no service. She'd quickly returned it to the hiding place in the lining of her knee-high boot, hoping that the truck had been moving through a dead zone and that Locke hadn't done something to purposely block the cell signal.

Her heart pounded in her chest as she tried again. Pulling the phone toward her in a smooth motion, she glanced down, tapping a finger on the partially exposed display.

The phone flashed to life, and Veronica could see from the time shown on the display that it had been almost twenty-four hours since she'd been abducted from Mackenzie Jensen's house.

The memory of the journalist's dead body caused Veronica's empty stomach to clench. She thought of the man who had taken her, wishing she'd had a chance to get a glimpse of his face behind his mask. His voice had seemed so familiar, and the way he had spoken made her think he knew her, and that he'd enjoyed scaring her.

Pulling the phone out further, she saw it now had a weak signal. She forced herself to stay still. If Locke was watching her, he might notice any little movement.

The truck suddenly came to a stop, and Veronica quickly pushed the phone back inside the boot, careful not to show alarm. She kept her head resting on her folded arms until the door to the hidden compartment swung open, and her father stood above her, staring down at her with eyes the same color green as her own.

He held out a plastic bag.

"Got these at the rest stop for you."

He dropped the bag on the floor by her boots, and Veronica could make out a plastic-wrapped sandwich and a bottle of water inside the bag. She turned her head away, ignoring the offered meal.

"Go on," he said, using his foot to nudge the bag closer to her. "It's safe to eat. It's all still wrapped and everything."

"I'm not hungry," Veronica muttered, knowing she'd have to talk to him if she hoped to find a way to escape.

"You best eat while you have the chance," Locke said, his voice hardening. "It might not be safe to stop again any time soon."

Looking back up at him, Veronica tried to gauge his strength, wondering what he would do if she tried to tackle him. He appeared hard and weathered, and while he was lean, she thought he still looked strong for a man that must be nearing sixty.

"Where are you taking us?" she finally asked.

She decided the cramped compartment wasn't the right place to try to overpower him. She'd need to take him by surprise, and she'd have to have a place to run in case she did manage to get away.

"I'm taking you back to my ranch," he said, folding his arms over his chest. "Where you should have been all these years."

"Is that where Skylar is?" she asked, watching his face.

His stern expression didn't change, but Veronica thought she saw a glint of surprise in his eyes. Maybe he didn't know about the message Astrid had sent after all.

"You'll find out soon enough," he said. "Now stop asking questions. All those questions will just get you in trouble."

"They're going to come after me," she warned, unable to help herself. "Ma won't let them ever stop looking for me."

Narrowing his eyes at her words, Locke shook his head.

"Your mother's dead," he said. "Or at least, she soon will be. I've got somebody hunting her down right now. By the time we get back to the ranch, she won't be able to betray anyone ever again."

"You'll never find her," Veronica insisted. "She's in hiding because of you. She won't come out until you're behind bars again."

Locke didn't react to her anger.

"So, your mother's gone into hiding again?" His voice was cold. "Guess that means she's turned her back on you, too, then."

Before Veronica could respond, Locke stepped back and closed the door to the compartment. She heard the latch click into place as she slumped back against the wall.

She pulled the bag toward her and looked inside. Taking out the bottle of water, she tested it and saw that it hadn't been opened. Unscrewing the cap, Veronica allowed herself a long swig of the water, then turned to Tenley.

Placing a hand on the unconscious woman's shoulder, Veronica shook her gently, hoping to rouse her enough to take a drink.

"Tenley? Wake up. I have some water."

Veronica checked her pulse again, then tipped the bottle to allow a few drops of water to drip into Tenley's slack mouth.

Stirring a little at the feel of the water on her lips, Tenley moaned and then murmured softly, her eyes still closed.

"Avery...my...little...girl..."

"I'm sure your daughter's fine," Veronica whispered, although she had no idea where the little girl was, or if she was okay. "She needs you to be strong right now, Tenley."

But Tenley had fallen back into a deep state of unconsciousness. Veronica tried tipping more water into her mouth, but it only dribbled back out onto the wooden floor.

Taking another swig of water, Veronica screwed the lid back on the bottle and set it to the side. She rested her hand casually on her boot, deciding she'd better switch off the phone to avoid running down the battery.

She would try to text Hunter once the truck had started moving again. She could tell him who she was with and that she was okay.

I've gotta let him know Locke has taken me and Tenley, and I have to warn him that he's sent someone to kill Ma.

CHAPTER THIRTY-EIGHT

Hunter opened his eyes and looked around, surprised to see snow falling on the windshield of the Chevy Tahoe. Sitting up, he adjusted his seatback and looked over to see Deputy Santino still asleep in the driver's seat. They'd finally pulled over at a rest stop just after three in the morning, knowing that neither of them was in any shape to keep driving.

"Where the hell are we?" he muttered, checking his phone as the events of the last few days began to trickle back into his mind.

Opening the door to the big SUV, Hunter jumped down and scanned the rest area for the nearest restroom. By the time he'd returned to the Chevy, Santino was awake and on the phone.

"We lost the signal in Kentucky," the deputy was saying into his phone as Hunter climbed back in the passenger's seat. "We're at a rest stop near the Illinois border. We're ready to roll but I'm still not seeing a signal."

The signal they'd been following from Willow Bay all the way to the Kentucky border had been coming from Veronica's phone.

After Veronica had been taken, Hunter remembered that Ling Lee could track down her daughter's phone using the *Find My Phone* app. He'd convinced Santino to stop by the safe house where Ling Lee was staying. They'd broken the news about Veronica's abduction and had picked up Ling's phone.

The men had been shocked to see the signal from Veronica's phone was showing her on Interstate 75 driving through Georgia. Santino had immediately requested help from local authorities in the area, but he couldn't provide them with a description of the vehicle they should be looking for, and then he'd lost the signal before any officers could be dispatched.

Undaunted at the thought of taking on an interstate manhunt, Santino had arranged for the Chevy Tahoe, and he and Hunter had set out with the intention of following the signal until they'd located the vehicle. Once they knew where Locke was and what vehicle he was driving, they could call in local back-up to help them take Locke down.

The main problem so far was that the signal had been going in and out, leaving them driving blind much of the time. But neither man was willing to give up. Veronica was out there on the road ahead of them, and if they persisted, they just might be able to find her.

And throughout the last twenty-four hours, Hunter had been tormented by the possibility that they might already be too late to save Veronica's life, or worse, that he might never know what had happened to her.

Now, as he sat in the Tahoe listening to Santino on the phone, Hunter's phone buzzed in his pocket. His eyes widened in excitement as he saw Veronica's number on the display.

"She sent me a text," Hunter said, putting out a hand to get Santino's attention. "Veronica sent me a text."

Tapping on the display, he held his breath as he read the words.

I'm okay. I'm in Locke's semi-truck. Tenley Frost is here, too. Locke says he's taking us to a ranch where no one will find us. Phone battery's almost dead. Please keep Ma safe. Locke has someone looking for her. Love you.

Relief flooded through him at the realization that Veronica was still alive. But as he read the words again, fear that they may never be able to track her down took over.

"I've got a signal," Santino said, his eyes bright as he looked at the little dot on the phone display. "Shit. They're in Missouri. Looks like they're heading for Kansas."

Hunter tapped in a response to Veronica's text message, then paused. He didn't want to send anything that could alert Locke that they were on his trail.

If Veronica's father were to find her phone, Hunter didn't want him to know they were using it to track the truck.

Editing the message, he tried to reassure her, while giving nothing away that might reveal their location or plan of attack to Locke.

Your mother is safe. Send me a text each hour if you can so I know you're okay. We will be together soon. Love you, too.

He tapped *Send*, then watched until the word *Delivered* appeared beside the text. He waited, hoping to see the word change to *Read*.

"Let's get going," Santino said, starting the Chevy's engine. "We're five hours behind them, but at least we know they're in a semi now, and we know they're heading toward Kansas."

Hunter sat forward in his seat, watching as the snow began to fall harder. He frowned up at the bleak Kentucky sky, then scrolled to the weather app on his phone.

It looked like the weather ahead was going to get a lot colder, and the snow would only get heavier.

"I haven't been in snow for a while," Hunter said, his eyes still on his phone. "I grew up in Florida, so I never did get used to it."

"I have a feeling Locke might end up taking us a lot further north than we'd like. Like maybe as far north as you can go in the US."

Santino glanced at Hunter as they sped along the icy interstate.

"Astrid Peterson was abducted in Montana," he said, turning his eyes back to the road. "And if my calculations are correct, we seem to be headed in that direction."

Shaking his head, Hunter looked out the window at the increasingly white landscape whipping by and shuddered. He wouldn't want to be out in the cold running around. Cold weather had never been his thing.

"Damn, the signal's gone again."

Wincing at Santino's words, Hunter dropped his eyes to his phone, a sense of dread filling his chest as they sped through the snow.

His message to Veronica was still unread.

CHAPTER THIRTY-NINE

Nessa nursed a bottle of water and tried to keep her eyes open and focused on the whiteboard. She'd asked Vanzinger and Jankowski to come in early to brief her ahead of the next interview they had scheduled with Garth Bixby.

She hadn't had any time off over the weekend, and it felt like it should be Friday afternoon, rather than Monday morning. Another week was starting, and a dizzying array of cases was still open and unsolved.

"We can conclude from the recording found at Mackenzie Jensen's house that the man who killed her and abducted Veronica Lee has been working with Donovan Locke," Jankowski said, drawing a line between the suspects' names he'd written on the whiteboard.

"Right, and our friends in the state cybercrime lab had no problem getting into Mackenzie's laptop," Vanzinger added. "She received an email with the information on Ling Lee last week. They're trying to track down the sender, but it was sent using an anonymous account, so it looks like a dead end."

"And what about your initial interrogation of Garth Bixby?" Nessa asked, stifling a yawn. "Did you guys get him to open up? Did he say anything interesting I should know about before we get in there?"

Folding his thick arms over his chest, Jankowski shot a frustrated look at Vanzinger, who just sighed and shook his head.

"We tried everything to get him to break," Vanzinger admitted, raking a big hand through his red crewcut. "I tried to buddy up to him, and Jank played the bad cop as usual, but Bixby didn't budge."

Nessa thought about the slimy campaign manager. Based on what they'd found out about his extramarital activities, he was likely well-practiced in deception.

"It seems Garth Bixby is an expert at sticking to his story in the face of all evidence to the contrary," Nessa said. "But for this next interview, I've asked someone to join us who just might be able to help break him."

Standing up and stretching, Nessa walked to the door.

"In fact, our special interrogator should already be here. I'll ask the desk sergeant to send her back."

"And Bixby's already in interview room three." Jankowski cracked his knuckles as if preparing for a fight. "I'll go get him warmed up."

Nessa picked up the phone and connected to the front desk

"Can you escort Barbie Bixby back to interview room three?" she asked, then put the handset back on the base.

Taking another long sip of water, she prepared herself for the interrogation. If Garth Bixby really was Diablo, she needed to get him to tell her where he'd taken Veronica, and what he knew about Tenley Frost's abduction. The lives of both women may count on it.

Garth Bixby sat at the interview table in a pristine shirt and tie. He was wearing his usual smile when Nessa entered.

"Where's your lawyer, Mr. Bixby?" Nessa asked, looking at the empty chair beside him. "If you don't have one, I can make arrangements to have the court appoint one for you."

"Oh, I don't need a lawyer," Bixby smirked. "And if I do decide to call in legal counsel, my wife will make the arrangements. She may even decide to sue your department for false arrest and slander."

Nessa stood and crossed to the door.

"Okay, well why don't we ask your wife about that."

Opening the door, Nessa motioned for Barbie Bixby to enter. The woman wore a cheerful red dress and matching lipstick, but her eyes told a different story.

"Barbs, what are you doing here?" Bixby asked, his cool façade slipping as his wife took a seat across from him.

"I've asked Mrs. Bixby here to enlighten us about your recent activities," Nessa explained. "She was kind enough to agree."

Bixby banged a fist on the wooden table and frowned up at Nessa.

"You can't force a wife to speak against her husband," he insisted, then turned outraged eyes to Barbie. "You don't have to say anything, baby. This is all just a big misunderstanding."

Nessa ignored the outburst, but Barbie raised a hand, as if to silence the room, and produced a thick file folder.

"No one is forcing me to do anything, Garth. It's my pleasure to provide Chief Ainsley with the evidence I've been collecting."

Bixby gaped at his wife, then looked down at the file, which she'd opened on the table. A photo of Bixby sitting at a dimly lit table with Tenley Frost was on top of a stack of other photos.

"These photos document your activity in the last month or so," Barbie said. "Underneath them, you'll find credit card records that add to the overall picture of your infidelity and lies."

"How did you get these?" Bixby asked, his eyes narrowing.

"I took that one myself," she said, pointing to the photo on top. "But after a while, I got tired of running around and hired a private investigation firm to follow you. I needed evidence for the divorce proceedings, and as you can see here, I now have plenty."

Bixby leaned back in his chair and produced a nasty smile.

"Those were all business meetings," he sneered over at Barbie. "Your insecurity is starting to show, dear. It really isn't attractive."

Jankowski, who had been looking through the photos, slapped one of them down in front of Bixby. It showed him in a car with Mackenzie Jensen. They were locked in an embrace.

"We found the Jetta in that picture abandoned off Highway 42," the big detective said, his voice hard. "Now, stop with the bullshit. You've been sleeping with Mackenzie Jensen and Tenley Frost."

"So, I like women," Bixby said, his smile widening. "That doesn't make me a killer."

"It doesn't make you a saint, either," Barbie said, standing up. "And I suggest you rethink your decision to retain a lawyer. You'll need a good one for the divorce."

Nessa followed Barbie out into the hall, watching her leave before crossing to interview room two. She rapped softly on the door before opening it. Ruby Chase sat across from Riley Odell. Peyton Bell stood next to Ruby, pointing down to a photo array of nine images.

"Just ignore me," Nessa said, stepping inside and shutting the door behind her. "Pretend I'm not here."

Looking down at the images in front of her, Ruby paused, then shook her head. She looked up at Peyton with a sullen expression.

"I've never seen any of them," she muttered. "Can I go now?"

"I think Ms. Odell wants to ask you a few more questions, Ruby," Peyton said. "I'll be back in just a minute."

The detective motioned for Nessa to follow her into the hall.

"I just got an update call from Deputy Santino," Peyton said, her voice hushed. "He's received a message from Veronica Lee."

A jolt of adrenaline flooded through Nessa at her words.

"Locke has her, and Tenley Frost, too," Peyton said in a grim whisper. "Santino is on the trail, but he's asked that we not share details with anyone at this stage, even inside the department."

Nessa nodded, her original excitement that Veronica and Tenley were still alive dampened by the realization that a cold-blooded killer had the women. A killer who had successfully evaded capture for almost three decades, and who had shot Astrid Peterson dead before dumping her body in Old Willow Square.

"Ruby saw the photo of Bixby in the lineup but didn't identify him," Peyton said. "If she really has seen Diablo, then it doesn't look like Bixby is our guy."

Turning back to interview room three, Nessa knew they had nothing solid to hold Garth Bixby on. Cheating on your wife wasn't against the law, and it didn't prove homicide.

Nessa opened the door and stepped inside. Bixby had dropped his nice-guy routine altogether. His face twisted into an ugly grimace as he turned on Nessa.

"You're on the wrong track, *Chief*," he said, his voice filled with disdain. "You should be looking for Avery Lynn's father. That's who Tenley was scared of. She would never tell me who the guy was, but she said he was a nasty bastard and that she'd never let him get his hands on her little girl."

The image of Tenley's tiny daughter flitted through Nessa's mind. Fear took hold of her, and she turned and headed toward the door, suddenly worried that Tenley's little girl might be a target, too.

* * *

Nora Fletcher's neat little house on Surrey Way was quiet when Nessa and Peyton arrived. Tenley's car had already been towed away to be searched by the crime scene team, and the driveway where it had been parked was now clear of mud and debris.

Walking to the door, Nessa tried to tell herself that she was wrong. The man who'd taken Tenley was long gone, and Deputy Santino was on Locke's trail as he fled Willow Bay.

There's no way Locke could have gotten back here to take Avery Lynn.

But Locke wasn't working alone. The man calling himself Diablo was still out there, and they had no idea who he was, although Nessa couldn't imagine what he'd want with a ten-month-old baby.

Unless she's his baby. Could Diablo be the father of Tenley's little girl?

Diablo had admitted on the recording to sleeping with Mackenzie. Could he have been in a relationship with Tenley, too?

Knocking on Nora Fletcher's door, Nessa glanced at Peyton as they waited. The detective looked as tired as she felt. It had been a hard week for both of them, and as they waited in vain for Nora to open the door, Nessa had the feeling it was about to get even harder.

"Mrs. Fletcher?" Nessa finally called out. "Nora? Are you in there? It's Chief Ainsley with the WBPD. I need to speak to you."

A deafening silence was the only response. Nessa tried to turn the doorknob, but it was locked. Hesitating only a second, she started around the side of the house, Peyton right behind her.

The sliding door to the patio was partially open. Nessa's heart began to thump in her chest as she approached.

"Mrs. Fletcher?" Nessa tried again, sticking her head through the sliding door. "Are you in here?"

A soft moan sounded from somewhere inside.

Drawing her Glock out of the holster under her jacket, Nessa motioned for Peyton to cover her. The detective pulled out her own weapon, and Nessa stepped into the room, holding her gun in a ready position.

The living room was dim, but the windows let in enough sunlight for Nessa to see that the room was empty. Making her way into the hall, she heard another moan.

Peyton came up behind her just as Nessa saw Nora Fletcher's crumpled body on the floor beside a crib. Her arms and legs had been bound with some kind of cord, but she was conscious.

Nora began to struggle when she saw Nessa and called out in a voice that was hoarse as if she'd been shouting for help.

"He took the baby," she said with a sob. "He's got Avery Lynn."

247

CHAPTER FORTY

Ruby Chase walked out of the police station and headed west toward the bus stop. She was in a hurry to get out of town as soon as possible now that the state prosecutor had explained that they'd decided not to pursue any charges against her for shoplifting or for the drug possession charges.

"But I do suggest you go back to Hope House and complete your rehabilitation program," the prosecutor had urged. "You can't let these men win, Ruby. You've got to take your life back."

Ruby knew Diablo's men would be watching the facility and waiting for her, and if she didn't want to wind up back behind the big walls and barbed wire, then she had to get out of town.

"Where do you think you're going?"

Detective Ingram stood on the sidewalk; he kept his little eyes pinned on her as she waited at the crosswalk.

"The prosecutor lady said I could leave."

Ruby inched closer to the curb, willing the light to turn green.

"So, Riley Odell and Nessa Ainsley are at it again," Ingram said, his voice bitter. "You must think you've gotten one over on me, but I'm pretty sure we'll see each other again. Your kind always turns up. Just like a bad penny."

The crosswalk light turned green, and several pedestrians on the other side of the road began to walk toward them. Ruby forced her feet to move, ignoring the feel of Ingram's eyes on her back as she stepped up onto the curb and hurried around the nearest corner.

When Ruby looked back, Ingram was out of sight, and she sucked in a deep breath, relieved to be out of the police station and free to leave town. She zipped up her hoodie and headed for the street ahead.

Keeping up a brisk pace, Ruby soon found herself on Townsend Road. The name sounded familiar, and after another ten minutes of walking, Ruby began to suspect she was on the road that led out of town. The same road that led to Diablo's base camp.

The urge to run in the other direction, or maybe to turn south and hitchhike down to Miami, came and went. She suddenly realized that she wanted to find the men who had held her, and who would do anything to stop her from leading the police to their hideout.

I'll find it and I'll call Chief Ainsley and tell her where it is. Then she can arrest Diablo and his men. Once they're in jail, maybe I can go back home. I might even be able to see Dad and Rory again.

The thought of seeing her father and little brother again kept Ruby's feet moving. By the time she'd found the turnoff to Diablo's camp an hour later, she was sweating. She took off her hoodie and tied it around her waist.

Creeping through the thick underbrush beside the dirt road, she saw the big concrete fence, topped by rusty barbed wire. She followed the fence around to the gate and peered in, wanting to make sure she was at the right place and that the men were still there.

Diablo's righthand man stood on the porch with a gun slung over one beefy shoulder. He was the same man she'd seen at Hope House. She couldn't mistake his massive chest and dark head of hair.

The big man watched as workers stacked small bags into the back of a black SUV. Ruby assumed the bags contained pills or some other kind of drugs. It was all just as she'd remembered it.

About to turn away, Ruby saw a young woman step out of the building onto the porch. The woman carried a baby in her arms, and as Ruby watched in shock, the baby began to cry.

"Get back inside," the big man yelled, motioning toward the door.

The woman shot him a dirty look but followed his orders. Moments later Diablo appeared. He looked nervous as he paced up and down, his expensive leather jacket flapping around him.

Ruby strained to hear what the men were saying, leaning closer, but trying to stay out of view.

"As soon as I get the call, I'm heading out," Diablo said. "You hold down the fort, and don't let anything happen to my little princess."

The big man scowled and shook his head.

"So now I'm a fucking babysitter?"

But Diablo wasn't listening. He turned back to go inside, and Ruby spun around and began making her way through the trees and underbrush to the road. She needed to get to a phone. She needed to tell someone that Diablo had kidnapped a baby. This time he'd gone too far.

Moving fast, Ruby took the same shortcut she had the last time she'd left the compound. Cutting through an empty pasture, she skirted around a citrus grove until she found the two-lane road that offered a more scenic route back to Willow Bay.

The convenience store she'd stopped at the last time was still there. When she walked inside, she saw the same manager working at the counter. Picturing the baby in the woman's arms, Ruby walked up to the man, knowing she didn't have time to waste.

"Can I use your phone? It's pretty important."

The man frowned at her and cocked his head.

"Do I know you?"

"I shop here all the time," Ruby answered without hesitation. "And I just need to make a call cause I'm having a little trouble with my car."

The man raised an eyebrow, then pointed to a phone on the counter. He turned away to ring up a customer's order as Ruby picked up the handset. She suddenly realized she didn't know Chief Ainsley's number.

If I call the police station, Detective Ingram might come for me.

Digging in her pocket, she pulled out the only number she had.

Frankie Dawson answered on the second ring.

"Barker and Dawson Investigations, this is Frankie."

"Frankie, this is Ruby. I know where Diablo is, and I need you to come now before he leaves."

The long pause on the other end of the line caused Ruby to panic. For a moment she thought he'd hung up. Then he was back.

"Okay, I got a pen. Give me an address and I'll be right there."

CHAPTER FORTY-ONE

Frankie pushed on the gas pedal, irritated that the Prius didn't seem to go over fifty miles an hour. He'd have to tell Barker to get a new car. But Frankie decided that could wait until he'd first told his partner that he'd borrowed the car without permission.

The fact that Frankie didn't have a license, and that he hadn't driven in more than ten years, probably meant that Barker wouldn't be happy to hear it. But Frankie had convinced himself he'd be fine.

It's just like riding a bicycle. Once you learn, you never forget.

Unfortunately, Frankie hadn't ridden a bicycle since he'd been a boy growing up in Memphis, so he wasn't sure how true that saying was. But his reason for not driving was, at least temporarily, not in effect. He hadn't had a drink for months, and he was feeling in control of his urges.

Besides, Ruby needed him, and he wasn't about to let her down. And he didn't think an Uber driver would agree to chase down a criminal kingpin. So, Barker's electric blue Prius would have to do.

Ruby was waiting outside the convenience store when Frankie pulled into the lot. She jumped into the passenger's seat without hesitation.

"What took you so long?"

Clicking on her seat belt, she pointed toward a little two-lane road that appeared to lead only to pastureland and citrus groves.

"Take that street back to Townsend Road and then take a right," she ordered. "Diablo's base camp is down a little dirt road."

Frankie got the Prius up to fifty-five when Ruby turned around in her seat with a frown.

"I think we just passed it back there. Make a U-turn."

Looking for a spot to pull over, Frankie saw a black SUV appear in his rearview mirror. The vehicle immediately began to speed closer, coming up fast behind him.

Before Frankie could panic, the big vehicle roared past him without slowing down.

"That's him!" Ruby shouted, making Frankie jump.

The sudden movement sent the Prius careening toward the ditch beside the road, and Frankie jerked the wheel back just in time to avoid an embarrassing explanation to Barker.

"Follow him," Ruby said, using a calmer voice. "Let's see where he's going. He may have the baby with him."

Frankie stared at her in confusion.

"Baby? What baby?"

"Just follow him," Ruby said, as the black SUV turned a corner and accelerated onto the highway.

Not sure the Prius would keep up with the speeding SUV, Frankie pushed his foot toward the ground, ignoring the rattling sound that started once the car had reached sixty miles per hour.

"I think we need to call the cops," Frankie said, keeping the SUV in sight. "I can call Peyton and have her meet up with us. She'll know what to do if these guys have guns."

Ruby shook her head.

"She might tell Detective Ingram, and I don't trust him."

Glancing over at Ruby's stubborn frown, Frankie sighed.

"If there's a baby in that car, we can't risk screwing this up."

The SUV suddenly veered onto an offramp without warning, and Frankie had to swerve into the right lane to follow it off the highway.

"Okay," Ruby said in a sulky voice that reminded him of Franny. "Call Detective Bell. But don't say I didn't warn you."

Picking up his phone, Frankie tapped on Peyton's name and waited. His stomach tightened when he heard her voice on the other end of the connection.

"I'm sharing my location with you now," he said, tapping on the *share location* option. "Ruby and I have Diablo in sight and we're following him on the interstate. We need you to meet us in case this turns ugly. Please hurry."

"Frankie, I don't think-"

But he'd already hung up, keeping his eyes on the black SUV as it turned into a subdivision. The big vehicle rolled slowly past a quiet house set back from the road, then came to a halt under a sprawling oak tree which hid the vehicle from view.

Frankie drove slowly past the neighborhood before making a wide U-turn and circling back. As the Prius turned into the subdivision, Frankie spotted a man in a black leather jacket and ski mask scale the fence and scurry around to the back of the house.

Driving past the SUV, Frankie strained his neck to look through the front windshield. The vehicle appeared to be empty. Bringing the Prius to a halt a few houses down, he and Ruby looked at each other.

"Should we wait here for Peyton?" he asked.

Ruby shook her head and opened the door.

"I want to find out who lives in that house."

She stepped out and walked casually toward the house, stopping at the mailbox facing the road. Frankie came up behind her, his heart pumping with adrenaline as she opened the box and pulled out a letter. She studied the name and address, then showed it to Frankie.

"Jack Carson," he whispered. "Isn't that the guy on Channel Ten News? The one that works with Veronica?"

Ruby shrugged and walked toward the gate.

"See, we can't get in," he said. "We'll have to wait for Peyton."

Rolling her eyes, Ruby jumped up and grabbed the top of the fence, then used her legs to propel her up and over. She turned back to Frankie and waved for him to join her, then began to hurry around the house in the same direction that the man in the mask had gone.

"Shit," he muttered, reaching for the top of the wall. "How did I get myself into this? I must have a death wish."

Dropping over on the other side of the fence, he followed Ruby around to the back of the house. He stopped short when he saw her crouching beside a sliding glass door, her eyes wide as an angry voice spilled out into the patio.

"I know she's here," a man snarled. "Turn her over and I'll let you live."

"I don't know what you're talking about."

Frankie recognized Jack Carson's voice as he crept up next to Ruby. The videographer stood with his hands raised in front of the man in the ski mask, who held a big gun.

Suddenly a muffled buzz sounded, and the man in the mask used his free hand to dig in the pocket of his jacket and pull out his phone.

"What do you want?" he barked into the phone.

He was quiet for a long beat.

"Okay, I'll be ready for them," he said, then stuck the phone back in his pocket.

"Looks like we might get some company," the masked man said. "My contact at the WBPD says we got some cops on the way, so I'm gonna need you to turn over Ling Lee now, or else I'm gonna have to use this."

He shoved the gun toward Jack, as Frankie tried to register what the masked man was saying.

Did he just get a tip-off that we called the cops? Could Peyton have hung up with me and called him?

The idea that Peyton could be working with Diablo and his men resurfaced in Frankie's mind, and he had to force his mind back on the situation unfolding in front of him. If he didn't act fast, he and Ruby may be about to witness a murder.

"I'm going in there," Frankie whispered to Ruby. "I'll wait until he looks away, and then I'll tackle him."

"No," Ruby hissed, but Frankie was already moving forward.

He stopped at the edge of the door and peered inside, his chest tightening as he saw the gun trained on Jack and noted the fear on the older man's face.

Preparing himself to charge into the room, Frankie froze in place as he heard the shrill ring of his phone echo across the quiet porch.

Frankie jammed his hand in his pocket to silence the phone, but it was too late. The man in the mask rushed to the door, and Frankie looked up to see the big gun pointed in his direction.

"I thought the real cops were coming," the man snapped, using the gun to wave Frankie into the room. "Go on, get inside."

The masked man backed up to make room for Frankie to pass, and Jack took the opportunity to spring forward, aiming a punch at the man, who stepped back out of range, then brought the gun down over Jack's head with a hard whack.

As the older man crumpled to the ground, Frankie felt a rough hand push him to the side, and a loud voice sounded in his ear.

"Police, put your weapon down!"

Falling to the ground, Frankie rolled to the side, then looked up to see Nessa Ainsley standing in the room holding a gun in front of her with both hands.

"I said put your weapon down."

The man aimed the gun at Jack's head and grinned.

"I've been expecting you," he said, moving behind Jack's cowering figure. "And I suggest you put *your* weapon down, or I'm going to blow this man's head off."

"Okay," Nessa said, her voice tight. "We can work this out."

The man shoved the gun closer to Jack and snarled.

"I said drop your fucking gun or I'll kill him."

Nessa bent to lay her gun on the ground, and the masked man shifted the gun in his hand toward Nessa.

A shot echoed through the room, and the man spun around and fell to the floor, his gun clattering to the ground next to him.

Staring over at the sliding glass door, Frankie saw Peyton step inside, her gun still at the ready.

"Is there anyone else in here?" she barked at Jack. "Is there anyone else in the house?"

Jack shook his head, but a small voice spoke up from beside Frankie. Ling Lee stood in a doorway Frankie hadn't even noticed. It looked like some kind of hidden entrance.

"I'm here," Ling said, swallowing hard. "Jack was trying to protect me. He let me stay in his safe room while they search for Locke."

Frankie's head was spinning as he sat up and looked around the room. He watched as Peyton walked over to the masked man sprawled on the floor. Peeling back his ski mask, she revealed a handsome face surrounded by thick dark hair.

"Nick Sargent," Nessa whispered as if she didn't believe her own words. "We've killed Nick Sargent."

* * *

Frankie stood on the patio and pulled a stick of gum out of his pocket. His hands were shaky as he peeled off the silver foil wrapper and stuck the gum in his mouth.

"You did good calling Peyton and sharing your location with her," Nessa said, coming up behind him. "Although why you tried to go inside...well, that's another story."

Hurried footsteps announced the arrival of Jankowski and Vanzinger. Nessa waved to the detectives as they came around the corner, her face pale but her voice steady.

"We have a suspect down. I've put in a call to Alma. Her team should be on the way," she said, pointing toward the house where Nick Sargent's body was sprawled on the floor.

"Chief Ainsley?" Ruby appeared beside Frankie. "I just wanted to...to see who was behind the mask. To make sure it was...him."

Nessa nodded and led Ruby into the room with Frankie following behind. Jack and Ling were talking quietly to Peyton, but they fell silent as the teenager approached the body on the floor.

She stared down at the dead man as voices sounded on the patio, and two figures appeared in the doorway. Special Agent Clint Marlowe's impressive frame stood next to Marc Ingram's scrawny figure. Nessa held up a hand to stop the men, then looked to Ruby.

"That's...him," Ruby said, her voice shaking as badly as Frankie's hands. "That's Diablo. He's the man in charge. His men...held me."

"She called me to pick her up when she went to find their base of operations," Frankie said, giving Ruby a smile. "We followed him back here. He was trying to find Ling Lee I guess."

Frankie suddenly remembered the call Nick had gotten when he'd been holding Jack at gunpoint. He turned to Nessa.

"Someone told Nick you were coming," Frankie said. "He got a call while we were listening in. He said it was a cop."

Vanzinger frowned, then crouched beside Nick's body and stuck his hand in the dead man's pocket. He pulled out a phone and looked at the display.

"It's locked."

He tapped on the display and shook his head, but Jankowski bent to pick up Nick's hand. He pulled off the glove Nick had been wearing and motioned for Vanzinger to hand him the phone.

Placing Nick's finger on the phone, he glanced at the display again and produced a grim smile.

"Now it's unlocked," he said. "Let's see who called him."

Pulling up the list of recent calls, he tapped on the last number and held the phone to his ear.

Frankie's eyes widened as a phone began to buzz in the room. Everyone turned to see where the noise was coming from. Agent Marlowe stepped to the side and stared at Ingram.

"Detective Ingram, I think your phone is ringing," he said, his voice cold. "Aren't you going to answer it?"

Nessa grabbed Nick's phone from Jankowski's hand and stared down at the number.

"It's his number all right," she said, looking up at Ingram's scowling face. "It seems you have some explaining to do, Detective."

Ingram's phone fell silent as he glared at Nessa.

"This is a set-up," he muttered between clenched teeth. "And I'm not saying anything else until I speak to my lawyer."

* * *

Frankie watched as Jankowski and Vanzinger shoved Ingram into the back of the cruiser. He looked over to see how Peyton was handling her partner's betrayal, but she was standing next to Agent Marlowe, looking down at the man they'd been searching for.

Frankie swallowed back the resentment that rose in his chest as he watched Peyton. The memory of her rejection still stung.

Although it looks like the task force needed my help after all.

He felt Ruby come up beside him, and they watched together as Ingram was driven away. Once the cruiser had disappeared, Ruby turned to Nessa.

"So, what are you going to do about the baby?" she asked.

259

Nessa and Frankie both stared at her and frowned.

"What baby?" they said at the same time.

"Diablo had a little baby with him at his camp. I guess he must have kidnapped her, but he called her his *princess.*"

First excitement, then panic crossed Nessa's face.

"Avery Lynn," she murmured, then turned and called to Peyton.

"I think they're holding Tenley's daughter at Diablo's hideout," she said in a rush. "And Ruby knows where it is."

Nessa and Peyton started for the Charger, but Ruby didn't move. They looked back and motioned for her to join them, but she looked at Frankie and shook her head.

"I'm not going back there without Frankie," she said. "He's the only one I can trust."

With Nessa and Peyton following in their Charger, Frankie drove Barker's Prius back to Townsend Road. Ruby sat in the passenger seat navigating. They waited at the end of the dusty road while Nessa and Peyton scouted out the area.

"Looks like this place is deserted," Nessa said, coming back to lean into the window of the Prius. "We don't see any cars or activity. You sure this was the place?"

Ruby nodded and then pointed down the road toward the gate.

The gate was open, and a big man stood with one hand in the air, and the other hand around a small girl wrapped in a pink blanket.

"I'm unarmed," the man called, stepping forward. "My name is Ivan Sokolov, and I believe you've been looking for this little girl."

Nessa rushed forward to take the baby from his arms while Peyton put the man in handcuffs and called for back-up.

Smiling down at the little girl, Frankie was surprised to see tears in Nessa's eyes.

"You caught the bad guy and you saved this little princess," he said. "So why the sad face?"

"There's another bad guy out there," Nessa said, her voice thick with emotion. "He's even worse than the one we just took down. He's taken Veronica Lee, and he's taken this little girl's mother, and I don't know if he'll ever let them go."

CHAPTER FORTY-TWO

Skylar had just swallowed the last bite of a protein bar when she saw the headlights coming along the winding road leading to the ranch. She'd been living off the bars for the last few days, wanting to keep her energy up for the Professor's return. The fear and dread had kept her stomach in knots, and the dry bars were the only thing she could keep down.

Moving to the kitchen table where she had the handgun laid out at the ready, she pulled on a warm jacket and slipped on a sturdy pair of snow boots. Taking a deep breath, she tried to calm the erratic beating of her heart as she ran a trembling finger over the barrel of the gun.

So, he's finally come back, and now I can end this once and for all.

By dawn, it would be finished. His reign of terror over her would end one way or another. She would either be free of him forever, or she would be dead.

Skylar knew she had no choice. Once she'd escaped the safe room and broken into the house, she'd known her options were to kill or be killed. The Professor had made it clear that he considered running away a betrayal, and that traitors received no mercy.

The death penalty is his only punishment for a woman who betrays him.

He'd taught her that lesson many times over the years, and now it was time for her to show him what she'd learned.

Listening to the rumbled of the big rig's engine, and the crunch of the heavy wheels over icy snow and broken branches, she picked up the weapon, holding it out in front of her just as she'd seen the Professor do so many times before.

He kept his guns locked and loaded, ready to use at a moment's notice, and she'd chosen the sleek handgun in his desk drawer over one of the heavy rifles on the rack. Rehearsing the scene in her mind many times, she'd convinced herself that she'd be ready when the time came.

Now, as the big rig jerked to a stop outside the barn, she watched from her viewpoint by the darkened window, sucking in a sharp breath as the driver's side door opened, and the Professor's long frame emerged from the cab.

Keeping her eyes trained on his hated figure, visible in the stark moonlight that shone overhead, Skylar held her breath as he approached the door and fumbled with the key in the lock.

She prepared to tighten her finger on the trigger as soon as he came through the door, but he only opened the door a crack, then jogged back to the truck. Unbolting the trailer door, he unfolded the step ladder and climbed inside to get whatever cargo he'd brought home with him.

Skylar's stomach squeezed at the thought of what, or who might be in the back of the trailer. Her finger loosened on the trigger with the fear she might end up shooting one of the scared, drugged women the Professor often brought home with him.

The Professor reappeared and climbed down from the trailer, then turned back to drag a limp form over the edge and into his arms. He grunted under the weight of the motionless figure, shuffling toward the back porch, and mounting the steps with difficulty.

Shouldering open the door, the Professor dumped the body in his arms onto the kitchen floor. Moonlight streamed in, illuminating the woman's slack face as the Professor turned back toward the trailer, oblivious to Skylar as she stood hidden in the shadows.

Aiming the gun at the Professor's retreating back, Skylar forced herself to wait. He was too far away, and she couldn't afford to miss what may be her only shot.

Expecting him to close and lock the trailer door, Skylar frowned when she saw him climb back up. When he reappeared at the edge of the trailer, she was shocked to see him struggling to drag another woman down.

Although he'd brought multiple women to the ranch on occasion before, they were usually compliant and restrained, and he rarely allowed them the opportunity to fight back as the woman on the edge of the trailer appeared to be doing.

Stepping closer to watch the Professor as he wrestled the woman off the trailer and onto the snowy ground, Skylar jumped when the woman's scream pierced the frigid air.

She cringed, expecting to see the Professor pull out a gun and end the woman's resistance on the spot. But instead, he grabbed the woman by the back of her red coat and yanked her toward the porch.

"You're gonna learn how to behave, girl," he muttered as he shoved the woman through the door, causing her to trip over the prone body on the floor.

As he pulled the woman to her feet and pushed her toward the hall, Skylar realized with a jolt of fear that the Professor was taking his captive to the saferoom, and that he would soon discover it was empty.

Holding the gun toward the two figures, Skylar stepped out of the shadows. The woman broke free from the Professor's grip and looked up at the gun with scared green eyes.

A calm certainty descended over Skylar as she aimed the weapon toward the man who had ruined her life. The man who had killed every woman she'd ever known.

She pulled the trigger without hesitation, but the Professor lunged to the side just in time, and the bullet blew a hole in the kitchen wall. Raising the gun again just as the Professor jumped up and charged toward her, she closed her eyes and pulled the trigger a second time.

This time the Professor spun around and slammed against the kitchen table, blood immediately seeping out from the bullet wound in his shoulder as he moaned on the floor.

Walking to stand over him, Skylar again lifted the gun and aimed it at the Professor's head. He lifted his hand in a feeble attempt to protect his face, and Skylar's eyes fell on the glove that concealed his missing fingers.

"Don't do it, Skylar," the man said in a breathless voice. "I taught you better than that, girl."

With cold determination, Skylar tightened her finger on the trigger. She stared down at the man who had taught her to show no mercy and knew if she let him live, she would never be free.

"You taught me to kill," Skylar whispered. "And to hate."

Squeezing the trigger, Skylar closed her eyes and waited for the explosion. But the gun only clicked, and the room fell silent. A gloved hand fell over her wrist, and the man below her shook his head.

"I told you not to betray me, girl. Now, look what you've done."

CHAPTER FORTY-THREE

The Professor wrenched the gun out of Skylar's hand and threw it to the side, surprised that there had been only two bullets in the Ruger's chamber. Wincing at the pain in his shoulder, he began to struggle to his feet. He'd have to make an example out of Skylar if he didn't want Veronica to get any ideas.

Sensing movement behind him, the Professor turned just as Veronica grabbed a saucepan off the counter and swung it toward his face. The jarring pain sent him falling backward, and he released Skylar's wrist to clutch at his bleeding nose.

"Come on, we've got to go now before he gets to the gun rack."

Skylar pulled on Veronica's arm, urging her toward the open door.

"But Tenley's still here," Veronica protested, shaking her head. "We can't just leave her like this."

Staunching the flow of blood from his nose with the sleeve of his jacket, Locke looked around for something to use to bind the bullet wound in his shoulder. He didn't think the bullet had punctured a major artery, but his jacket was already soaked with blood, and he couldn't afford to lose much more.

And he needed to get to the gun rack. If he had a working gun in hand, he could get Veronica into the saferoom, and give Skylar her due. Pushing himself into a sitting position, he grabbed the dishtowel off the stove and wrapped it around his shoulder, pulling it tight enough to make him gasp in pain.

"The Professor killed Astrid, and he'll kill us, too," Skylar insisted, rushing to the door. "Unless you want to end up in a hole in the ground, you better run."

Veronica hesitated, looking around the room for something else to use as a weapon. The Professor ignored her as he forced himself to his feet and staggered toward the hall.

Grabbing a lightweight rifle off the rack, he returned to the kitchen, enraged to see that both Skylar and Veronica were gone and that the door stood open, revealing only the swirl of wind and snow in the dark night outside.

Tenley Frost lay motionless on the floor, and as the Professor moved past her, he wondered if the Fentanyl would kill her after all.

I should've only given her half a pill. Next time I'll know better.

Stepping out onto the porch, he looked to the ground, his eyes following the footprints in the snow that led around the house toward the gate. The wound in his shoulder throbbed as he descended the stairs, and he gritted his teeth against the pain.

He wasn't in any shape to be running around the freezing woods at night, and the girls already had a head start on him.

I think it's time to go for a little ride.

Slinging the rifle over his good shoulder, he moved across the backyard toward the barn. The stiff wind and cold air revived him, and he began to move faster, wanting to get to the girls before they got into too much trouble.

My ungrateful daughter is just as bad as her traitorous mother, but it's still my job to protect her. And to teach her a lesson.

Unbolting the big barn door, he threw it open and slipped inside, crossing to a bulky tarp in the corner. Throwing back the tarp, he gazed at the bright red Arctic Cat

He hadn't had much of a chance to use it lately, but he'd kept the snowmobile fueled and ready to go just in case he ever needed to make a quick getaway.

The Professor had lived the last twenty-eight years looking over his shoulder, prepared for a SWAT team to descend on his doorstep at any moment. He'd purchased the ranch from a survivalist who'd built the original safe room as a shelter from nuclear war, natural disasters, or civil unrest.

Deciding he could put the underground room to better use, the Professor had soon changed it from a safe haven that protected its occupants from outside dangers getting in, to a hidden cell that would keep the women he collected from getting out.

He'd always known someday he might be discovered, and that the authorities would try to lock him away in a cell much like the one he'd devised for his unwilling guests.

But the Professor had promised himself he wouldn't be taken alive. He'd die before living like an animal in a cage.

Gritting his teeth against the shooting pain in his shoulder, he picked up the black helmet on the snowmobile's seat and pulled it on, making sure not to let the face shield touch his throbbing nose.

He climbed onto the Arctic Cat and started it up, surprised to hear the engine begin to hum on the first try. Accelerating slowly out of the barn, he switched on the headlights and steered back toward the house, following the girls' tracks in the snow.

The gate was wide open, and he cursed himself again for being too lazy to get out and bolt it behind him once he'd driven the semi through. After decades of doing everything right, he'd started making mistakes.

Maybe I really am getting too old for this. Maybe I should just sell the ranch and retire down in Florida for good.

He allowed himself a half-smile at the thought, guessing the folks down in Willow Bay had had enough of him already. Hopefully, by now they were finding Ling Lee's dead body and realizing they'd need to find another candidate for mayor.

He'd have to contact Diablo as soon as he'd taken care of the girls. He'd have to make sure the man had fulfilled his part of their bargain. Otherwise, he really would need to go back down to Florida and finish the job himself.

Gliding over the powdery snow, the Professor let his eyes roam over the bare trees as the headlight lit up the forest beyond. A soft hoot and a flutter of movement in one of the trees proved to be a gray owl, its eyes blinking in the moonlight as he passed by.

He settled back on his seat and circled back the way he'd come, searching again for tracks in the snow. Veronica and Skylar were out there somewhere, and he had no doubt that with a little perseverance he would find them, and he would bring them home

CHAPTER FORTY-FOUR

Hunter had never seen so much snow, and he'd never been so tired. But according to Ling Lee's phone, he and Deputy Santino were only a mile away from the location where Veronica's phone had last been detected. And although the signal had gone out again, Hunter knew they had to be close. He wasn't about to give up now.

"Try again," Santino said, nodding to the phone in Hunter's hand. "See if you can pick up something because it looks like we're out in the middle of nowhere, and I'm not sure where to go."

For the last hour, they'd driven down lonely roads lit only by the moonlight overhead, not knowing where they might end up, and who might be there waiting for them.

Reloading the *Find My Phone* app, Hunter watched anxiously to see if the dot that represented Veronica's phone would show up on the map.

After leaving the rest stop in Kentucky, they'd followed the signal off and on through Missouri, Iowa, and South Dakota, taking turns driving, and slowly making up time, and getting closer and closer to Locke's truck.

Neither of the men had been surprised to find themselves crossing the Montana state border into Big Sky Country, and they suspected they were nearing their final destination.

After all, Astrid Peterson had been abducted in Montana, and Locke most likely had acted on an opportunity that presented itself close to home.

The killer's compulsion to get revenge on Ling Lee had taken him all the way down to Willow Bay, but now he'd turned tail and was running back home. If they were lucky, they would find him before he could go to ground and hole up in his lair.

"I don't see a signal," Hunter muttered, his eyes on the phone. "From the looks of it we're close to the Bitterroot Valley, but I can't see any houses or buildings on this map. Just a bunch of trees."

A sudden light in the forest ahead flashed across the windshield, then disappeared behind another cluster of trees.

"What was that?" Hunter asked, staring out the Chevy's window into the icy forest. "Were those headlights?"

Santino lifted his foot off the gas, letting the Tahoe roll slowly down the road, while they both kept their eyes glued to the trees. They almost drove past the little road leading off into the forest, but another flash of light drew their attention just in time.

"There it was again. Someone's down there," Hunter said, pointing to the narrow road. "And there are track marks in the snow."

Glancing down at the phone in his hand, it took Hunter a minute to realize that the dot for Veronica's phone was back on the map. It was so close to the dot for the phone in his hand, that the two dots were almost touching.

"She's here," Hunter said, his voice cracking. "Her phone is to the north of us just up that way."

They both looked toward the dark road, then at each other.

"You ready for this?" Santino said, his eyes suddenly cautious. "I thought I'd have time to pull together a team before going in after him. I mean, I still could. It might just take a while."

Hunter shook his head just as a gunshot sounded in the dark beyond, followed by a high-pitched scream.

Stepping on the gas, Santino steered the SUV down the little road, keeping the vehicle at a steady speed to avoid slipping on the icy surface. Hunter kept his eyes glued on the phone screen, his heart pumping faster as he saw they were getting closer to Veronica.

"Hold on!" Santino shouted, stepping hard on the brake to avoid a white gate that swung back and forth in the wind.

"There's a house up there," Hunter said, his mouth dry with fear and hope. "Come on, let's go. I see a light on."

Santino hesitated, then flipped off the Chevy's headlights.

"If we can see their light, they'll be able to see ours," he warned. "And I don't think we want to announce our arrival. Besides, the moon's pretty bright. I think I can see where I'm going."

Driving slowly toward the big house, Santino saw the track marks from the road continued through the gate and around to the back of the house. Opening the console between them, he took out a heavy handgun and held it out toward Hunter.

"You familiar with one of these?" the deputy asked as Hunter took the weapon from him. "It's loaded and ready to go, so be careful."

"Veronica's been teaching me how to shoot," Hunter said, gripping the handle of the Glock. "This is a lot like the one she has."

Santino pulled out the gun in his holster and checked it, then put his hand on the door.

"Okay, on a count of three I'll get out and head up to the back door. You cover me from here. If it's clear, I'll signal you to join me."

Hunter nodded, not sure he knew what to do, but anxious to get in the house and see if Veronica was there and if she was still alive. His pulse pounded in his ears as Santino opened the Chevy's door and stepped down into the snow.

Watching with bated breath, he kept his eyes on Santino's lean figure and dark hair as the deputy scurried across the dark yard and onto the porch. Looking around, Hunter could see no movement, and no sign that anyone was in the house, or the barn beyond.

Seconds ticked by, and just when Hunter was starting to fear something had happened to Santino inside the house, the deputy motioned for Hunter to join him on the porch.

The cold air hit Hunter like a slap as soon as he opened the door and jumped to the ground. Bending his head down, he ran through the snow to meet Santino, who kept his gun at the ready and his eyes darting around the yard.

"Come on, get inside," Santino muttered, looking over Hunter's shoulder. "It doesn't look like Locke is here, but–"

Hunter stopped short as he saw Tenley Frost sitting on the kitchen floor, her face deathly pale as she shivered under her navy-blue coat. Looking up at him with glassy eyes, Tenley tried to speak.

"I think she needs some water," Santino said, picking up a mug off the counter and holding it under the tap.

Kneeling next to Tenley, the deputy held the mug to her mouth, letting her take several small sips before she pushed it away.

"My daughter," she whispered. "Where's my little girl?"

Hunter's heart squeezed at the look of fear in Tenley's eyes, but he managed a smile, glad that he'd gotten the message from Nessa that Ling Lee was safe, and that Avery Lynn was being cared for.

"Your little girl is fine," Hunter said, sensing Santino growing impatient beside him. "But we're trying to find Veronica. Wasn't she with you and Donovan Locke?"

Tenley's eyes widened in fear at the name and nodded.

"He was here," she said. "I pretended to be asleep so he would leave me alone. He ran out after them."

Heart pounding at her words, Hunter forced himself to keep his voice calm as he exchanged a look with Santino.

"Them? Was there someone else with Veronica?"

Giving a stiff nod of her head, Tenley began to cough. Santino handed her the mug, and she managed to grip it with trembling hands and bring it to her lips for another sip.

"A girl he called Skylar. She shot him."

Motioning toward the wall, Tenley shivered again at the sight of the bullet hole and the blood on the floor.

"And then they ran away, and he...he went after them."

Tenley's voice broke, and she looked to the door.

"He might come back. He has a gun. Lots of guns..."

Hunter crossed back to the door, but before he could open it Santino put his hand out, holding it shut.

"Locke's injured, and he's armed," Santino said with a heavy sigh. "There's no telling what he'll do next. I think you should stay here and guard Tenley. Locke may come back before I do."

Shaking his head in protest, Hunter glared at Santino.

"No. I didn't drive across the whole damn country to sit in here while Veronica's out there," he said, putting his hand on the doorknob. "Now, get out of my way."

Santino stepped to the side and let Hunter yank open the door and walk through. Once he got out on the porch, Hunter looked to the ground and activated the flashlight on his phone, still clutching the Glock in his other hand. He would follow the tracks around the house and see where they led. With any luck, he'd find Veronica before Locke did.

CHAPTER FORTY-FIVE

Veronica huddled behind the thick trunk of a towering pine tree, her teeth chattering as she listened to the snowmobile's engine sputter past them in the night. Skylar turned to stare up at her with wide eyes that were luminous in the moonlight.

"Who are you?" the girl asked, a frown creasing the delicate skin between her pale eyebrows. "Why doesn't the Professor treat you like the others?"

"The Professor?" Veronica asked, pulling her coat tighter around her. "Why do you call him that?"

Skylar shrugged.

"That's what I've always called him."

"How long have you been with him?" Veronica asked, trying to keep the pity out of her voice. "When did he bring you here?"

A faraway look entered Skylar's eyes, and Veronica thought for a minute she'd gone into some kind of trance. When she spoke, her voice had a dreamy quality that made Veronica uneasy.

"I've always been here, and he said I'd never leave."

"Well he was wrong," Veronica replied, putting a hand on Skylar's small arm and squeezing. "You and I are both going to be leaving very soon. We just have to find our way to the road."

Turning to the south, Skylar pointed past the trees.

"Oh, the road's over that way," she said. "But the Professor will be looking for us over there. He's never going to let us get that far."

Veronica thought of the phone in her boot and wondered how far away Hunter might be now. He'd been following Locke's truck all the way from Willow Bay, and she'd tried to save her battery as much as possible, hoping it would last long enough for him to find her.

Deciding she couldn't wait anymore, Veronica bent to take the phone out of her boot. She tapped on the display, but nothing happened. The screen didn't light up. The phone was dead.

Suddenly realizing that the snowmobile's engine was silent, Veronica raised a finger to her lips and motioned for Skylar to stay quiet.

"Skylar! Come out here, girl!"

The voice came from only yards away.

Fear filled the girl's thin face, but Veronica thought she could see something else, too. Something that looked like anger.

A soft hooting came from behind them, and Veronica looked back to see an owl sitting on a branch several yards away. The bird stared at Veronica with wide eyes, before spreading its pale wings and silently taking flight.

As she watched the owl disappear beyond the trees, Veronica heard footsteps behind her. A light shone in her face, and she looked up to see Donovan Locke standing before her, his face twisted into an angry scowl, and a rifle cradled in the crook of his arm.

"I thought you were dead all these years, you know," he said, shaking his head. "I thought both you and your mother were dead."

He stepped closer, and Veronica could feel Skylar's small body begin to shake next to her.

"Maybe it would have been for the best if that had been true," he continued, swinging the rifle so that it pointed in her direction. "Maybe you think being dead would be better than being with me."

The moonlight revealed his narrowed green eyes, and Veronica was struck by how much they resembled her own. After all the years of wondering about her father, she now stood in front of him, and she didn't have to wonder anymore.

And now I know exactly why my mother never told me about him. The truth is worse than anything I could have ever imagined.

Locke studied the emotions playing over Veronica's face, and his voice hardened with resolve.

"But none of that matters now. You're here and you're gonna stay here. Dead or alive, you're staying here with me."

Turning his angry gaze toward Skylar, he scoffed.

"And you...I guess you're just like your mother after all," he muttered. "She never would follow the rules. That's why she ended up as fertilizer for that garden you spend so much time in."

His eyes glinted with remembered satisfaction.

"And there's plenty of room for you next to her if you don't get back to that house."

Veronica gaped in disbelief at Locke's callous words. Her outrage turned to surprise as she saw Hunter's tall figure rise up behind Locke, a gun in his hand.

An involuntary gasp from Skylar alerted Locke that someone was behind him. He ducked and twisted out of the way, narrowly avoiding the butt of the gun Hunter had swung toward his head.

Wrenching the rifle around, Locke saw Hunter duck behind the big pine tree, and he scrambled to his feet. Lunging toward Skylar, Locke held the muzzle of the gun to her head.

"Come out now, or I'll blow her head off."

Hunter stepped out from behind the tree, the gun still in his hand. As Locke swung the barrel of the rifle in his direction, Veronica flung herself forward, grabbing at his wounded shoulder and knocking the rifle to the ground.

Locke reached for the gun, but a deep voice spoke up from the shadows before he could grab hold of it.

"Donovan Locke, I'm Deputy Marshall Vic Santino with the U.S. Marshals Service, and you're under arrest."

Santino stepped out of the shadows, his Glock pointing at Locke's head as he kicked the rifle out of his reach

"Now, lay face down and put your hands behind your back."

Locke sneered over at Santino.

"You're about twenty-odd years too late, I'd say, *Deputy*."

He looked down at his shoulder, which had started oozing blood again, and shook his head.

"First you guys shoot off my fingers, and now that girl gets me in the shoulder," he muttered. "Maybe you should just shoot me in the head and be done with it."

Without warning Locke kicked out toward Santino's feet, then rolled to the side, attempting to get to the underbrush. But a shot rang out before he'd gotten more than a few feet away, and blood sprayed out onto the snow in front of him.

Veronica stared at the hole in Locke's back, too shocked to scream as he fell forward and lay still on the ground.

Turning to Skylar, she saw that the girl was holding the rifle in front of her, the faraway look in her eyes again.

"I couldn't let him get away," she said in a soft voice. "He killed Astrid, and he put my mother in the garden."

Santino moved forward and took the rifle from Skylar's hand, then led her back toward the house, as Veronica turned to Hunter, who was running toward her in the dark.

"Be careful with the gun," she called out, having seen enough guns and blood for a lifetime. "It's slippery out here."

Pulling her toward him, Hunter wrapped Veronica in a warm hug, lifting her off her feet and burying his face in her long, dark hair.

"I didn't know if I'd ever see you again," he murmured, leaning back to look down into her eyes. "Now, let's get you home."

CHAPTER FORTY-SIX

Hope House was quiet as Peyton walked through the front door and headed to the reception desk. It had been almost two weeks since Ruby had found her way back to Diablo's base camp. Her actions had helped bring down Nick Sargent and his trafficking operation and had likely saved Ling Lee's life. Peyton wanted to see the brave teenager again before she was released from the rehabilitation program.

"Detective Bell, I wasn't expecting to see you here today."

Reggie Horn appeared beside Peyton. The counselor's bright smile matched the fuchsia wrap dress she was wearing, and her strappy sandals reflected the warmer weather that had returned to Willow Bay after the recent cold snap.

"I heard that Ruby might be leaving the program today," Peyton said, looking around the lobby. "She hasn't already left has she?"

"Oh, no, Ruby's still here. I can take you back to the rec room," Reggie offered, leading Peyton toward the hall. "She's just saying goodbye to a few of the friends she's made here."

Peyton almost didn't recognize Ruby as she looked around the room. The formerly sullen girl was sitting by the window, her face lit up with a smile as she spoke to the girl next to her.

"Ruby, there's someone here to see you."

Smiling at Peyton's obvious surprise at the change in Ruby, Reggie turned to the girl sitting beside her.

"Skylar, it's about time for our morning session. Why don't you come along with me and we'll leave these two to catch up."

The girl's name sounded familiar, and with a jolt, Peyton realized that Ruby's companion was the girl Santino had saved from Donovan Locke's ranch. She hadn't known Skylar was in Willow Bay, much less at Hope House getting treatment with Dr. Horn.

But if anybody can help the poor girl overcome the trauma she must have gone through, it'll be Dr. Horn.

Peyton turned curious eyes to the frail girl with long, blonde hair that appeared almost silvery in the bright sunlight coming through the window. She watched as Skylar followed Reggie down the hall, then turned back to Ruby.

"So, how does it feel to be a hero?"

An embarrassed grin spread over Ruby's face, and she shrugged.

"It's a lot better than feeling like a criminal, that's for sure."

A pang of guilt started in Peyton's stomach as she sank into the chair that Skylar had vacated.

"I'm sorry for not believing you," Peyton said, meeting Ruby's eyes. "And I want to thank you for doing what you did. You risked everything by going up against Diablo. That was really brave."

Ruby's grin faded a little at the mention of the man who'd tried to ruin her life, as well as the lives of so many others.

"It's okay," Ruby finally said. "I wasn't the most reliable of witnesses I'm sure. Most people didn't believe me."

After a moment of silence, Ruby smiled again.

"Although Frankie did," she said, her eyes bright as she stared over at Peyton. "So, I should be thanking you for calling him and asking him to help get me in here. He saved me a few times."

The mention of Frankie caused another pang of guilt to stir.

"Have you seen Frankie lately?"

Peyton tried to sound casual.

"Oh, yeah, he's come to see me a bunch of times."

Ruby sighed and dropped her eyes.

"I probably shouldn't say this, but I think he's kind of lonely. He says I remind him of his sister, but I'm not sure that's a good thing."

Peyton swallowed hard, trying not to picture Frankie's hurt eyes when she'd told him not to get involved with her case.

"I'm sure it's a very good thing," Peyton said, hoping she sounded convincing. "It's always good to be reminded of the people we love."

Looking out the window, Ruby's face suddenly erupted into a happy grin. She jumped up and rushed out of the room, leaving Peyton to scurry after her. Peyton stepped into the lobby just in time to hear Ruby's peal of laughter.

"Dad! Rory!"

A heavy-set man with a receding hairline and worried eyes was coming through the door. He turned toward Ruby's excited voice as the small boy next to him broke into a run, crashing into Ruby as he wrapped his arms around her in a big bear hug.

"Is this where you've been staying, Ruby?" the little boy asked, looking around the room with wide eyes. "Can you come home now?"

"Yes, little bug," Ruby said, her voice hoarse. "I'm coming home."

* * *

Peyton drove back to the police station in a thoughtful mood, happy that Ruby was healthy and on her way home but knowing that other girls out there weren't so lucky.

The idea that Nick Sargent had done so much damage in such a short amount of time was depressing. There would always be men like Nick Sargent out there trying to take advantage of vulnerable girls like Ruby.

Approaching the station, Peyton saw Nessa and Special Agent Marlowe talking on the steps. She'd been working with the FBI agent and the task force in the aftermath of the shootout at Jack Carson's house, and she'd come to see the agent was very good at what he did, even if he did have a hard veneer.

Maybe you have to be hard to do what we do. Otherwise, it'll just tear away at your heart until there's nothing left.

Dropping her eyes, Peyton attempted to pass by Nessa and Marlowe without disturbing them, but Nessa called her over.

"You're officially without a partner for the time being," Nessa said, raising a hand to shield her eyes from the sun. "Ingram's been suspended without pay pending investigation of the allegations against him. If anyone asks about it, tell them to come see me."

Peyton nodded, glad that Ingram would no longer be a thorn in her side but at a loss as to what would happen next.

"So, when will I be getting a new partner?"

Nessa looked at her and shrugged.

"It could take a while," she admitted. "But in the meantime, I've agreed to let you work with Agent Marlowe on the joint task force."

Marlowe crossed his arms over his chest and pinned Peyton with a hard stare.

"Nick Sargent and the Diablo Syndicate was just a small cog in a very big wheel," he said with a frown. "Operation Stolen Angels won't wrap up until we find every player and every organization involved in the larger trafficking network, and we're going to need good people on board to do it."

A thrill rolled through Peyton. Getting the chance to track down the lowlifes that preyed on girls like Ruby and Skylar was just the opportunity she'd been hoping for.

Trying to retain her composure, Peyton nodded and smiled.

"You can count me in, Agent Marlowe. That'll suit me just fine."

CHAPTER FORTY-SEVEN

The final report on Garth Bixby's extramarital activities sat on Frankie's desk, waiting for Barbie Bixby to arrive. The soon-to-be ex-wife of Mayor Hadley's campaign manager had insisted on picking up the file that afternoon, even though it was a Saturday, and Barker had agreed to her demand without asking Frankie.

"You think we're running a twenty-four-hour operation around here, or something, Barker?"

Frankie propped his long legs on the desk.

"Yeah, I thought that's why you're always spending the night on that cot in the back," Barker said, taking a swig of coffee.

"No, I sleep back there because my mother watches too many reality shows," Frankie said. "Her hearing has kind of gone so she turns it up way loud. All that shouting messes with my beauty sleep."

The front door swung open before Barker could reply. Barbie Bixby breezed into the room, her form-fitting dress and high heels making her appear ready for a night out rather than an afternoon of preparations for her divorce hearing.

"Thanks for getting this ready over the weekend," she trilled, taking the folder and sticking it under her arm without looking inside. "Send the bill to my accountant. He's working today, too, so we can have everything ready for Monday's hearing."

Shooting a suggestive look at Barker, Barbie paused at the door.

"I am looking forward to putting this all behind me. And now that I'm on the market again, I plan to look for someone more stable and law-abiding."

She glanced at Barker with a knowing smile.

"And I'm done with younger men. I need someone *experienced*."

Looking back and forth between Barbie and Barker, Frankie shook his head and frowned.

"Oh, no. Barker's taken," he said bluntly. "He's off the market."

Barker shot Frankie an angry glare but didn't contradict him as Barbie sniffed and disappeared through the door.

"Speaking of me being taken," Barker said, getting to his feet. "Reggie and I have plans this afternoon, so I need to get going."

As the door closed behind Barker, Frankie felt a stab of envy.

Must be nice to have someone to have plans with.

The thought brought Peyton's amber eyes to mind. They hadn't spoken since the day they'd taken down the Diablo Syndicate, and he wasn't sure they were even still friends.

Feeling restless, Frankie powered up his computer, deciding to search online for a new car. Ever since he'd taken Barker's Prius on the wild ride to Diablo's hideout, he'd wanted to get back behind the wheel. He had his drinking under control, so maybe it was time to start driving again.

He'd just clicked on an article about top-rated sports cars when he heard a soft knock on the door. He looked up as Peyton stepped into the office wearing a shy smile.

"How'd you think I'd look in a Ferrari?" he asked with a nervous grin. "Or would that just be showing off?"

Peyton laughed and sank into the chair across from him. Her laugh was soft and pleasingly familiar, and Frankie couldn't help thinking how much he'd missed hearing it.

"I saw Ruby today," she said. "She really appreciates everything you've done for her, and she seems happy now. I think she's going to be okay. Or at least, as okay as any teenager can be."

"She's a good kid," Frankie agreed, wondering why Peyton had come. "I'm proud of her for doing the right thing."

After a pause, Frankie leaned back in his chair.

"So, is that why you stopped by? To tell me about Ruby?"

Peyton hesitated, then shook her head.

"No, not really," she admitted. "It's just, I got some good news today, and realized I didn't have anyone to share it with."

A pretty blush colored her cheeks.

"Then I thought of you, and, well, I know you probably don't feel like talking to me after what I said about not wanting you on the investigation, but...I thought I'd stop by just to make sure."

Absorbing her words, Frankie felt his chest tighten.

"I thought you didn't want to talk to me after my reaction," Frankie countered, feeling his face growing hot. "And I have to admit, I was starting to think you were in cahoots with Diablo."

Peyton seemed surprised.

"I never thought of myself as someone who went into *cahoots* with anyone," she teased. "Although, it does sound kind of fun."

Frankie couldn't hold back a smile.

"So, what's your good news?"

He crossed his arms over his chest and stared at her, unable to take his eyes off Peyton's face. She seemed so happy, so lit up from within.

If I was a romantic guy, I'd think maybe she's in love.

Her next words sent his heart plummeting.

"Agent Marlowe invited me to be a member of the joint task force between the FBI and the WBPD."

She dropped her eyes, suddenly self-conscious.

"It may not seem that important to anyone else, but it's a pretty big deal to me, and it felt pretty good."

A lump settled in Frankie's throat. So, the glow had been lit by some other guy. She'd gotten all excited because she would be working with hunky Agent Marlowe.

I'm such a fucking fool. I actually thought she might be falling for me.

Frankie forced the stupid thought from his mind. Why would a woman like Peyton want anything to do with him? He should be glad to have her as a friend and stop making an ass of himself by always wanting more.

"That Agent Marlowe's a pretty handsome dude," Frankie finally managed to say, trying to keep his voice casual. "I mean, he must be a real lady-killer."

"I've had my fill of killers lately."

Peyton rolled her eyes and smiled.

"And that goes for any kind."

"Well, Marlowe's a pretty important guy, and all macho and..."

He let his voice fade away, deciding he was laying it on too thick.

"I'm not looking for macho," she said, frowning at his comment.

"What are you looking for?"

Frankie couldn't help asking the question, but he winced at the hope he heard in his voice, knowing she could hear it, too.

"Actually, I'm not looking for anything."

Her words were soft, but they knocked the wind out of Frankie's lungs in one sickening gush of air.

"Okay. Got it," Frankie said, slumping in his chair. "You need to focus on work now. What with the task force thing, and all that."

He dug his hand into his pocket and pulled out a stick of gum, dropping his eyes as he carefully removed the silver foil.

"That's not what I meant." Peyton's mouth turned up in a sheepish smile. "I meant that I already found someone I want to spend time with. Someone I'm hoping to get to know a little better."

The shy revelation was too much.

"You really know how to hurt a guy."

Frankie pushed back his chair and stood up.

"I mean, I may just be friend material, but you don't have to rub my nose in it. I wish you luck and all that with this guy, but I don't really need to hear the details."

Jumping out of her chair, Peyton's eyes widened in confusion.

"*You're* the guy, Frankie," she said. "If you want to be."

Frankie stared into her wide, amber eyes, his mouth dry.

"You're not screwing with me, are you?" He cleared his throat. "You mean...you're serious?"

"Yep."

Circling the desk, Peyton stood in front of him and lifted a hand to rest on his chest. For once he didn't worry about being too skinny, or not having enough muscles to impress her. He just let himself enjoy the warmth of her hand on him. It had been too long since he'd felt something so good. So right.

"I've been trying to give you hints for a while," she murmured, biting her lip. "And you are a PI so I thought eventually you would figure it out, but..."

Frankie stood completely still, worried that if he moved, she might take her hand away.

"My grandmother always told me if something was too good to be true, it probably *wasn't* true."

Frankie's voice dropped to a whisper.

"And from where I'm standing, you look too good to actually be standing here looking at me like...like..."

"Like what?"

Frankie couldn't find the right words. Instead, he reached for Peyton's hand and drew her to him, his heart pounding hard against his bony ribcage, as her soft, warm body molded against him.

Her lips on his sent a spark of electricity down his spine, and she lifted a hand to pull him closer.

"Did that feel like a lie?" she teased.

"I think you just proved my grandmother wrong."

Frankie bent his head for another kiss.

"But don't tell her I said that."

"Don't worry," Peyton whispered. "Your secret is safe with me."

CHAPTER FORTY-EIGHT

The *Ling Lee for Mayor* signs had all been restored in Old Willow Square as Nessa passed through. She tried to keep her eyes off the bench under the old willow oak tree. The memory of Astrid Peterson's body, and the man who had killed her, was still too raw.

Turning the corner toward City Hall, she saw Riley and Vanzinger coming down the front steps.

"You two in there getting your marriage license?' she teased.

"No, but we still haven't finished making plans and the wedding is in a few weeks," Riley said. "Hopefully, Tucker will have a little more time to focus on me now that things have settled down."

A hint of irritation crossed the state prosecutor's face.

"Although, I think I might be a little busy come to think of it."

"You have any luck getting Ivan Sokolov to make a deal?" Nessa asked, picturing Nick Sargent's hulking cousin holding little Avery Lynn. "Will he give evidence against the network he and Nick were working with?"

Nodding, Riley lowered her voice.

"Sokolov has agreed to plead guilty to trafficking charges, and says he'll cooperate, but he denies knowing anything about Mackenzie's murder or Veronica and Tenley's kidnapping."

Nessa thought for a minute, then shrugged.

"Well, Nick Sargent was capable of lying about anything and deceiving anyone, so why not his own cousin?"

She was just about to continue up the stairs when she thought of another question and turned back to Riley.

"What about Marc Ingram?" she asked. "He wouldn't talk to me, was he any better with you?"

"He finally got a lawyer, and now they're claiming Nick was trying to set him up. That he was a victim in the whole thing."

Pushing back a wave of anger, Nessa sighed.

"I guess I shouldn't be surprised."

"Well, it looks like it'll end up in court in any case," Riley said in a glum voice. "And Judge Eldredge is presiding over the bail hearing on Monday, so it's likely Ingram will be out on the street while we go through the trial."

Stewing over Ingram's refusal to admit to what he'd done, Nessa watched Riley and Vanzinger walk away, then turned back to continue up the stairs. But her eyes fell on a familiar figure standing at the entrance to Old Willow Square.

"I didn't know you were back in town, Deputy Santino."

Santino turned to her with a start.

"Oh, Chief Ainsley, how's it going?"

The deputy's usually cheerful voice was subdued.

"I'm just back for a day or two. I came to see Skylar over at Hope House. I need to give her an update on something related to the case, and I thought I'd stop by and see where Astrid Peterson was found."

The sad look in his eyes reminded Nessa of how many people Donovan Locke had impacted. He'd spread so much evil and suffering for so long. But at least he was gone for good, and the people he'd left behind could now start to heal.

"You did a good job bringing down Locke," Nessa said, feeling like she and the town were in his debt. "It's good to know he won't be coming back here."

"Yes, hopefully, we all can sleep better now that Donovan Locke is no longer a threat."

An awkward pause followed, then Nessa looked at the duffle bag by his feet and cocked her head.

"Are you headed home after this?" Nessa said, pointing to the bag. "Or do you have another fugitive from justice to chase down?"

Santino looked down and produced a wry grin.

"Actually, I do," he said. "A bad guy fled to Canada, and I'm about to go somewhere colder than Montana if you can picture it."

Nessa shook her head and lifted her face to the blue sky.

"Oh no, I don't even want to think of that."

She was glad that the brief cold spell was over and that warmer weather had returned to Willow Bay.

"But I wish you luck, Deputy Santino. You go get the bad guys. And try to keep them out of my town next time if you can."

* * *

Nessa steered the Charger out of the parking garage, anxious to get home by the time the boys got back from the matinee with Jerry. She'd been trying to spend more time with the family, although it never seemed easy.

And it's only going to get harder from here.

Ignoring the little voice of worry in her head, Nessa thought about her conversation with Riley. Talking about Ivan Sokolov had brought up memories of Avery Lynn and her mother, and Nessa suddenly decided she needed to make one final stop before she could go home.

Tenley opened the door with a questioning frown.

"Nessa, there isn't anything wrong is there?"

"Oh no, nothing's wrong," Nessa said, giving her a reassuring smile. "I just wanted to check and see how you and little Avery Lynn are doing."

Stepping back from the door, Tenley motioned for Nessa to come inside. She immediately saw Avery Lynn playing on a mat on the living room floor. The little girl smiled up at Nessa, chewing on her chubby fingers.

"Well, somebody seems to be happy," Nessa said, kneeling down next to Avery Lynn. "I'm glad to see it."

"Thanks to you," Tenley said. "Avery and I owe you and the rest of the team our lives. If Nick had gotten his way, I'd be dead and who knows where my little girl would be right now."

Keeping her focus on the baby, Nessa pretended not to see Tenley wiping at her eyes.

"Nick was Avery Lynn's biological father, you know."

Nessa nodded.

"Ivan Sokolov told us that," she admitted, sickened that a father could do what Nick had done to the mother of his child.

"I didn't know Nick was...well, what he was," Tenley said. "At least, not at first. He was a reporter at Channel Six when I was reporting for Channel Ten."

Her voice faded away as if she was recalling a day long gone.

"What can I say? He was persistent, and I was lonely. When I told Nick I was pregnant, he didn't handle it well. By the time he decided he wanted to be a part of his daughter's life, the truth about him had been revealed."

She raised pleading eyes to Nessa.

"I couldn't let a man who would do those terrible things be near my daughter, could I? But I never suspected he was involved with organized crime. Or that he hated me so much."

Nessa reached out to touch Avery Lynn's plump arm, then smiled up at Tenley.

"You did what any mother would," she said softly. "You tried to protect your child. That's what mothers do."

Tenley dried her eyes and nodded.

"Well, I can't thank you enough for saving my little girl."

"It's my job," Nessa said lightly. "Besides, I know how I'd feel if anything ever happened to my little girl."

Resting a hand on her stomach, Nessa met Tenley's eyes.

"You're *pregnant*?"

Tenley's voice rose with excitement, and Nessa was happy to see a genuine smile spread across her face.

Nessa grinned and nodded.

"You're the first person I've told, actually," Nessa said, feeling her cheeks grow warm. "I just hope my husband is as happy as you are about it."

"And you already know it's a...a girl?" Tenley said, confused.

"Not officially," Nessa admitted. "Let's just say I have a hunch that I'm gonna need to start liking pink."

CHAPTER FORTY-NINE

Hunter had been hoping for a slow news day so that he could get to Veronica's house early, but the mayoral campaigns were heating up, and several rallies and campaign events had been scheduled on the last Saturday before the election.

"I've got to get out of here," he said to Jack as soon as the news van had finally pulled to a stop outside the station. "I want to get over to Veronica's and see how's she's doing."

Jack nodded his head, which still bore a fading bruise from the blow Nick Sargent had delivered.

"She feeling any better?"

The older man began to unload the van.

"I know her mother's been awful worried."

The last few weeks had been difficult for Veronica, and Hunter wasn't sure how to answer Jack's question.

Although she wouldn't admit to feeling down, Veronica hadn't been herself lately and Hunter couldn't figure out how to help her.

"I'll take Gracie over there and see if she can cheer her up."

Hunter led the white Lab out of the van, then bent to rub the soft fur behind her ears.

"She's the only one who seems to do the trick."

"I hope it works," Jack said. "That girl's been through a lot."

He hefted his camera out of the van.

"Last time I was over there even the polls that showed her mother is leading in the race couldn't get a smile out of her."

Hunter crossed to where his Audi was parked in the station lot, surprised to see Deputy Santino leaning against a Chevy Tahoe that looked a lot like the one they'd driven up to Montana.

"Deputy Santino? What are you doing here?"

Their long road trip together now seemed like it had happened a lifetime ago. But they'd formed a bond over the many miles they'd traveled together, and the deputy's face was a welcome sight.

Reaching out to shake Santino's hand, Hunter felt a surge of emotion at the thought of what could have happened, if Santino hadn't been there.

"You saved Veronica's life," Hunter said, suddenly choked up. "I don't know how to thank you."

"It's my job," Santino said. "But, you're welcome. I'm glad this case had a happy ending. Not all of them do."

Running a big hand through his hair, Hunter sighed.

"That trip was...intense," he said, unable to find the words.

He thought Santino might be the only one who could understand how he'd been feeling.

"Being out on the road like that again...it brought back memories. I used to travel to the other side of the world to get a story. Back then it felt like what I was doing mattered. That's how our trip felt. It was hard, and it was dangerous, but it mattered."

Santino raised a finger in warning.

"It's easy to get addicted to the thrill of the chase," he said, his eyes serious. "But take it from me, if you spend all your time chasing down bad guys, or in your case chasing down a story, you give up a lot."

The look in Santino's eyes told Hunter that the deputy was talking from personal experience and that he'd sacrificed a great deal in order to do his job.

Hunter still carried his own baggage from his days in the Middle East, and he could see a kindred pain underneath Santino's tough exterior.

"So, what brings you back to Willow Bay?" Hunter asked, wanting to lighten the mood. "You missed the warm weather?"

"Actually, I'm here to see Skylar, and then I wanted to go by and speak to Veronica as well."

Santino looked uncomfortable, and a sense of uneasiness settled over Hunter. The U.S. Marshal wouldn't come down unless it was something pretty important.

"I'm heading over to Veronica's house now," Hunter said.

He wondered how Veronica would respond to the deputy's sudden appearance.

"I can let her know you're coming by."

"Okay," Santino agreed. "Once I stop by and speak with Skylar, I'll head over there."

Hunter watched the Chevy Tahoe pull out of the station lot, then opened the door of the Audi and let Gracie jump into the passenger seat. Within minutes he was speeding down Baymont, heading toward Marigold Lane.

He looked over at Gracie, who was staring out the window. The dog's quiet presence had a calming effect, and he was grateful she'd been able to help Veronica during the last few weeks.

"I just hope whatever Deputy Santino has to say to Veronica will cheer her up."

He said the words aloud, then glanced hopefully at the Lab, but Gracie just continued staring out the window.

"She's been through a lot. It can't be easy finding out your dad is a serial killer and then seeing him shot down in front of you."

Gracie finally looked at him, her big eyes curious, and he ruffled her fur, feeling foolish.

But as he neared Veronica's neighborhood, Hunter wondered again what it was going to take for Veronica to find the part of herself she seemed to have lost in the cold forest of the Bitterroot Valley.

CHAPTER FIFTY

Veronica sat at the little desk in her bedroom, trying to finish the script for her upcoming special report. The recent takedown of Nick Sargent and the Diablo Crime Syndicate had been big news across the state, and as one of Nick's victims, Veronica had already been the subject of multiple reports and had even had her picture on the front page of the *Willow Bay Gazette*.

But she'd decided it was time she told her own story, hoping that the process would be cathartic and that it might help her come to terms with everything that had happened.

Stifling a yawn, Veronica found herself struggling to keep her eyes open after another restless night of not enough sleep and too many dreams. Her father seemed to haunt her, as did the ranch up in Montana where too many bodies still lay buried.

She had just started to drift off again when she heard a soft knock at her door and turned to see Ling Lee.

"Hunter and Gracie are here," her mother said, taking in Veronica's sleepy eyes and somber expression. "And I'm going to put on a pot of coffee. Might help you wake up."

"Okay, Ma, I'll be right down."

The dejected tone in her voice caused her mother to look back.

"I thought for sure those two would be able to lift your spirits," Ling said. "But you still look like you've lost your best friend."

"I'm sorry," Veronica said, standing up and turning to her mother. "I know it doesn't make sense, but I can't help feeling like I'm somehow responsible for all the terrible things my father did. I keep thinking about the women he killed, and about Skylar."

Walking back into the room, Ling took Veronica's hand.

"None of that is your fault, Ronnie. And Skylar is getting the best care available over at Hope House," she insisted. "I just wish you would go see Dr. Horn, too. She could help you...deal with things."

"I'll think about it," Veronica said, trying to smile.

She knew her mother had been through a lot, too. And moping around the house would just make things worse.

Bending to scoop Winston off the foot of her bed, she carried the big tabby cat down the stairs with her.

The sight of Hunter standing in the hall with a hopeful expression on his handsome face lifted her mood, as did the white Lab sitting patiently next to him.

Dropping Winston to the ground, she watched the big cat disappear into the front room, then turned to Hunter.

"You look tired," he said, pulling her against him. "Are you still having trouble sleeping?"

She nodded, and let herself melt into his arms, not wanting to talk about the reason she couldn't sleep. Talking about it made it hard to forget, and everyone wanted to do nothing else.

She couldn't leave the house without someone asking her about her abduction and her narrow escape. One reporter had even asked Veronica if she considered her father a serial killer or a spree killer.

"I'm fine," she finally said, looking down at Gracie. "And I'm glad you both are here."

She was just about to offer Hunter a drink when a loud knock at the door made them both look around.

"Oh, I was going to tell you," Hunter said. "Deputy Santino's in town and he wants to speak with you."

Panic blossomed in Veronica's chest as she thought of the last time she'd seen the U.S. Marshal, and wondered why he would need to see her now.

Could he be coming to tell me my father isn't really dead? Was Locke's death in the forest just another one of his tricks?

Her throat tightened as she opened the door, and she could barely bring herself to speak when she saw Santino standing on the doorstep.

"Deputy Santino. Come in."

She stepped back to let the deputy inside, then froze as she saw the thin girl standing behind him.

Skylar's long blonde hair shone in the sunlight, and her face was painfully pale as she looked at Veronica with wide, frightened eyes.

"Skylar?"

Taking the girl's small hand, Veronica led her into the house, worried by her fragile appearance.

"Is everything okay?" she asked, turning to Santino.

Ling appeared in the kitchen doorway, her eyes widening as she saw Skylar in the hall. She rushed forward and took Skylar's other hand, and together Ling and Veronica led her to the sofa in the living room.

"There's been a development in the case," Santino said, clearing his throat. "I've already explained the situation to Skylar, and now we'd like to discuss it with you."

He looked at the sofa and raised his eyebrows.

"You may want to sit down."

Sinking onto the sofa next to Skylar, Veronica reached out for the girl's hand, feeling it tremble slightly under her own as Santino settled onto an armchair across from them.

"Donovan Locke's autopsy has revealed important information that I believe will be of interest to you both."

The deputy's words sent a shiver of apprehension through Veronica, and she squeezed Skylar's hand tighter, preparing herself for more bad news.

"Donovan Locke is Skylar's biological father."

Ling Lee gasped at Santino's words, but Veronica remained still, her mind reeling with the implications.

"We're still trying to determine who her mother was. We've found multiple remains on the ranch in the Bitterroot Valley, but we haven't managed to link any of them to Skylar yet."

Shifting on the sofa, Skylar turned to face Veronica.

"Deputy Santino told me that the Professor...I mean Donovan Locke, is...was your father, too."

Veronica nodded, hearing the confusion and pain in Skylar's voice.

"That's right," Veronica whispered, holding back tears. "So, that makes us sisters, doesn't it?"

Skylar glanced at Veronica; her green eyes were hopeful.

"I...I was hoping...well, I don't have any family, and..."

"You have me, now," Veronica corrected. "You have a sister."

Looking up, Veronica met her mother's eyes and smiled.

"*I* have a sister."

Ling sank onto the sofa next to Skylar and put a hand on her arm.

"And you have a family here...with us," Ling said. "If you want."

Santino cleared his throat and stood, clearly relieved that his mission had been completed.

"I can give Skylar a ride back to Hope House once you've had a chance to talk," he offered, but Veronica shook her head.

"I'll take her back when she's ready to go."

Veronica stood and looked at Santino, sensing this might be the last time they saw each other, and the last time she would get a chance to thank him in person.

"When I left the ranch, I felt like something was wrong. Now I know what that was." She looked down at Skylar and smiled. "I'd left my sister behind, but now you've brought her home to me."

When Santino walked out to the Chevy a few minutes later, Veronica pulled Skylar with her to stand on the porch, and Ling followed behind them.

Feeling Hunter step up next to her, Veronica leaned her head against his strong shoulder, smiling when she saw Gracie come out to say goodbye as well.

And as the Chevy drove out of sight, Veronica thought of the report she'd been writing upstairs only an hour before. She'd wanted to tell her own version of her own story, but she didn't know then it would have such a happy ending.

If you enjoyed *Her Winter of Darkness*,
You won't want to miss the next book in the series:
Her Silent Spring: A Veronica Lee Thriller, Book Four

ACKNOWLEDGEMENTS

I GREW-UP READING NANCY DREW MYSTERIES and often tried to lose myself in the make-believe world between those wonderful covers when the real world was too much to face without a little help.

Now that I'm all grown up with five children of my own, I find myself turning again to the pages within a story to escape the reality of this new world we are living in, if only for a while. But this time, I find respite by writing the mystery instead of reading it.

Determined to finish this third book in the Veronica Lee Thriller series on schedule, I relied on my wonderful husband, Giles, and my five amazing children, Michael, Joey, Linda, Owen, and Juliet, who make me proud every day with their kindness and compassion.

I'm also incredibly lucky to be blessed with an extended family I can always count on, including Melissa Romero, Leopoldo Romero, Melanie Arvin Kutz, David Woodhall, and Tessa Woodhall.

Reading books helped me get through the difficult days after my mother's death, and now writing my own books helps me feel close to her all these years later. I'm grateful to always have her with me in memory whenever I write.

ABOUT THE AUTHOR

Melinda Woodhall is the author of the new *Veronica Lee Thriller* series, as well as the page-turning *Mercy Harbor Thriller* series. In addition to writing romantic thrillers and police procedurals, Melinda also writes women's contemporary fiction as M.M. Arvin.

When she's not writing, Melinda can be found reading, gardening, chauffeuring her children around town, and updating her vegetarian lifestyle website.

Melinda is a native Floridian and the proud mother of five children. She lives with her family in Orlando.

Visit Melinda's website at www.melindawoodhall.com

Other Books by Melinda Woodhall

Her Last Summer
Her Final Fall
Her Silent Spring
Her Day to Die
The River Girls
Girl Eight
Catch the Girl
Girls Who Lie

Made in the USA
Columbia, SC
26 September 2024

43153357R00186